The Last Secret

a novel

by

Pam Royl

blue denim press

Cover Design by Shane Joseph
Cover image: iStock/beeldlab

Library and Archives Canada Cataloguing in Publication

Title: The last secret / a novel by Pam Royl.
Names: Royl, Pam, author.
Identifiers: Canadiana (print) 20220263507 | Canadiana (ebook) 20220263558 | ISBN 9781927882733
   (softcover) | ISBN 9781927882740 (Kindle) | ISBN 9781927882757 (EPUB)
Classification: LCC PS8635.O9585 L37 2022 | DDC C813/.6—dc23

Dedication

To my husband and true love, Ian.

1860

Chapter 1

The day the Prince of Wales came to visit, I met my first husband. His Royal Highness was to open Victoria Hall in our small town, one of many such towns carved out of the dense pine forest lining the north shore of Lake Ontario, in the Province of Canada West. With new railways snaking across the region, our town leaders had convinced themselves of a prosperous future, borrowing funds to build a magnificent new town hall and naming it in honour of the Queen.

Despite the threat from overcast grey clouds that autumn day, the crowd was exuberant. The entire population of over five thousand souls lined the main road. Well-dressed gentlemen and ladies crowded dry, clean boardwalks while the less fortunate crammed filthy sides of the muddy road, pushing and shoving for a clear view. Young men hung from posts and railings and small children darted about hoping to be the first to see, while parents shrieked.

I reached over to touch Father's sleeve.

Turning toward me, he smiled. Ever since I was a little girl, I loved his broad smile, slowly sloping sideways, teeth barely visible behind big rosy lips. "Excited, my dear?"

I smiled back at him and nodded. Fortunately, his tall angular body created a welcome barrier between Mother and me. Mother's delight at the royal visit was irritating me more than it should. It annoyed me that she couldn't leave England behind. We had come across the ocean to this North American colony, at her insistence, ten years ago when I was just six years old. Since then, she had become obsessed with recreating an English way of life she only imagined existed in the tiny hamlet we left behind.

Today, the air was filled with smells of flowers, sweet meats, horse dung, damp wood, and mud. Above it all, Mother's lavender cologne wafted over us in the light breeze. I nudged past my older sister, Tabitha, in the hope of a better view, stepping on her best boots. She muttered that I should stop behaving like a child, but when I smiled sweetly at her, she let me stand in front.

The road had been dragged to remove horse dung and smooth out wagon wheel ruts, the wooden plank boardwalk upon which we stood had been scrubbed clean, and a grand floral archway with an enormous crown fashioned in its centre was erected across the road. A great roar went up as an elaborate carriage came into view. The draft horses that typically pulled such a carriage had been replaced by ten young men who honoured the Prince by pulling his royal carriage to the hall.

"Oh, how vulgar," Mother said, far too loudly, causing others in the crowd to turn their heads towards us. Father tried to quiet her. "Do not shush me, Bertie. This was meant to be a grand occasion. Not a reminder that we remain a crude colony." When she noticed the sophisticated ladies openly glaring at us, she managed an apologetic smile.

Since our arrival in this *crude colony* Father had transformed himself from a village blacksmith to the owner of a thriving iron foundry, and this *crude colony* was on the verge of becoming a country. With Father's rise, we had become part of a fortunate class; an odd mixture of well-heeled English immigrants and wealthy United Empire Loyalists, intermingled with ambitious entrepreneurs like Father. They all shared one common value: seeking fortune.

The young men pulling the royal carriage were farmers, not the educated, wealthy gentlemen Mother considered the best prospects for her daughters. When the procession drew near, I stared curiously at the muscular men sweating beneath their ill-fitting Sunday shirts and tunics. As a proper young girl living in town, I seldom watched men at work. I giggled—how silly they looked, sweat dampening the backs of their clothing. Tabitha poked me in the back, a sharp reminder to behave myself.

To make matters worse for Mother, the lead men pulling the carriage were Drurys, one of the first Scottish families to settle this land, and held in high regard by most of the community. Except Mother, of course. She thought all Scots were uncivilized savages. I continued staring. Until now I had never seen a Drury up close, just heard of them in idle conversation tossed around our dinner table. They were large burly men, hairy and unshaven and, judging by the sighs rippling through the ladies around me, viscerally attractive. Especially the young man in the lead position who appeared, by the muscles bulging up his neck and forearms, to be taking much of the load. He was head and shoulders above the others, with straggly black curls tumbling over his face. As the grunting men drew nearer, my head swam with the animal smell of them. Tabitha covered her nose with a silk handkerchief and poked at me to do the same. I leaned closer.

The Royal procession halted. The conspicuous young man stood directly in front of me, adjusting the harness biting into his broad shoulders. He swept ragged curls off his face, sending a spray of moisture into the air. I was gawking rudely but could not stop myself. His large roman nose which should have been ugly, curled sensuously around his flaring nostrils. Unexpectedly, he turned to look directly at me. His eyes were the same blue as the bluebirds I so loved. One of those blue orbs winked at me, and I broke into a smile so wide my cheeks hurt. A rush of heat tinted my face.

I felt a sharp pain as Mother pinched my arm. "Stop that, you stupid girl."

***

Later that afternoon, I burst into Tabitha's bedroom.

"Really, Sarah, could you please knock," she said, irritably. "We've separate rooms, now." Still not used to her new room I admired the exuberant pink and red flowered wallpaper, matching thick drapes, and bedspread with pillows mounded high on the white framed bed. She even had white bedside tables, a filigreed vanity, two wardrobes, and a carved

4

full-length mirror. Just last month, we had moved from a cramped cottage to the grand manor house that Father built adjacent to his foundry. Better to oversee his thriving business, he claimed, but we all knew that the grand manor was built to appease Mother's burning desire to climb socially. I was fairly certain Father loathed the pretentiousness of it all.

Tabitha perched upon her new vanity stool, brushing her chestnut-coloured hair. Three years older than my sixteen years, she should have been courting a young gentleman by now. Mother had become anxious about her prospects, openly worrying that she might become an old maid.

I sat on the edge of her bed and let out a long sigh wishing I could spend the afternoon riding, instead of preparing for the evening ahead. "Are you excited for the ball tonight?" I said, pretending to be interested, when actually I would have preferred to stay home. But it was a very important night for Tabitha.

"Mother said it will be my coming out, of sorts," she said, the eagerness in her voice conveying her deepest hope that her luck was about to change. I struggled not to laugh at the preposterous notions Mother put into her head: that Tabitha could be a debutante, as if we lived in London.

"Have you ever thought of not obeying Mother?"

She turned to me, eyes darkening. "When will you come to your senses. We have to do as Mother dictates. She knows best. As she says, 'The success of one's husband and the children we give him are the most sought-after achievements for a young woman.' We have no choice."

"But why? It's absolutely ridiculous to think that way here in the colonies. We left England. Why can't a woman achieve something in her own right?"

"And what would that be, dear sister? Pray tell."

"I'm not interested in a ladies' life. My desire is…" I hesitated, then straightened my back and continued, "to run my own enterprise. I don't know what it'll be yet, but I know I can do it. Father discusses the foundry's affairs with me all the time."

A tiny chuckle of laughter grew in my sister's throat, but she strangled it, once realizing by the set of my jaw, that I was deadly serious. Her eyes softened, her mouth composing into the all-knowing superior smile of an older-much-wiser sister.

"You know that would be impossible. Do you expect to take over the foundry one day?" She looked at me with startled eyes.

"No, of course not, that's not what I meant," I said, frantically searching for a way to express my ambition, while knowing full-well that I had no idea what I wanted.

Taking advantage of my hesitation, she jumped in to argue her side of our long-standing debate about a woman's role in society. "You can't possibly own a business. As a woman you can't own property. And men won't do business with you, it is just not done. The only women who have small enterprises are those in the lower classes who do laundry and other household tasks. Or dressmakers. You can't possibly be thinking of doing that!"

"No, of course not. Although I would enjoy the look on Mother's face if I announced I was running a laundry out of the house." My joke managed to break the tension, allowing me a moment to arrange my thoughts. "I'm fully aware of the restrictions of being a woman, but I feel capable of so much more, if only I could free myself of Mother's ridiculous expectations."

Her brow creased and I rushed on to explain. "I'm so sorry, I didn't mean to be insulting. Being a wife and mother are perfect for you. It was all you ever talked about when we were little girls. You were the one who played with dolls and hosted pretend tea parties, while I was outside in the mud playing with neighbourhood boys."

She laughed at the childhood memories, but her mouth returned to its taut thin-lipped expression of concern. "It's not just Mother. It's what everyone expects of us. It's a reflection of the important standards we brought with us from England, standards that are re-enforced by the minister every Sunday. You know what Mother says—"

Cutting her off, I leapt to my feet, my chin jutted out and my chest thrust upward, "'We left England; however, we must never leave the best of British ways behind us,'" I said, using Mother's most pretentious accent.

"Oh really. Must you be so disrespectful?" Tabitha scolded, but the edges of her mouth turned upward.

Sighing, I flung myself onto her bed. "What rubbish. In England, we lived in a small two-room cottage. We weren't part of society at all. I loathe the idea of becoming a perfect lady. But don't mistake me, I'm not so naïve as to think I can do this on my own. I will need the support of a husband. I'm determined to get what I want, if only I can find the right man willing to help me." Simply hearing my ambition stated out loud made it sound possible.

Without warning, Mother burst into Tabitha's room.

"Really, does anyone knock," Tabitha said, muttering quietly to herself.

"Girls, I have wonderful news," Mother said, in the acquired accent she believed reflected well upon her as an authentic high society lady. "The Prince of Wales will be attending the ball tonight." Mother was extremely short and rather stout. Her choice of a multi-paneled, multi-coloured gown with a high-necked ruffled bodice made her look like a chubby court jester. All she needed was the pointed hat with a bell attached.

"Sarah, will you ever stop finding everything so silly. This is a serious matter."

She turned to Tabitha who had adopted her familiar supplicant posture in Mother's presence—slightly bent shoulders and head bowed. Mother snatched the hairbrush out of Tabitha's hand and proceeded to vigorously brush her hair, causing my sister to flinch with every stroke. "Now, Tabitha, this is your big opportunity. Sit up straight and listen to me. I have identified the most interesting gentlemen prospects for you to meet. And with the Prince making an appearance at the ball, they are *all* bound to be attending." Unbeknownst to herself, Mother's accent kept slipping back to her native, not-so-fine Yorkshire, "The pretty girls will be competing to dance with the Prince, hoping to become the next Princess of Wales. So, while they are distracted, you have a much better chance of attracting a suitor."

I winced at her cruel assumption that the Prince would never be interested in my sister, but I was far too familiar with the litany of shortcomings frequently noted about Tabitha. Mother would often exclaim in puzzlement, "Goodness, my dear, you are taller than most men now. And those wide shoulders and big feet..." Then she would remind us that Tabitha had an attractive face even though her jaw and forehead were slightly too broad, but her full figure held enough allure to attract the courtship of a wealthy gentleman.

As usual, completely unaware of the insult to Tabitha, Mother continued, "...in particular, you must meet Albert Whittingham, newly arrived from England. His family is very wealthy, I hear, investing heavily in the new railway, the one running north. He is building a mansion overlooking the river *and* the lake. I hear it will be the grandest estate in the region. He must be looking for a wife to share such a big home." Each point of Mother's lecture was emphasized by a rough stroke of the brush.

I half-listened. We felt sorry for Mother. When we had crossed the ocean our older brother, William, died during the voyage. The loss of her only male child consumed Mother with guilt. It had been her idea to immigrate here. I often found her staring out the window with tears in her eyes, and, when I reached out my hand to console her, she would swat it away and dab at her eyes, then start lecturing about how we girls must marry well to generate the right successor for the family's growing enterprise. But I suspected she yearned more for her own elevated status. It wasn't clear where Father stood on the matter of succession. The one time I overheard him respond to Mother's badgering about an heir, he snapped that he was far too busy working to worry about what happened after he was dead.

"Now girls, please dress for the evening," Mother said, stroking Tabitha's shoulder gently and then turning toward me. "Sarah, you are to be a respectable young lady tonight. Do not do anything to threaten your reputation." She walked over to me, her eyes softening, wrinkling gently at the corners, an expression she reserved for me alone. "Remember, you are the pretty one. I have high hopes for you. Is that clear?"

I sat up straight and met her controlling stare. "Of course, Mother."

She scurried out of the room, her bustle bobbing dangerously from side to side. I collapsed onto the bed, smothering my face in a pillow to stifle a strange desire to laugh and cry at the same time.

My sister was now struggling to pin her hair.

"You know, we have a maid who could do that for you, Tabby."

"I'd rather not ask. Really, why do we need so many servants? Help me instead, please, darling."

Moving behind her where she sat at the vanity, I twisted her hair into a tight bun and started pinning it in place, laughter bubbling up. "And, the other day, when Father refused to hire footmen, she said, 'Very well, I will wait until we have a new carriage, then I'll insist, Bertrand.' The look on Father's face."

Now laughing too, Tabitha spluttered as she tried mimicking our father. "'For God's sake Alice, I need to build a stable first. And no one has footmen! Where do you think we live?'"

Sobering, I met her gaze in the mirror. "I absolutely must choose the man I marry." My thoughts drifted back to the parade earlier today. "And I might just find a husband who truly excites me."

She patted the vanity stool beside her, then draped an arm around my shoulders. "Is this because of what happened today, with that Scot? I saw you staring."

"What? No, of course not. But, tell me something." I pulled away from her, looking into her eyes. "Does it hurt you terribly when Mother says I am the pretty one?"

She sighed. "Oh, I'm used to it by now. I know I've failed her. Yes, I have," she said, ignoring my protest. "Not pretty enough, not smart enough, not Godly enough, not good enough. I will never attract the right husband. But you . . ." She held me by the chin and turned both our faces to the mirror, "Look at you."

I never paid much attention to my appearance, much to Mother's chagrin. Now, forced to look at my reflection, I frowned at my unruly hair, upturned nose and pouting lips.

Tabitha met my eyes in the reflection. "Once I am married, Mother's attention will turn to you. You are beautiful. And you are to be her finest achievement."

***

That evening, we stood at the entrance to the new ballroom.

"Mr. and Mrs. Bertrand Benjamin Denton and daughters," the herald announced, as my parents entered the grand ballroom of Victoria Hall. A few heads turned in our direction and glanced away. Mother, compressed into her ornate bejeweled ball gown with the assistance of a straining corset, led us in on Father's arm, acting as if she were Queen Victoria herself. I overheard him mutter to her, "*Bertrand*! My name is *Bertie*, for God's sake."

Head held high she whispered loudly, "You would not want anyone mistaking you for the Prince."

Flabbergasted by the ridiculous notion that anyone would use the family nickname of *Bertie* to address His Royal Highness in public, Father looked around anxiously to see if anyone else had overheard his wife's remark.

As Tabitha and I crossed the threshold behind our parents, heads turned back toward us, lingering, making me feel ill at ease. My hands fluttered to my waist to make sure the embroidered shawl Mother had hastily found remained in place, concealing my breasts. At first, Mother had been shocked to see the snugness of my new gown, and further inspected me as if I were her prized mare. A broad smile crept over her face. "This is not the time for you to shine my dear. Tonight is Tabitha's night," she said, securing the shawl and smiling with self-satisfaction.

The ominous message in that smile stayed with me as I now walked, tentatively, beside my sister into the ballroom. Tabitha slipped her hand into the crook of my arm, reassuring me. "Here we go, darling."

The gown I had been forced to wear was so awkward, I thought I might stumble. Made of a soft purple silk with multiple crinolines that created a conical swirl of shimmering fabric, the gown cascaded from my waist down to the floor. The bodice, now hidden under the shawl, was pleated with a modest neckline and delicate lace-trimmed cap sleeves. I wore matching full-length evening gloves.

Awkward and completely out of place, I followed my parents into the magnificent ballroom as graciously as I could manage, while my sturdy sister held me steady. My gaze was immediately drawn upward by the tall pale-paneled walls and vertical windows, rising high to the ceiling, all of which created a sensation of soaring. The ceiling was painted with large circles of floral patterns. Stunning chandeliers hung low, thousands of candles casting sparkling light upon all of us below. Over each of the large entry doors, dark wood trim culminated in a sharp peak. An honour guard stood at attention on either side of each entrance. Hundreds of excited voices created an atmosphere of anticipation in the ballroom redolent with the smells of lavender, cigars, whisky, and nervous sweat.

I caught a glimpse of the Drury men, even more striking in their dress kilts. My stomach jumped at the possibility of seeing the one who had winked at me.

Mother swept to the centre of the room on Father's arm, nodding acknowledgment to anyone who had the misfortune to catch her eye. "Oh, this is glorious," she said, nodding her head regally toward Mrs. Gilbert, one of the finer ladies in town. Visibly caught off-guard, Mrs. Gilbert looked past Mother, pretending she hadn't noticed her. Undaunted, Mother continued her progress, with Father acquiescent at her side, while we dutiful daughters trailed behind like dressed-up dolls.

Our procession came to an abrupt halt, causing me to bump into Father's back. He turned to smile at me, just as Mother poked him with her fan to get his attention. "Here we are, this will do splendidly." She had positioned the two of them in line with the mayor and other local dignitaries, making it appear as if they were part of the formal receiving line for the Prince. Father looked mortified by her presumptive behaviour.

As instructed earlier by Mother, Tabitha and I joined the other young girls clustered along one of the walls. I stood outside the group, bored by their silly chatter.

Unlike me, Tabitha joined in eagerly, soon surrounded by her many friends. We all attended the grammar school run by the Anglican Church, where only the daughters of the finer families were allowed to attend.

Much to Mother's disappointment, I didn't have any friends. "But Sarah, darling," she would say, more times than I could count, "you must make friends of the daughters of the best families. Many of those girls have brothers, one of whom may one day be interested in courting you." Perhaps it was Mother's persistent nagging that made me resist friendships, or perhaps it was much more basic than that—I simply could not accept the superficial life they held so dear.

From my distant vantage point, I watched my sister. She was radiant in her gown made of the most stunning gold satin, overlaid with lace and embroidery. The fitted bodice with the small cap sleeves had a low-cut neckline that flattered her full figure and drew the eye away from her broad shoulders.

A sudden fanfare made me jump, and the orchestra fell silent. We all turned in unison toward the sound. From where I stood, all I could see was the top of the Prince's head, while the Town Crier's voice boomed across the room. "His Royal Highness, the Prince of Wales." The trumpets blasted another tribute, and His Royal Highness proceeded down the receiving line of bowing and curtseying dignitaries. The crowd shifted a little to reveal Mother nudging Father into position closer to the Mayor. At school, girls made fun of Mother's blatant attempts at social climbing. No doubt, after this performance tonight, I would be the target, yet again, of their rude comments.

I slipped away from the line of girls and circled the back of the hall where the crowd was thinner. With no better idea about what to do, I stood admiring the desserts table and idly fingered its fine tablecloth.

I felt the air move around me and a whiff of cedar and pine scented the air. It was him. Thrilled more than startled, I spun around and looked up into his eyes. He bent forward to speak softly, nearly touching my ear. "You're the most beautiful woman I've ever laid my eyes upon."

My face burning, I was stunned into silence. All I could do was stare into those penetrating eyes and marvel at the candlelight dancing like tiny little stars within them.

"Sarah, what are you doing?" The unexpected sound of my sister's voice made me jump, just as it always does when she catches me doing something wrong.

A little shaken, I retreated to her side. The two of us gaped at the magnificent Scot standing before us. His broad shoulders were emphasized by the wide cut of his formal Prince Charlie jacket and vest. His long black curls, captured loosely in a red satin ribbon, framed his firm, clean shaven jaw line and high cheek bones.

I furtively glanced at the muscled thick legs revealed below the hem of his kilt and wondered about what lay beneath the tartan cloth. I realized, too late, that he had followed my glance and was flashing that wicked smile at me again, causing my blush to grow to a deep dark red. I heard my sister gasp. She grasped my arm.

"Allow me to introduce myself, ladies. I'm Joseph Drury. Joe to my friends. So pleased to make the acquaintance of the lovely Denton daughters," he said, over the swelling sound of the orchestra now playing, nodding to each of us in turn. His voice was deep and resonant, with a slight Scottish lilt.

"Pleased to meet you, sir, now we must return to our parents." Tabitha spoke politely, but assertively, while trying to push me further away from him.

I remained fixed to the floor, unable to move or think.

"Beg your pardon. I was hopin' Sarah might do me the honour of a dance. If, of course, you'd allow it, Tabitha?" Joe extended a huge, calloused hand toward me.

Much to my surprise, I allowed my delicate hand to be swallowed up within his hot flesh.

Tabitha squeezed my arm until it hurt, trying to free my hand from his grasp. "How dare he speak to us in such a familiar way," she whispered harshly in my ear, "when we've not been properly introduced. Let go of his hand."

It was not Tabitha's urgent whispers, but the sight of Mother rapidly approaching that made me snatch my hand back.

"There you are." Mother grabbed our arms, pinching so hard we both flinched. Squaring off in front of Joe, she looked up the entire height of him, disgust etched onto her pinched face. "Pardon us, Mr...?"

"Mr. Joseph Drury." Joe met her eyes and gallantly offered his hand.

Mother refused his hand, staring at it as if it were a snake. "I want to make myself perfectly clear, young man. Stay away from my daughters." Her face was florid. I stared at the floor and allowed myself to be dragged back to the center of the ballroom and deposited at Father's side.

"Do not let her out of your sight. I must find Mr. Whittingham, so Tabitha can be properly introduced. Keep Sarah away from the likes of that Drury *person,* or her reputation will be ruined. He is uncouth, uneducated and... a Presbyterian, for God's sake!" A devoted Anglican, Mother's eyes rounded at the horrible taint of being associated with such a lesser religion. She turned to my sister and said, "Come Tabitha."

As Mother and Tabitha disappeared into the crowd, Father put his arm around me. I sunk into his embrace, a welcome salve after a confrontation with Mother. He steered me to a quiet corner away from the orchestra, finding comfortable chairs for us. He sighed, but there was a twinkle in his eyes. "Darling daughter, what have you been up to?"

Feeling rather wobbly, it felt good to sit down. "Nothing," I said, looking beseechingly into his eyes.

"I doubt that. Why is Mother so upset?" He tried to look stern, but his mouth curled up.

Twisting in the chair to face him, I grabbed his hand. "It wasn't my fault, he surprised me…and then, I was just being polite. Just as Mother taught us." My voice sounded much too childish.

"Joseph Drury, you mean?" His faint smile had disappeared.

"Yes, I can't help it if he spoke to me. What was I supposed to do, kick him in the shin and run away?"

Father broke into the full deep laugh he was known for. "No, I don't suppose that would have been appropriate, but you know how Mother feels about farmers, and a Scot to boot?"

"The Drurys are very successful."

"But Joe doesn't have a very good reputation."

"Since when do you listen to gossip?"

"Your mother has extensive knowledge about all the eligible men. I believe it's her main purpose at the tea socials."

I giggled, hoping he wouldn't say more. "Don't make me laugh."

We sat in silence for a few moments as we watched Mother and Tabitha approaching Mrs. Gilbert, who appeared to be monopolizing a young gentleman. "What have you learned about this Mr. Whittingham Mother is hunting down for Tabitha?"

"Not much. But your mother would be happy with any gentleman who is willing to court your sister."

I sighed deeply and watched as Tabitha smiled at this stranger. Mercifully, he was as tall as my sister, but with a surprising slight build for his height. I didn't like the look of him: his narrow face hosted a pointy nose and long mutton chops that emphasized his tight little mouth. The way he leaned down over her outstretched hand made me tense that he might bite it.

Father grasped my hand. "Stay away from that Joseph Drury. He will bring you nothing but grief."

Chapter 2

Not long after that evening, I stopped Father at our back door on his way to the farmer's market.

"What is it, dear? I'm in a hurry."

"Father, may I go with you?" The market was the place where farmers and townsfolk mingled the most.

He glanced out the door and fiddled with his hat. "Please be quick about it. I don't want to miss the best prices." I had to walk quickly to keep up with him as he dashed toward the old wagon kept behind a shed in the back yard, well-hidden from nosy neighbours, and sparing Mother being embarrassed by its shabbiness. Most gentlemen sent a servant, but father insisted upon negotiating with the farmers himself.

A short while later, as we approached the town hall, we heard the din of the crowd and smelled smoke. Arriving at the well-trodden earth behind Victoria Hall, a riot of colours and smells welcomed us: stalls of green, yellow, and red vegetables; stacks of wheat, barley, and hay; the sharp burnt smell of roasting chestnuts, the spiced scent of hot cider, and the acrid smoke from small bonfires. Shielding my eyes from the bright sun, I scanned the long lines of overflowing wagons and the corrals of chickens and ducks, hoping I might catch a glimpse of his wild black hair.

"Is there anything in particular that interests you?" For a moment I thought my father might have read my mind and could not answer.

"Oh… I was interested in finding some new hair ribbons," I said, smoothing my windblown locks and glancing around for a likely vendor. "Oh look, I see a woman over there."

I was off the wagon and on my way before he could say anything. Pushing through the crowd, I reached a plump rosy-cheeked woman with baskets full of colourful ribbons. Smiling at her in greeting, I fingered though the silky fabrics, all the while glancing around.

"There you are my beauty."

I turned to gaze into his rugged face. His dark beard had grown in and his neck was smeared with fresh-smelling dirt; his penetrating eyes and wicked smile rendered me speechless again. All I could do was grin at him, feeling the heat reddening my cheeks.

"I tried to find you, I even stopped by your house." At my startled look, he nodded. "And I saw you the other day, out ridin' but gone before I could chase you."

Leaning down toward me, I thought he was about to kiss my cheek. Instead, he reached behind me—his breath hot on my face and smelling faintly of whisky—to select a vibrant red ribbon. "Turn 'round."

I obeyed him.

He stepped in close. His woodsy smell mingling with whisky was a scent that would always make me think of him. He captured my curls in his big hands and wrapped the scarlet ribbon around them, the scratch of his rough hands on my neck sending shivers down my spine.

"There. A beautiful ribbon for a beautiful woman." He laid his hands upon my shoulders and turned me to face him.

Instead of his face, it was Mother's that I saw, some distance away, getting out of her carriage, her finger jabbing towards me as she shouted at my stricken father.

Finally, finding my voice, I said, "Please go. My father is coming."

"Good. I can have a word with him. I'm very serious 'bout my intentions." He turned toward Father, with an eager smile.

I pushed my hands against his solid chest. "No, please, my parents will never allow it. Speaking to my father will only make matters worse."

I thought he might stride towards my father; instead he quickly whispered in my ear, "Meet me in the forest. I'll send word," then disappeared into the crowd.

I allowed Father to take my arm and push me roughly towards Mother who was holding open the carriage door as though waiting to trap a wild animal. *How had she known?* She flung herself into the carriage behind me, scolding me as though I were five years old and caught playing in the mud. I proclaimed my innocence all the way home under her threats to lock me in the house if I were to ever see Joe again.

When we finally reached home, I ran upstairs to Tabitha's room, seeking the comfort only my sister could give. Forgetting to knock, I flung open the door. She was reclined upon her flowered bedspread, and I was struck by the contrast between its exuberant colours and my sister's pale skin.

"Oh, really. Could you please knock."

"Oh right, sorry." I flopped onto the mound of soft pillows beside her, a puff of lavender wafting around us.

She scanned my face, reading me like a book. "You are in trouble with Mother again."

"It wasn't my fault, he surprised me."

"Who surprised you?" She sat up. "Not that Joe Drury person?"

"Well, he is better than your dreadful catch."

"You're such a child." She lurched off the bed and stomped over to stare out a window.

I leapt off the bed and grabbed her arm. "Please tell me you're not serious about courting that revolting Albert."

She yanked her arm free, staring at me. "Of course, I am. Mother is delighted that I have the potential for such a good match and so am I." She returned her gaze to the window, her chin lifted with determination.

I shoved her away from the window, forcing her to look at me. "Do not do this to please Mother. Find a man who thrills you every time you see him. There's still time for you to find true love."

"What do you know of love?" she snapped at me.

My face reddened and gave my feelings away. "My God, do you imagine yourself in love with that…that…*farmer*?" she asked in a shocked whisper.

I immediately dropped my gaze and ran from her room.

***

One week later, I paced my bedroom, not understanding why Joe had not contacted me. I peeked out the window hoping to catch a glimpse of him. Then thinking myself ridiculous, I marched to the opposite wall to glare at the climbing rose wallpaper, my eyes following it to the ceiling, my head falling back, and my mouth wide open in a silent scream.

At the sound of a gentle knock, I sprang to open my bedroom door.

"A wee lad just delivered this for ye, Miss Sarah," said a young maid as she handed me a note.

Snatching it away from her, I closed the door rudely. I ripped open the note. *"Take the north road and meet me at the forest by the creek."*

***

I galloped through the town streets, my riding skirt flapping up over my knees and my bonnet thrown back. I could sense the fluttering of curtains as the town's gossips judged my unseemly behaviour of sitting astride a horse instead of the more ladylike side-saddle posture. I could just imagine the shaking of heads and murmured comments to Mother at the next tea social.

Reaching the forest's edge, I slowed my horse to a walk and waited by the babbling creek, watching the road for him. A sudden cracking sound startled me. Turning around I saw him there, standing by his horse.

"There you are my darlin'." His arms were spread wide, and he flashed his wicked grin. "Follow me, I've found a place for us."

I let Joe take the reins and lead us along a forest trail into a small clearing with tall grass and fallen leaves, hidden amongst the dense pine trees. He tied our horses to a tree and reached up for me. I fell into his arms. When my feet touched the ground, he did not let me go, instead pulling me into a tight embrace.

"Oh, my darlin', I've dreamt of how you'd feel when I first held you," Joe whispered in my ear, the sound of his Scottish lilt curling around my heart.

I eagerly wrapped my trembling arms around the breadth of him, my hands barely able to reach beyond his waist, and inhaled his now familiar scent.

Breaking our embrace, he gestured behind him. "Please sit, my darlin'. I have brought some bread an' cheese."

I sat on a blanket he had spread over the ground, a soft layer of leaves and branches beneath it to cushion us from the damp ground. A wiser girl might have been afraid to be hidden in the woods with this man. Instead, its secret nature made it all the more thrilling.

"Would you like a drop of whisky? It's marvelous with this cheese," he said, gesturing with a flask held toward me. Father allowed us a taste of whisky on occasion, but this early in the day, it was unthinkable. Joe was looking at me as if it was the most normal thing in the world.

It suddenly struck me that he must be a lot older than me. Maybe ten years? That would explain his drinking in the morning. Wishing to appear grown-up, I nodded enthusiastically. When he handed me a rough pewter cup filled to the brim, I downed it all. The burning in my throat caused me to erupt into a fit of coughing and gasping.

Handing me a dirty handkerchief, he patted me softly on my back. "Are you all right?"

Unable to speak, I nodded, enjoying the warmth of the whisky in my belly. It was relaxing me. I gave him my cup for a refill.

"Now, what shall we talk about?" he said, while he poured.

I looked away from him so I could talk and blathered on and on about whatever came to mind. "Father had the most extraordinary thing happen yesterday. No doubt you've heard of Crossen Car, they produce the highest quality railway cars in the land. Just marvelous, elegant and well appointed. Well, Father just received an enormous order for iron fittings from the company. It will keep our foundry running for some time to come. Father shares much of his business dealings with me. And I help him keep his account records. He says I have a fine mind for enterprise."

I kept on babbling, trying to prevent myself from reaching out to touch his thick dark curls as he sat so close. The air simmered between us.

When he touched my shoulder, I looked into his eyes. "A rare beauty, and clever too." He leaned in close to me, his eyes brimming with desire. Slowly, he put my cup down and reached for me, pulling me toward him. He kissed me gently on the mouth.

Relaxed by the whisky, I let him kiss me again, and I kissed him back. He paused, stroking my cheek. I gazed into the blue of his eyes, flushing to the roots of my hair. An image of my mother flashed before me, her face shocked and horrified at my sitting on a blanket in the pine forest, kissing Joseph Drury.

Yet, I cared for nothing, only for Joe.

Chapter 3

During the weeks that followed, I walked around in a daze, and scolded myself for being unable to resist each time the maid brought his note to me. No matter how many times I told myself I would not do it, I still found myself hidden in the forest with this forbidden man. As winter took hold, the deep snowfalls made it impossible to meet. Missing him so, my nights became consumed by dreaming of loving him—hot and restless—frustrated as such strange desires took over my body whenever I thought of his kisses.

Finally, spring arrived, and we were able to resume our forest courtship. By summertime I had fallen deeply in love. Now, there was no way forward and, certainly, no way back.

One hot summer morning, we lay upon a blanket wrapped in each other's arms, kissing and caressing. When I felt his hardness against me, I froze. "Stop Joe, please."

He let out a shuddering sigh, raising himself onto one elbow to look into my face.

I tried to smile, but started to cry instead, surprised at how quickly my emotions got away from me. "It just seems so impossible."

He stood slowly and raised me up to join him. He took my shoulders and stared deeply into my eyes. "I love you. I would never hurt you."

A slight quiver crept into my stomach. This was the first time he had spoken words of love to me. I clasped his huge hand in mine and started running my fingers over the rough callouses. "It's just that…oh, you know."

"Your mother doesn't think I'm good enough."

I felt like choking and my jaw hurt. I hated acknowledging the impossibility of our future, its reality poisoning our otherwise idyllic times together. Life was completely unfair. If only Joe were an English gentleman, Mother would be salivating behind the drawing room doors, eager for a proposal of marriage.

"Listen. I've an idea that might change her mind. No, no listen. Just please, listen for once," he said, gently touching a wide finger to my lips to stop any protest. "My da has given me some land, well not exactly given it to me, but he says I can work it 'til I earn enough to buy it from him, at a fair price, mind. It's prime land, right by the water, the railway runs straight through the bottom of it. It's marvelous land."

A tiny glimmer of hope began to stir in my heart. Perhaps if he became a wealthy landowner, Mother could be appeased. "How wonderful. I'm happy for you."

"You see, I don't meet with you just to feel your body pressed up against mine." He winked. "I've grown to love you and to realize how bright and able you are—a woman with a strong will of her own. I'm a hard worker. I can do anythin' when it comes to farmin'. And I think I'm really good at it. But I'm not good at keepin' track of things. I can't figure out my sums and I'm hopeless at plannin' very far ahead. . ." Joe abruptly knelt in front of me. He took my hands in his and gazed at me with his blue eyes. I struggled to catch my breath. "I'm not doing a very good job of makin' this sound appealin'. My darlin', I can't live without you. You'll make all the difference. You'll make me so much better than I'd ever be on my own. And you'll accomplish anythin' you set your heart on, I'm certain of it. Please, marry me, Sarah."

Had I really found a man who saw me capable of so much more than being a mere wife? Joe made it sound easy. I started to imagine building my own dreams within his dream of this promised land. He sounded so certain of success, that I was swept up in his excitement. My nagging doubts began to whither. Just for a moment, I was convinced that we could be together, and that I could have it all.

Then I thought of Mother. And Father. Their direction had been more than clear, and I had defied them both. Meeting his intense gaze, I placed a hand gently on either side of his face and looked deeply into his eyes so bright with visions of our future together. "Joe, I love you, too. And I love the idea of the life we could build together. I want to marry you, and if the decision was mine to make, I would say *yes*."

He held me at arms' length, his eager eyes searching my face. "Then say *yes*."

"I don't think Mother would be convinced no matter what you promise."

"Then come with me. Right now. I'll show you my land. You'll see."

***

Taking forest trails to avoid the public roads, I followed behind Joe through the thick woods until we finally arrived at the lands of the Drury family. The sun was now at its full height and the heat of the day was upon us. My underarms felt wet, and my hair stuck to my head under my bonnet.

We halted our horses in the shade of the forest's edge, protecting ourselves from the sun. I cast my eyes over lush fields of grain swaying lazily in the gentle breeze. My nostrils filled with the earthy, sweet smell of ripening barley as I took in the enormity of the land. No wonder the Drurys were rumoured to be wealthy. "Oh, my Lord. It's magnificent."

"It's a marvelous sight, isn't it," he said, sitting high in his saddle, justifiably proud of what lay before us. "Da exports barley to American distilleries and breweries across the lake. He got the idea from farmers in the next county. My da always says, as long as men drink whisky and beer, we'll make money."

"And this is the land you farm?" It was incredible, Joe must be a wealthy man already.

"Well… actually, that land is farther over." He pointed past the fields, in the direction of another pine forest. "This is my da's land. But it shows you what can be done." With a wink of an eye, he kicked his horse and was off, yelling over his shoulder, "Follow me, and I'll show you my land."

Eager for a run, my horse broke into a full gallop with only the slightest touch of my heels. I gained on Joe quickly and flew past him, laughing, nearly losing my bonnet to the wind. Accepting the challenge, Joe galloped past me a moment later, heading toward the forest. In no time at all, we crossed the field and reached the other side. We slowed, crossing a railway line that cut through the land and entered another heavily wooded area.

Riding behind him, watching the undulating sway of his horse, I began to doubt we would ever find his promised land. We followed another barely visible trail to reach a lake. Hot and tired, we dismounted and walked through huge tree trunks to the water's edge. This close to the water, ancient pine trees had grown to massive proportions. I felt dwarfed and somewhat humbled by their majesty.

After watering the horses and filling our canteens, we stood on the shoreline, while we drank deeply and admired the gentle rippling of the lake. Joe pulled out his whisky flask and added some to the water in his canteen, gesturing for me to do the same.

I was getting increasingly agitated by his behaviour. "Where exactly is this land?"

"We're standing on it!"

I stared at him quizzically, then spun around, seeing nothing but huge pines.

"The land starts here and goes for miles to the west and north. It's acres of land," he said, as he pointed in a less than precise manner, slightly encumbered by drinking from his canteen at the same time. "Did you think my da would give me land that'd been cleared?" He laughed heartily and winked at me again.

My jaw clenched, and I suddenly realized how little I knew about what life with Joe would be like. "How long will it take to clear and start farming?" I leaned back to look up the entire length of a giant tree nearby, making myself dizzy. How could such a tree be felled?

"Well, let's see," he said, scratching his head and taking another drink. "We have to fell the trees, that could take a year or two, then we burn the stumps and let them rot. That takes several years. So, I'm guessin' four, maybe five years."

I threw up my arms. This whole idea was futile. My parents would never agree to me marrying a farmer without a working farm, no matter what promise the land might hold. I should get back on my horse, head straight for home, and forget about this fanciful man. Instead, I remained staring at him. Tears brimmed my eyes. It was hopeless. My love for him was hopeless.

Finally realizing I was angry and upset, Joe drew me into his arms and chuckled. I struggled to free myself. "Calm down, my darlin'. I guess I went too far. My brothers and I have been clearin' the land for years. We'll each farm a section. I was just havin' you on."

Scrubbing tears from my eyes, I slapped his chest. "Joseph Drury, you are impossible. I demand to see this so-called farmland of yours. Right now."

A short while later, we emerged out the other side of what I now realized was a thick stand of pine forest between fields. A great expanse of burnt stumps spread out before us. The deep blue of the lake bordered it, a slash of railway tracks cut across it and it sloped upward to a stand of maple trees.

"I left the maples, it'll make a grand place for our manor," he said, gesturing up the hill, a broad smile on his face, one hand shading his eyes. "For now, I live in a settler's cottage my granda built years ago, over the other side of the hill. It'll take only a season or two to plough the land and yield crops. Come with me. Wait 'til you see the view from atop the hill."

Following behind Joe's horse, I carefully picked my way across the fields. At one point we dismounted, so I could feel the richness of the soil. When we reached the hilltop, we stood in the shade of the giant maples, holding hands. Even with the charred stumps, I could easily imagine the cultivated fields that would soon yield an abundance of crops.

"How long has your father owned this land?" I said, wondering why this felt too good to be true.

"Oh, for years, it was my granda who first acquired it. Now he's passed, my da owns it. This is the last of its kind for miles and miles around."

"Why doesn't he want it for himself?"

"Oh, my darlin', he has enough."

I resisted the urge to ask why he had not simply given the land to Joe. Why make him buy it? Perhaps the answer was obvious. This rich land with its close proximity to town and the harbour would be worth a small fortune. If I were to fall into Mother's bias against the Scots, I would have to assume his da was too miserly to give his land away to anyone, not even his own son. As I stood upon the hill, I decided that the intricacies of how Joe acquired this land would never be my concern, so I put it out of my mind. My thoughts shifted back to the land's potential. Gazing over the fields of black stumps, I imagined the possibilities. Such a vast acreage could support much more than barley crops. All sorts of enterprises could blossom here, including one of my own invention.

Suddenly, it dawned on me that I was looking at my destiny. My dreams could be born here and thrive. But I was no fool. An extremely difficult challenge remained: how to convince my parents to give me their permission to marry Joseph Drury, the very man they forbade me to see? Mother would never be convinced that a Scottish farmer was my best choice for a husband, no matter how impressive the land he had, nor how rich his family. Above all, she would be too furious at my disobedience to even listen to me.

My father, on the other hand, would likely come around to support my decision. He had often commented on the value of farmland. "After all, everyone needs to eat. Farmers with vision will become very wealthy as this country grows," he would often say, sounding wistful. Casting my eyes over this fertile land, my ambition started to take form. With Joe's knowledge of the land and my imagination, our success would be assured. We would create a farming empire out of this land. Father was sure to grasp its promise. But even if my father were convinced, he would not take on the inevitable battle with Mother. Nor should he. That battle was mine to fight and win.

Turning toward Joe, I took his rough hands in mine and stared into his eyes, their blue vibrant in the summer sun. "Yes, I will marry you."

He crushed me into him, smothering my face with kisses, tears brimming in his eyes. "I will ride in today and ask your father for your hand?"

"No. Not yet," I said, suddenly needing to take control of the situation. My parents would be outraged if he simply knocked on their door and asked whether he could marry me. The answer was sure to be a resounding *No*. "First, I must work on a plan to give them no choice but to agree. For now, let us keep our commitment to marry a secret."

***

Returning home that day, I found the household in an uproar. Albert Whittingham had proposed to Tabitha, and the wedding planning was already in full swing. Mother was in her glory, sending servants in all directions with messages and errands. I took the stairs two at a time, my skirt held up to my waist to avoid tripping, eager to learn if she was truly happy. Perhaps I had been wrong about Albert—wealthy, Oxford-educated with a plummy accent, and always impeccably dressed—he was beyond Mother's wildest expectations for Tabitha. Even Father had formed a bond with Albert over a shared passion for the rail industry. Yet, my sister remained uneasy in Albert's presence, neither of them expressing the tiniest bit of affection toward the other. Too distracted by my own love affair, I had lost interest in their courtship. If they were now engaged, things must have changed.

Reaching my sister's bedroom door, I thought it might just be the right time to finally share my secret with her. There was so much more to tell her now; all my dreams were coming true. I was about to create a farming empire with the man I loved. Tabitha was sure to understand. Especially now that she had seemingly found love. Maybe she could even help convince Mother and Father that Joe was the right choice for me.

After all, she was about to fulfil Mother's dream of having a wealthy son-in-law from a prestigious English family. Surely, one successful daughter was enough.

Bursting in, I came to an abrupt halt at the sight of Tabitha. She sat at her vanity, staring blankly into the mirror, while holding a hairbrush before her as though it were a weapon, the grip so tight her knuckles were white and her arm rigid.

"What's the matter?"

As if someone had slapped her face, she lowered the brush and forced a smile. It was more of a grimace than a genuine smile. "Nothing. You've heard?" Her voice was hollow. She stared at me, her eyes vacant. "Yes, I am... to wed Albert." She faltered, her shoulders collapsing.

I rushed across the room and reached out to her. "It is not too late. You don't have to marry him."

She flung the hairbrush onto the vanity, then rounded on me. "Stop being so impossibly naïve. Of course, I *have* to marry Albert. Can't you see how pleased Mother is with me? Now stop all this nonsense. Be happy for me, I am getting married."

Chapter 4

On her wedding day, Tabitha wore an imported English wedding gown of white satin silk, with appliquéd lace overtop a bustle and crinoline under-structure, which forced the skirt into an enormous circle of fabric floating just above the floor. A crown of delicate pink flowers adorned her head, topping a white organza wedding veil cascading down her back and trailing along the floor. Father helped Tabitha maneuver the heavy, unwieldy gown and veil down the aisle, no easy feat as he could barely reach her hand over the expanse of rigid crinoline.

Mother beamed with pride, fanning her flushed face and savouring the admiring glances of the elite society she so adored. I imagined a sturdy rope hauling her prodigious bulk up her precious social ladder as my father handed their eldest daughter over to a man Tabitha clearly loathed. At least, she could suffer in comfort, I thought, peevishly.

At the altar, standing beside Tabitha as her maid of honour, I noticed her hands trembled as she handed me her pink flower bouquet to hold. After the minister had welcomed the congregants and mumbled a few prayers and homilies, he proceeded with the marriage ceremony. When her turn came, Tabitha cast her eyes to the floor and began to stumble over her marriage vows. "I take thee, Albert Bartholomew Whittingham, to be my lawfully wedded h…husband, to have and to…to hold, and to…obey…" unable to continue, Tabitha lapsed into a shaky silence.

Albert's grip tightened on her hand. From my vantage point I had a clear view of his face. His narrowed eyes scrutinized the top of Tabitha's head as though she were some strange creature presented before him.

The tension became unbearable, forcing the minister to gently prod Tabitha to continue. Slowly, she raised her head to meet her betrothed's gaze. "Until death do us part."

"You may kiss the bride," the Minister said, clearly concerned about this new bride faltering before him. Albert leaned toward his new wife, tentatively. Tabitha shuddered slightly when their lips met. The church organ burst into a rapturous rendition of Mendelssohn's Wedding March, and the congregation applauded the newly married couple.

Oh, how I wished I could have helped her resist our mother, to understand that love was more important than wealth and prestige, and insist that if she waited for the right man, she could have it all. I had kept the news of my betrothal to Joe a secret from Tabitha. Now the sight of her so unhappy made me more determined than ever to marry the man I loved.

***

Later that evening, everyone had forgotten about me. Mother was consumed by the spectacle of Tabitha's wedding reception at the Arlington Hotel and Father was pre-occupied with host duties. I slipped away from the festivities to meet Joe. It was prearranged that we would meet for a few moments. He wanted to see me in my finery, as he called it. Given the excitement leading up to the wedding, we had not seen each other in two weeks, the longest we had ever gone without touching each other. I was excited to see him. And I had a plan.

"Just follow me," I said, as he stepped out of the darkness, reaching for me. Leading him through the dark town, we walked without speaking to my family home. On this warm August night, the house stood empty, the entire household attending or on duty at the reception. We stopped at the base of the stone path.

Joe turned toward me and cupped my face in his hands, gently tilting my head up to meet his gaze. "I know what you are planning, my darlin'. Is this the only way?"

The moonlight illuminated his handsome features and made his eyes sparkle.

"With Tabitha married, Mother will turn her attention to me," I said, my voice a little shaky. Despite being certain there was no other way, I hesitated, but just for a moment. Once done, there was no turning back. "We must make our move tonight. Before it is too late."

"And this is the only way to get them to agree?" he said, his voice full of trepidation. "It's just... why does it matter now? Tabitha has married a very rich man. Can't your mother be happy with that? What about your father? Can't we talk to him? I'd rather that, than have him furious with me for violating his daughter."

"Mother will never agree. By doing this," I gestured toward my house, "she'll have no choice." And hopefully, she would soon get over my betrayal.

I grasped his hand and guided him up the pathway and we entered my parents' home. I slammed the large oak front door shut, my heart pounding in my ears.

Joe pulled back, his apprehension growing as I drew him towards the intimacy of the stairway leading to our bedrooms. "But why here? Can't we meet in our place? We can take a blanket—"

I shook my head. "No. It must be tonight. And please Joe, let me pretend it is *our* wedding night, and I want you to make love to me in the sweetness of my own bed."

Joe pulled me against him. "My darlin', please don't look so scared. I won't hurt you." He consumed my mouth with his kiss. His newly found certainty steadied my resolve. Taking his hand again, I pulled him up the staircase toward my bedroom. He looked around in wonder at a house he would never be welcomed into, certainly not after we announced our news in a few months' time. Pushing him ahead of me, I closed the door and sucked in a quivering breath when he drew me into his arms.

Moonlight flooded in through my open windows providing a soft glow in the room. Gently, but firmly, he guided me backward toward the bed, kissing my mouth and face. When my legs butted up against the bed, I came to an abrupt stop, and he pressed into me. "Lie down, my darlin'."

Reclining amid the familiar smell of my bed, I gazed up at the forbidden man who would soon be my husband. He unbuttoned my bodice, lifting me gently to remove it. With tender care, he removed my gown and undergarments, his darkened eyes taking in every part of my trembling body. By the time I lay naked before him, my breath had quickened to such a degree I feared I would faint.

He leaned back to take in the full length of me. "You are more beautiful than I ever imagined." His voice was deep yet hushed. He began to remove his own clothes in a slow and deliberate manner, his gaze never leaving me.

In the light of the full moon, I watched as the secrets of what lay beneath his clothes were finally revealed. For a moment I wondered whether he was truly standing at the foot of my bed, or had I simply conjured him up as I had so often on those fevered sleepless nights. My gaze lingered on his muscled chest and arms, hesitating to drop downward and take in the fullness of his nakedness.

I gasped when I did.

Joe laughed and reached down to take hold of himself. "That's not the reaction I was hopin' for. Does the sight of it not please you?"

My face flushed with heat. "I had no idea…it is so…" I could not say that it was uglier than I had ever imagined. And so big. "I mean, I just don't see how this is… possible."

"My darlin', how I wish you'd stop sayin' that everythin' is impossible. We are here, aren't we? About to create our first child. I feel certain it will happen tonight. And I know it will be a boy."

1874

Chapter 5

The summer's day was unbearably hot, the air inside the shed thick with humidity and smelling of manure. Wiping sweat off my forehead with the sleeve of my filthy dress, I dug out another pitchfork of straw and shook it over the rotting, smelly floor. The fat sow was noisily eating her slops on the far side, and the chickens were fighting over the grain I had just scattered. Laying aside the pitchfork, I went outside, envying the cows out in the pasture lying motionless in the shade of the border trees. Opening the gate, I trudged across the hard-packed earth of the barnyard, lowered my sore body onto a rough bench in the shade of our half-finished dairy barn, and rubbed my aching back. The baby moved, and I quickly ran my dirty hands over the bulge under my threadbare skirt, worried about how I would keep working once I grew bigger. If only Joe would stay home more.

I glanced down the laneway hoping to see him. He made frequent trips into town, claiming he must have a commercial presence there. It was never clear what that meant, and why those trips were becoming more and more frequent, with him oftentimes spending the night. To keep the peace, I never challenged him, at least not too much. Lately, I was becoming more and more frustrated with his absences.

Leaning back against the rough barnboard, I stared at the rundown settler's cottage where we still lived. When I married Joe, I happily moved into this miserable shack, believing we would soon be building a beautiful manor house. It had been a fun and exciting adventure at first, living in such limited and primitive space, the novelty of it invigorating after the stifling preciousness of my parents' house. The ill-equipped kitchen, cramped parlour, and two slip rooms—each one barely wide enough for a bed—seemed quaint at first, as though we were truly pioneers. Now, the peeling front door and the dark hallway leading from it into the dreary parlour were grating to me. When our family kept growing, Joe added two extra bedrooms that helped us make room for a girl, recently arrived from Ireland, willing to work without pay, happy to have a roof over her head.

I sighed with relief at the sudden breeze cooling my face and watched as it rippled over the barley growing in the nearby field. These fields were the only part of Joe's promises that had come true; within two years, the burnt stumps and brush had been ploughed and planted and now produced abundant crops, fetching high prices from American distilleries and breweries. While Joe sowed the land, I learned how to run a dairy farm—milking the cows, making cheese, butter, and buttermilk, and selling the surplus. I grew more deeply into my little dairy and recently thought of a way of expanding it. But a year ago, Joe had stopped building the dairy barn upon which I now leaned, and had yet to give me a good reason why.

There were other things. I kept the farm records and knew that we made a good income each year. Why were our lives not better? I did not even know if we owned this land. Joe's father, Duff, used to visit often at first, despite his resentment and anger that Joe had married a spoiled town girl who was completely wrong for farm life. When his father stopped visiting last year, I asked my husband if something was wrong. He shrugged and walked away. I confess, at first it was a relief that Duff had stopped coming. His dour presence put us all on edge, and we were happy when he left.

Now, it seemed as if Joe, too, was relieved at his father's absence. As though he no longer had to prove himself to his father or measure up to his standards. It was dawning slowly upon me that Joe had given up on our dreams. I felt my cheeks burning. I could not stand it any longer.

Readying myself to rise, I sat back down as my eldest son, Joe Junior, came around the corner of the barn carrying a pail of water, the barnyard dogs trailing behind him.

"There you are, Ma," he said upon catching sight of me. He had just turned twelve; his long legs seemed to grow every day, as did his nose—

the cute little upturn of it was now lengthening out and broadening—destined to become the striking profile of his da.

"Sit with me, my love." I patted the bench.

It creaked and groaned as he sat down. He spoke harshly to the dogs, telling them to get lost.

"Is something bothering you?" I asked.

"When will Da be home? We need to repair that fence line; the cows keep wandering off."

"Perhaps, today."

We sat in a troubled silence, neither of us wanting to share our thoughts. I lifted my hand and stroked his hair. I remembered my excitement when Joe made the cedar wood cradle for his arrival. We were so happy then.

Of course, Mother had an apoplectic fit when she learned I was pregnant by a *Scottish Presbyterian farmer*. She adamantly refused to attend the wedding and for twelve years had refused to meet my children. But nothing could keep my father away; he quickly forgave my defiance, choosing to not let spite keep him from his grandchildren.

Junior gave an irritated shrug. "He keeps promisin' to help. But he's always too busy in town." He leaned down, scooping up some of the water from his pail, and splashed it over his face, as though trying to cool down his thoughts as well as his skin. The water clung to his dark black curls and eyelashes, making the bluebird colour of his eyes more vibrant.

I leaned down too, and scooped up a handful of water, patting my brow. "It'll be dark soon. If he plans to return today, we should soon see him." And when he does come home, I will insist upon answers.

We both looked up when the dogs started barking. "Speak of the devil," I muttered.

Junior and I continued sitting there, watching Joe approach. In the summer's heat, his horse walked slowly with head hanging low, Joe's body swaying from side to side with each step. His thin shirt was soaked with sweat, his trousers covered in a layer of dust and his hat pulled down to shade his eyes. When he looked toward me, all I could see of his face was the wide grin I so loved.

When he drew near, he turned the weary horse sideways and lifted the brim of his sweat-stained hat in salute. "Well, good evenin' my beautiful wife."

My heart still jumped at the sound of his voice.

"And my boy," Joe continued, looking at Junior. "Every time I lay eyes upon you, I think I'm lookin' in a mirror."

Junior sighed beside me, sounding irritated.

Joe swung off his horse and came to me, his eyes sparkling in the sun. I eased into his embrace. "Take this sad fella to the shed and wash him down, my boy."

Without a word, Junior took the reins, and boy and horse sloped off to the shed.

"No word for your da?" Joe called after him. "What's wrong with him?" he asked me as Junior continued walking, not looking back.

"Repairing the fence line in this heat is getting to him. He needs *help.*" I said.

Joe's response was to drape his heavy arm over my shoulder and rub my growing belly. "How is my baby comin'? Is he givin' you any trouble?"

I felt myself softening and hated that I let go of my frustration so easily, even for a minute, but I needed to feel him near me. He still smelled of cedar and pine, even though he no longer spent his days felling trees to clear the land. There was that whiff of stale whisky and a faint trace of something else.

"And what makes you so sure this is another boy?" I said, looking up at him.

He squeezed me against his hot body and gave me a lingering kiss. I wished we could stay like this forever, that I could forget everything else and never again confront him about our lives together.

But maybe now was the right time… "Joe, I…"

The cottage door banged open, and our six-year-old twins ran toward us. "Dada, look at the rock I found by the stream. See how it sparkles?" said Bertie, the more outspoken one. Willie stopped just behind him, their striking blue eyes alight with discovery, and their sweet little mouths gaping open as they looked up at Joe.

"It might be gold." Kneeling, he fingered their treasure and winked up at me, then hugged them in a crushing embrace.

"Oh, I doubt that." Cameron, ten years old, came up behind the twins, a borrowed book from his grandfather tucked under his arm. "The rock formations around here don't contain real gold."

"Cameron, are you sure you're mine? You have no imagination."

Cameron shrugged and headed back inside, colliding with Freddie, one year older, yet so small in comparison. "Sorry," exclaimed Cameron, catching his brother before he toppled. Then he ran off, while Freddie steadied himself.

"Hello, Da." Freddie reached for his father as though to hug him, but Joe punched him a little too roughly in the shoulder instead. Freddie stumbled sideways again. "Still no meat on those bones, boy? Let's get inside so we can have our supper and fatten you up." Freddie flushed bright red, and I had to stop myself from scolding Joe, again.

Soon, seated around our pine table, we ate a meal of cheese, ham, and carrots, and listened to Joe. He poured whisky into a cup and looked around the table at his sons, stopping at Junior sitting beside him. "Would you like a drink, my boy?"

"No, Joe, please. He's too young." I felt a knot form at the back of my neck.

"You really have to stop babyin' the boy."

Junior stiffened his spine and nodded at his father. Joe poured a large portion into the boy's cup and then laughed when his son choked on it.

After he stopped sputtering, Junior grew serious, brow furrowing and eyes stabbing at his father. "Da, you must help with the fence line. I spent most of the day chasing cows."

"And I can see it has made you lose your good sense. You don't speak to your da like that." Junior ducked as his father took a mock punch at him, Joe's laugh causing the others to giggle.

"Awe, come here." He grabbed Junior's head and rubbed his hair roughly. "You know it won't be long before I give you a section of land. You're near a man."

Now brimming with curiosity, Junior nodded. "Really?" A burn was rising up my neck.

Freddie squirmed on the other side of Joe. "Me too, Da?"

Joe pinched Freddie's thin arm, searching for a muscle. "You need to get stronger first. Then we'll see."

Cameron pushed his hair back over his brow and tapped his brother's hand. "You can study with me, if you like. There's other ways of being strong."

"You need to get your nose out of those books and help your ma 'round here," said Joe. He leaned back on his chair, smiling down the table at me.

"I was thinkin' I might get each of 'em a horse of their own. What do you say, Mother?"

Bertie and Willie popped out of their seats, saying in unison, "Us too?"

"Ponies for the little ones," said Joe. "But for the rest of you…" he added, as the twins hugged each other in delight, "… a fine horse each."

Junior's face brightened. He looked up at his father with sudden hope, Cameron smiled politely, while Freddie sought me out with wet eyes; just the thought of riding a horse made him throw up, but Joe kept forcing him to ride.

I could hardly keep from smashing Joe's plate against his head as I cleared it away.

***

Later that night, after everyone else had gone to bed, Joe and I settled onto the kitchen porch bench under the light of a full moon, enjoying the cooler air now that the humidity had gone. The night was alive with the shrill of cicadas and the clicking of crickets, and the sweet smells of ripening vegetables coming from my garden. It was such a tranquil moment, I hesitated to disturb it. But his promises to the children at dinner urged me on. "Joe, why are we still living like this?"

"What do you mean?" he said, slurring his words slightly. He slapped at a mosquito.

"I am tired."

"Of what, me wee hen?" I hated him calling me by the old Scottish slang for wife, and he knew it. The smell of whisky on his breath and his flippant manner only caused my fists to clench.

"I am tired of working so hard. It never seems to improve the way we live."

"Stop fussin'. We live just fine."

I pulled on his arm. "Listen. I'm fed up with working this land. And I still don't know if we even own it. And I'm tired of living like paupers in this overcrowded cottage. Remember our dreams, Joe?"

He sat rigidly on the bench. After a few moments of silence, he spoke, "Well, you know I plan to buy the land from my da."

"Really? All these years and how much do you own?"

Joe went silent.

"And where is Duff? Has something happened between the two of you?"

"Aw for God's sake Sarah, you're makin' things up now. What has my da got to do with anythin'?"

I looked out at the dark fields. "He owns this land. Unless you tell me differently."

Joe took a long drink out of a bottle stashed at his side, refusing to look at me or answer.

"And you stopped building the dairy barn. We should be buying more cows by now, instead of you promising horses and ponies to the boys." I spoke louder than intended and tried to hush my voice to avoid waking the children. "And where is that manor house you promised?"

I was suddenly nauseous. Remembering the baby, I caressed my stomach. "Joe? Please talk to me. I know how much we have earned. Enough to buy this land, finish the new barn, and build a grand manor. Tell me, where is our money?"

"In the strongbox, of course."

"All I know is that you pull out that strongbox from under our bed, unlock it, and drop in our new earnings. Then you place the key back into your pocket."

"Are you sayin' you don't trust me?"

I shook my head out of habit.

He reached for my hand.

I snatched it away before he could grasp it. "You promised me a better life than this. I want my mother to visit me in a fine-looking house. A house that would prove how wrong she was about you." Unwanted tears sprang to my eyes. I sounded like a child. "It has been twelve years now, twelve years of living in this shabby cottage while we earned a small fortune. I don't understand."

He finally turned to meet my gaze. His eyes were blood-shot and rimmed with puffy lids. "I built an addition."

"That was six years ago!"

"And we brought in Jessie to help with the cookin' and the children. She has a way with our boys. And she's a damn fine cook."

I stared at him, astonished he had no idea how close to the edge I was. "Yes, I appreciate that." My jaw ached. We sat in silence, and I looked up at the blanket of stars for guidance. "I just want to know what you are doing with our money, Joe. I have a right."

Nothing. Joe said nothing. He just lowered his head into his hands.

I erupted. "Fine. Perhaps I will take the boys in to my parents, then, shall I?"

Never before had I made such a threat. Joe lifted his head from his hands very slowly and turned to me. "Go then. But leave the boys and don't come back."

I had gone too far. Damn my temper. His pride was hurt, and he always struck out when that happened. "I'm sorry. I didn't mean it. And the last place I'd flee to would be my parents." My attempt at laughter sounded more like a cackle. He knew Mother would never take me back. "I just don't understand why we continue to live like this." My voice trailed off and I sank into silence.

Joe heaved a great sigh, his shoulders relaxing. He reached for my hand, bringing it into his lap. "I didn't mean it either, but you shouldn't be threatenin' your husband like that. I can't have my wife leavin' me and takin' my sons with her. So, don't be so foolish again. And remember how much I love you." He pressed a kiss onto my cracked knuckles.

I let him draw me closer. Bringing our marriage to the brink had unsettled me, it felt so much safer to let my anger go and just hold his hand.

Anyway, there was no choice. If I left him, my boys would stay behind. I would have nowhere to go, and I would lose everyone I loved. "I love you, too," I whispered.

Chapter 6

In the weeks that followed that awful argument, the hot weather gave way to cooler temperatures and the barley turned brown. It would soon be harvest time, and Joe stayed home to prepare. On a cool crisp day with the sun shining brilliantly, I worked in my vegetable garden, relieved I could still bend down over my growing belly and kneel on the ground. My sons had just left with Jessie to collect supplies in town, and Joe was in the corral. The sound of horses riding up our laneway surprised me. I struggled to my feet to see who it was.

It was Duff, with a group of Drury men riding behind him, our dogs yipping at their horses.

Joe came out of the corral when he heard his father and brothers approaching, and looked to me, beckoning, a wide grin on his face.

"Is it time to harvest?" I asked, coming up to him. "The barley doesn't look ready yet."

"No. But I have a surprise, my darlin'." Gesturing towards the men now getting off their horses, he said, "The Drury boys will finish your dairy barn today!"

"But? Why didn't you tell me?"

"I had to be sure they'd come. You'd be sure to bite my head off if they hadn't."

I smiled, embarrassed by my short temper ever since the night we fought. "Oh, Joe, I'm sorry. This is wonderful. Thank you," I said, my faith in him restored. I smiled and waved at Duff, but he did not acknowledge me. It was Duff who had given me the idea to expand my dairy when I overheard him bragging about his own expansion and how he now had a reliable source of income should the demand for barley fall. I wanted to tell him that and ask his advice. It was time he got past his ridiculous belief that I was not cut out for farm life.

I hugged Joe and started towards Duff. "I want to ask him what to buy first."

Joe kept hold of my arm, his breath on my face smelling of whisky. "Leave him be. Let us build the barn first."

Looking into his eyes, I saw something akin to discomfort. "Why?"

"You know he doesn't like a woman to speak out. Just let me deal with him for now."

"He's never known how to treat a woman. And he has only gotten worse since your mother died." The only time I had heard Duff speak of his deceased wife, he called her a hard-wearing woman, as if she had been his horse.

"Off with you, go on inside," Joe said as his father headed toward us. Duff's face looked like thunder.

I stayed put.

"Fer God's sake, have ye no work to do?" Duff called out to Joe. "I do na have time to waste."

I offered Duff a tentative smile, but he ignored me, coming to a stop before Joe, sniffing at him like a surly dog.

Duff's blue eyes were dull compared to Joe's, and the deep crease between them made him look perpetually angry. His curved nose overpowered a grizzled face that was a mess of black pores and broken veins. Avoiding his father's gaze, Joe walked past him to the shed.

Struggling to not snap at my father-in-law and his belligerence, I said, "Thank you for helping, Duff. I'll prepare some food for later."

He grunted and followed his son.

I strode to the cottage, heading into our bedroom to wash up and find cleaner clothes. Joe's trousers lay on the floor. While picking them up, I heard the clatter of something hitting the floor. It was the key to the strongbox.

I stared at it. In all our years, I had never known Joe to not have that key with him. I picked it up and fingered it for a moment, feeling all its edges. Then I knelt beside the bed and dragged the strongbox out from underneath. Inserting the key, I turned it, opened the lid, and stopped.

It was empty.

For a moment, I stayed on my knees beside the empty box, unable to move. The ground shifted beneath me.

A shadow fell across me. Joe stood in the bedroom doorway, staring at the empty box.

"Where? Where is it?" I demanded.

"What're you doin' opening that box without askin' me first?" He crossed his arms over his chest, staring at me indignantly.

"I've every right to open this box." His accusing stare made me feel sick.

"But now, look what you've done."

"What I have done? What have *you* done, Joe? Where is our damn money?" I ran at him and raised my arms to strike his chest. Instead, unable to bear his presence, I tore past him and out onto the porch.

Duff was standing there.

"Tell me. Has your son bought even one acre of this land?" I yelled at him.

Duff gave me a piteous look. He glanced behind me at Joe and shook his head. Then walked away.

Rounding on Joe, I shouted, "Have you got anything to say?"

Hanging his head, he walked past, not even offering a lie as an answer.

Fearing I might run after him and beg for the truth, I held my belly and ran towards the barley fields. I walked until I reached the stand of maples on top of the hill. Finding a flat boulder deep within the trees, I sat, trying to slow my breathing and steady my trembling hands now circling the swell of my belly to sooth the baby. Then, frozen by the enormity of it all, I sat on that rock for two or more hours, wishing for a miracle that would make his horrible lie disappear. For a moment, I thought of never going back, of leaving forever. Tabitha might take me in. But just as quickly, I dashed the thought away, knowing I would never leave my children. But how? How to live with Joe? And his lie? And what did he do with our money?

There was a sudden chill, the salty tears wetting my lips turning cold. I glanced westward and noticed storm clouds gathering on the horizon with the sun fading behind them. I should go inside.

Returning through the fields, I saw Joe high up on the roof of the dairy barn. When he caught sight of me, he stood up and staggered in my direction, seeming to forget where he was. There was something in the expression on his face that made me gasp. I had hoped for remorse, or regret. Instead, his face was slack, drawn downward, his eyes bleary and wet, his lips quivering. Seeming to forget he was high off the ground, he staggered toward me and shouted, "I'm sorry. . ." His voice was cracked. He ran his hands roughly through his hair, as if he wished to tear it out.

Junior suddenly appeared below and shouted up at him, "Da, please!"

After a lingering wretched stare at our son, Joe abruptly turned away, staggered, and then teetered on the very edge of the roof. Reaching up to the sky, it appeared as if he deliberately leaned back and fell in a graceful arc—with outstretched hands resembling our Lord Jesus dying on the cross—landing headfirst upon the trodden ground below.

By the time I reached him, a tight circle of Drury men had formed around the spot where Joe had landed. I shoved them out of my way and saw Duff kneeling beside his son. I fell upon Joe's broken body. The reek of sweat, whisky and blood overwhelmed me. Bile rose in my throat, and I felt faint. I shook Joe's shoulders, not understanding why his blue eyes stared up at the sky and not at me. I begged him to say something.

Duff grasped me firmly by the shoulders, pulling me away. I leant against him, watching in utter disbelief as the brilliant light of Joe's blue eyes faded, a pool of deep red blood seeping from beneath his head.

Junior dropped to his knees beside me, his eyes wild.

Duff stood up, giving me a small nudge toward my son. "Take yer ma away, lad."

I tried to pull away from Junior, watching the Drury men close in around Joe's body. Stumbling along in stunned silence I saw my children running toward me, and my knees buckled. Junior half carried me, stopping the others. Cameron took the other side of me, and Freddie held fast to the twins. Together we struggled into the bedroom and huddled on the bed. In a stupor, I told them their father was dead. Only Freddie cried, the rest of us stared at each other in disbelief. Jessie appeared and took charge of my children, leading them away after I hugged each one numbly.

Alone, the light now fading in the room, I curled into a ball around my belly and cried softly into a pillow.

***

The next morning, I lay in a heap, exhausted and spent, praying sleep would take me, and obliterate the guilt seeping within the tendrils of my grief. It was my fault. I should have trusted him. Leaving him in anger, only to return and cause him to fall. If only I had not opened that strongbox.

Sunlight poured through the bedroom window. I was alone, and had no sense of the children, where they might be. I tried to get up, but was locked into a stony silence. My body felt like an abandoned ship that had been wrecked in a violent storm, lying gutted and keeled over on its side. Rubbing my belly, I finally felt a kick. After a night of utter quiet, I feared the baby had died too.

Outside, the sounds of the world continued on without Joe—chickens squawked, our pig squealed, birds sang, cows mooed, and flies buzzed in and out through an opening of the small bedroom window. A soft breeze brushed my face, and I smelled the hollyhocks just outside. *The morning after Joe died.* The morning did not know there was a giant gaping hole within the very heart of it.

I heard my sons' voices through the closed bedroom door, and felt a sudden urge to comfort them, but seeing me in this numbed state might be so much worse than simply hearing me crying. For the moment, they were better off with Jessie—I could trust her to remain calm while I fought my way through this.

Suddenly, I heard a woman's voice, familiar yet out of place in my home. Then, the noise of a gown swishing side to side. I would know that step anywhere, even after all this time. *Mother!* I pulled the thin sheet over my bloated body and the dirtied dress I was still wearing from yesterday.

The door creaked open and the room was filled with the sound of rustling crinoline as she bore down on my bed, wafts of lavender engulfing me. "Sarah, dear." I sensed a hand hovering over me, but remained still, pretending to be asleep. Her voice grew more insistent. "Sarah, wake up. We need to talk."

Even now, in this moment of my greatest grief, her superior attitude made me bristle. Peering from beneath my cover, I caught her surveying the room, disapproval etched across her pinched face. I reluctantly sat up, adjusting the sheet to hide my stained dress. I had hoped for that special way she once looked at me when I was younger, when she believed I was to be her triumph. Instead, her look of utter disappointment sank me further. "It is time you came home."

All I could think to say was, "Why?"

Another look of disdain cast around my room. "Because you cannot possibly stay here. You must think of your children. And I see you are having another. Let me take care of you and your children. After all, they are my grandchildren. I can't simply abandon you." Her chin wobbled slightly and her eyes softened.

Kept away by her anger, yet here she stood, ready to step in now that my husband was dead.

"But *this* is our home."

Father's ashen face peered around from behind Mother, his trembling mouth clamped shut, not knowing what to do or say. Perhaps, he was afraid of revealing too much in front of her. If he opened his mouth, the truth might spill out—that he visited my family whenever he could sneak away from her.

I stared at my parents with an odd sense of disbelief that they stood in the bedroom where I had slept with Joe just one night ago. I noticed how formally Mother was dressed, in full corset, bustle, and hat. But her clothes could not hide the truth that she had aged poorly. Deep creases etched either side of her mouth and forehead, from frowning at everyone in disapproval, no doubt.

"Do not look at me that way," she said, backing up slightly under the intensity of my gaze, "I am only looking out for your best interests. It's all I've ever done. Not that I have received any appreciation for it." Mother sniffed the air, while securing the tiny black hat perched in a ridiculous fashion atop her head. Then her eyes softened again, and she reached for my hand. "Sarah, darling, I've met your boys. Such sweet ones," she said, patting my hand. "It's too soon for you to see what is best. We'll be back to discuss it further."

Chin up, shoulders back, she turned away and nearly collided with Father. "Come, Bertrand. I have done my best." Then she headed for the door, expecting him to follow.

"Be there soon." Coming close, he said, "May I sit, dear?" The tenderness of his voice caused my lips to tremble. Father embraced me, the warmth of him thawing my frozen state and allowing my tears to fall. After a moment, he lifted my chin gently. "Your mother means well, dear girl. Please come home with us. We'll take care of you, just for a while, then you can get back on your feet."

His words were meant to be kind, but they simply fueled this helplessness. I hated being this fallen-apart woman I had suddenly become, completely unable to cope. I forced my tears back, forced myself to speak. "I will never do that. This is my home. You understand that, don't you?"

"Bertrand, come. Now!" Mother's voice was harried and starting to rise.

Father embraced me. "Take time to get better, now. I will help you in any way I can."

After he left the room, I was relieved he had not demanded I abandon the farm immediately and return to town.

When I heard their carriage leaving, I released my breath and lay down again, exhausted. I should rush to my sons. God only knows what Mother, a complete stranger to them, had been saying. I heard Jessie's soft voice reassuring them, encouraging them to return to their food. Just a few more minutes, to pull myself together, then I would be ready to face them. To face what was coming. Mother, no doubt, trying to take over my life. And what of Duff? He would likely throw us off this land without another thought. I half sat up and saw the strongbox on the floor.

How long had it been empty?

Death has stolen the answer, making my sorrow so much harder to bear, so infested with an unspeakable anger toward my dead husband, and the guilt that I had caused it all. Why had I looked in that infernal strongbox?

But if I let this burden defeat me, my sons and I would be forced into a very different way of life. Right now, I could not let that happen without first trying to save us.

Determined to carry on, I yanked the sheets back and lifted my legs over the edge of the bed. The bed boards creaked in protest. Hoisting myself up, I splashed my face with water, tied back my hair, and put on the clean linen dress left on the chair. I glanced at the empty strongbox once more before opening the bedroom door and walking outside to face a new life.

The twins rushed at me when I stepped into the kitchen. Their uncertain smiles tore at my heart, they were too young to grasp the depth of yesterday's tragedy, but they felt the wrongness of it. I gathered them into my arms, burying my nose in each auburn mop and inhaling deeply. "How are you, my darlings?"

"Grandma gave me a coin," said Bertie laying it in my hand. Willie piped up, "Do you think it's gold—?"

"Grandma said it wasn't," Bertie cut in.

They were both silenced by Cameron. He was sitting at the kitchen table, studying from one of his schoolbooks. "You must call her Grandmama," he said irritably to the twins. Turning to me, he said, "She said we were moving to town to live with her."

A lump formed in my throat, thinking of how easily he would leave here.

"Can we still have ponies in town?" asked Bertie.

"Yes, can we?" asked Willie.

Cameron slammed his book shut. "Will you two ever stop worrying?" My studious boy was not coping well.

Freddie appeared in the doorway, his grief evident in his wet, imploring eyes. "Do we have to live with Grandmama?" Pulling him into my embrace, I tried to sooth him. "She scares me," he mumbled into my shoulder.

Junior came up behind his brother. "Well, I plan to stay," he said, his face so like his father's when Joe was intent upon getting something done. "I can run this place, Da said I know how." He lowered his eyes. "I'm so sorry, Mother."

He never called me Mother.

"What, love?"

He came to me, burying his head into my hair and leaning gently against Freddie. The twins squiggled in, and Junior tried to embrace all of us. Cameron sprang to his feet to join us, and we remained there for a moment, all of us, weeping as one.

Suddenly there was the loud clatter of a carriage outside. Bertie wriggled free and bounded to the window. "It's Auntie Tabitha."

Never before had she come here. I sent the boys to greet her, then stood frozen in the doorway, overwhelmed by the sight of my elegant sister walking up my tangled, weedy path, reaching out, hugging each of the boys.

She looked up at me, her eyes brimming. "Sarah, oh Sarah, darling."

I grasped her to me, with the sudden realization of how much I needed her.

We soon settled in the parlour. After much consoling and drying of tears, I sent the boys outside to find distraction so I could speak privately with Tabitha.

"How was your journey here?" I asked, unsure of how to talk to her any more. My sister and I had seldom seen each other over the years. To avoid her incurring Mother's wrath, I travelled to Grandview, the mansion Albert had built, once or twice a year, bringing my sons along. These occasions were stilted and guarded, focused on local gossip and trivia, with the boys eager to leave the minute we got there. I had hidden the truth about the mean life I lived here. Today was the first time she would set foot in my crude home. I wondered what she would think.

"My buttocks are sore from the carriage bouncing on the plank road, but I had to reach you," she said. For a moment, she sounded like the old Tabitha.

I moved my chair beside her and leaned into her, savouring this tiny, tentative connection. Sitting so close together, I longed to tell her about the horrible circumstances surrounding Joe's death.

"I can hardly think, the shock of it all. The grief is overwhelming," I said, my voice sounding weak, trembling in my throat.

She gently lifted my hand, placing it securely between hers. They felt so strong and soft. "This will pass. And once you and the boys move back with Mother and Father, perhaps you can find some way forward, after the baby is born, of course."

I felt a sharp stab in my throat. "I will not move back there!"

Tabitha drew back. "I don't see what choice you have. And why would you want to stay here?" She glanced around the small room with its rough-hewn furnishings, grimacing as if it were mud beneath her soft leather boots.

My voice hardened.

"Because this is my home! My sons' home." I tried to say more, but looking at her, dressed in her pretty silk gown, coiffed hair, and jewelry glinting around her throat, I stopped. She would never understand my life, nor would she be sympathetic toward my situation.

"Of course, you and I have never talked about it, but you made an unfortunate mistake that forced you to marry Joe. Now, you might be able to overcome that, there's no reason for you to struggle like this any more."

"But I loved Joe. I always will. Marrying him was *not* a mistake." The last words faltered on my tongue. I grasped her hands, willing the fury out of my voice. "It was no accident that I got pregnant. I knew what I was doing. It was the only way I'd ever get Mother and Father to agree to me marrying Joe. Didn't you see that?" She looked stunned. "How could you think I'd been so completely smitten by Joe that I'd throw away everything just for love? This is what I wanted. Well," I glanced around, quickly adding, "not this exactly. There's so much more we planned. This was my dream. I could see it, all those years ago when Joe first showed me this land. I can still see it. And we were almost there—" I broke off, unable to finish the sentence. How could I now confess to her that my husband had been lying to me?

The way my sister was looking at me now reminded me of our mother with eyebrows knitted and lips clamped tightly as she peered down her nose at me. Then she softened. "Please don't be angry. I only want what's best for you."

"*This* is best for me, and for my sons," I exclaimed. "Why are the women in my family so convinced they know what is best for me. Did Mother send you?"

Averting her eyes, she said, "No, of course not."

"Things haven't turned out that well for you either," I snapped.

"Because I can't have a child? You, it appears, can't stop having them." Immediately, her face fell. "Oh, I'm sorry. Poor Mother. It appears we have both disappointed her."

Before I could apologize too, Tabitha spoke again, "I doubt I'll ever have a baby." Her lower lip started to tremble.

She had come all this way to support me when my life had fallen apart. Even if I could not tell her the truth about Joe, I should be extremely grateful for her being here.

I reached for her hand. "Oh, I feel terrible for saying that. I'm so sorry."

She grasped my hand and squeezed it. "I'm sorry too. I shouldn't be so critical of your choice to live here. It's just…well, I was so surprised when I saw…this place. I had no idea. Please forgive me."

Tabitha looked at me imploringly and my anger disappeared.

"Well, *this* wasn't exactly what I'd imagined when I married Joe. And, dear sister, one day you'll have a child, I just know it." I was trying to be kind and make amends, hoping we could grow close enough to share more secrets.

"Oh, I doubt that." Her words caught me off guard.

"Aren't you trying?"

Tabitha's eyes were now downcast, a slight blush on her cheeks. "Never mind." She stiffened beside me, and I felt the distance grow between us once again.

"Let's agree that we'll never press each other about our respective lives. However, know that when you're ready to confide in me, I promise to not judge you. Nor tell you what to do," I said, softly.

"Of course, darling." She pulled me close. "Now, if only we could convince Mother to stay out of our lives."

Chapter 7

They buried Joe two days later in the graveyard behind the Presbyterian church near our farm. Father stood solemnly beside my broken family. Thankfully, Mother avoided the hypocrisy of attending. Tabitha agreed to stay away, her elegant appearance would only remind Duff of my soft upbringing. Flanking their father, Joe's four brothers and their wives stood in finely tailored clothes that sharply contrasted with the worn clothes my sons and I wore. Over the lowering casket, I met Duff's gaze, his eyes hard and unyielding. I refused to look away or bow my head.

Afterwards, Father took the boys to his wagon, while the Drurys expressed their condolences to me. They moved away quickly, afraid to linger too long under Duff's watchful gaze. At my side again, Father was about to lead me to my sons, when Duff unexpectedly appeared beside us. "Bertie, we must have a word."

"Here? Right now? Good God, man, can it not wait?" Father steadied me, a strong arm across my shoulders.

"No, it can na. Yer daughter must go with her boys."

I had no patience for his belittling attitude toward me, on this of all days. "Duff, if you plan to force us off the land, at least have the decency to tell me to my face," I said, immediately regretting such harshness when the man must surely be grieving too. But looking closer, there were none of the red-rimmed eyes or drawn mouth of a father mourning his son. The man was made of stone.

Duff walked away, as if expecting my father to follow.

"It'll be all right. Join the boys." Father squeezed my arm, then walked off to join him under a tree.

Back at the wagon, I struggled to read their faces, fearing the one thing they would agree upon was that my family had to leave the farm. They talked for a long time, then parted with a handshake.

Father's face was drawn when he reached us.

"Please, just tell me." I shook my head when he glanced over my shoulder at the boys, all leaning in to hear, concern clouding their eyes, Junior the most eager. "I see no point in hiding anything from them."

He sighed. "Very well, then. Duff will let you stay on the farm. But only if one of his older grandsons works it."

"Who would that be, Grandfather?" Junior's eyes went from expressing concern, to immediate suspicion.

"Hamish. He's Joe's eldest brother's son, I believe."

Junior threw his hat to the ground in a flash of anger so like Joe that my throat caught. "Why do we need him?" he demanded of Father.

My father took his arm. "It's for the best. You'll need the help to get through the winter. Be calm, think clearly. Now, help me get your mother home. She's had enough for one day."

***

In the following days, the reality of life without Joe set in. Junior struggled to tend to the livestock, milk cows, and stow vegetables in the root cellar for the long winter ahead. Freddie and Cameron tried to help, but they were just boys. And there was so much more to be done—harvest the barley, finish the dairy barn. Junior couldn't possibly do it all.

Two weeks after Joe's funeral, on a dull afternoon, I trudged into the kitchen in a daze of exhaustion and grief. Through the dirty window appeared an apparition of Joe walking toward the cottage. His black curls cut short, with the clean-shaven look of his youth. I blindly flung open the door and gasped. Then, drew back, shaken. It was Hamish, Duff's grandson.

Seeing how I wobbled, he rushed to grasp my hand. "You look faint." His resonant voice had a slight lilt to it, not as pronounced as Joe's, but just enough to unsettle me.

I shook off his hand and invited him in, while trying to recall the last time I had seen him. Perhaps in church last Christmas. I did remember he was the same age as me.

"Thanks, but we've come to harvest."

Looking past him toward the barns, I saw the Drury men. But not Duff.

Hamish threw a large sack down on the porch.

"What's that for?"

"I'm moving in."

"Oh? Why?" I fumbled with my loose shawl, drawing it around me.

"I need to live here to work the farm."

I shook my head. So, this is how Duff sees it, sending a man to live here, expecting me to fail otherwise in the harsh reality of a winter without Joe.

"Well, you're not staying in this cottage. Sleep in the barn. You're here to work, and the barn needs to be finished before winter."

"Will I?" An eyebrow raised, he shrugged. His look of defiance reminded me of Joe when he thought he knew better. Slinging the sack over his shoulder, he walked away.

He was at the end of the path before I yelled after him. "Wait, Hamish. I'm sorry. I didn't mean to be so rude. It's just—"

"I know. We'll work it out as we go along." He returned, the sway of his hips and smile on his face so familiar that it would surely break me every time he was near.

When he reached the porch, I leaned weakly against the doorframe. "You see, Junior and I have been managing this farm for quite some time."

He took off his hat and rifled his fingers through his hair. "I expect you've had to," he said with a knowing look.

Thrown by his meaning, it took a moment to continue. "Listen, we'll all get along better if you wait for us to ask you for help. Do you know anything about running a dairy?"

He nodded.

"Wonderful. That'll be a great help."

"Right after I harvest the barley and finish the barn. Then, I'll build your new dairy?" He gave me a playful smile.

"Well...yes...I mean..."

He slowly put his hat back on. "Anythin' else, Boss?" He grinned and sauntered off.

I yelled after him. "Actually, there is. Make sure you give me all the money you get from selling my barley."

Ambling away, his back turned to me, he left behind the distinct impression that he took nothing I said seriously.

∗∗∗

One day dragged into another as the autumn deepened. Nothing in particular distinguishing each one from the other. Hamish had been true to his word, sleeping in the barn and finishing it, handing over the barley money, and working hard to prepare us for winter. He would sometimes eat a meal with us, but mostly he preferred to keep to himself. Everyone tried to get along, but Junior grew quieter and more belligerent with each passing day.

On a rainy afternoon a gentle knock at my bedroom door surprised me out of a deep sleep. Jessie's face peered around the cracked door, apple-cheeked face screwed up with worry, unruly red hair escaping her maid's bonnet. "Yer parents are in the parlour. I told'em you were restin', but they insisted. Should I say ye wouldn't wake, that you're not feelin' t'all well? T'is not proper for folk to just drop in like that without word—"

I cut her off before she continued her nervous babble, "Not to worry. Tell them I'll be there shortly, please." It had taken me some time to get used to her thick Irish accent, but I still grew impatient at her prattling.

Taking my time, I washed my face and put on the only dress that still fit me. Mother must have a new plan to bend me to her will. We had not spoken since the day after Joe died. Leaving my room, I felt wobbly and slightly faint from my nap. Seeing Jessie in the hallway outside the parlour, her face crimson from, no doubt, another confrontation with Mother, I whispered to her, "Where are the boys?"

"In the kitchen, workin' on der readin' and grammar." Bless her soul, she made certain the boys kept up their lessons, even though she couldn't read or write a word.

"Kindly keep them there. I don't want Mother filling their heads again."

With a quick smile and a reassuring squeeze of her rough hand, she went back to the boys.

The rain was falling so hard it rattled the windows at the end of the dark hallway to the parlour. Mother must be determined to have travelled here on such a dreadful day.

I hastily ran a hand through knotted hair and smoothed my worn wool dress over the expanse of a protruding middle and strode into the parlour, interrupting Mother as she argued with Father. "She needs to think of the boys first and foremost…" Seeing me, she became speechless for a moment, her chin uplifted, revealing the trembling saggy throat as she stared critically at my heavy belly, puffy face, and swollen eyes. The rain lashed harder at the windows.

"Greetings, Father." I embraced him warmly. Then I turned on my mother. "Deciding my fate again, Mother?"

"Sarah, you must learn how to put your grief aside and help your boys. For once, you must stop being so selfish."

I tensed, my jaw clenching, at a loss for words.

Father intervened. "That is completely unfair, Alice. She won't see beyond her grief for some time to come."

"I think she will," Mother said, her voice rising higher in pitch, eyes still on me. "She is strong-minded. And she'll do exactly as she pleases. We must ensure she doesn't make another mistake."

"But she's facing a tragedy. We must give her time. I only agreed to bringing you here because you promised not to argue with her. That you wouldn't force her to come home."

"Stop it, both of you. I will decide my fate," I said, my voice strong.

Mother rounded on me. "Now he's dead, you can move on. You cannot run this farm. It's just not done. And the boys need to attend school and be properly educated, with the opportunity to become gentlemen instead of crude farmers. And that Hamish person living here…"

"So, you would have the boys lose their father, their home, and their whole way of life, all at once?" I said.

"You imply that I don't hold their best interests to heart?" For a moment, all I heard was the rain lashing against the window. She turned toward Father. "You know I am right, Bertrand."

"You cannot undo the past, no matter how hard you try," Father said.

"So, we let her stay here. And do what? Run this place?"

"I would like to help her stay on the farm, for a while anyway."

"Whatever for?"

"Because I believe in her. She could build a wonderful legacy for her sons."

"Her sons? You mean *my* grandsons. They might be the only males in our family to inherit the foundry and our fortune. How can we possibly allow them to remain lowly farmers?" She flicked her gaze at me.

Finally, I saw what Mother was really doing.

She opened her mouth, but I spoke first, "Let me make myself absolutely clear. I will never live in your house again. I would sooner die."

Chapter 8

The trees shed their dead leaves and the days grew short. On a chilly cloudless day, I sat on the kitchen porch, with a heavy shawl over my shoulders, the knitting balanced atop the enormous bump of my belly. Yawning, my eyes drooped, and I struggled to not fall asleep.

The dogs had been snoozing in the midday sun, when suddenly they sprang to their feet and started barking, jolting me awake. I anxiously looked down the laneway, hoping to see Father. Instead, it was Hamish and Junior riding the wagon, piled with firewood, coming in from the fields. Junior held the reins of the two giant work horses, with Hamish on the seat beside him. My son pulled back on the reins, with all his might, struggling to stop the powerful beasts. Steam snorted from their nostrils into the cold crisp air, their huge hooves stomping the ground. I watched, with a lump in my throat, as Hamish grasped Junior's hands to help halt the horses. How easy it was to imagine it was Joe with our son. Did Junior feel the same at this moment? As if it could be his da? He refuses to talk about his feelings, claiming to have dealt with his grief. But it seems too quick to be real. He had watched his father die, maybe even thought he should have stopped his fall. How could he so quickly be over that?

Before I could move, Freddie slipped in beside me. "Are you warm enough?" he asked in his soft voice. "Can I get anything for you, Mother?"

I hugged him into me. "I'm just fine," I said speaking into his unruly mop of hair. "Although I don't like sitting here knitting while watching all of you do the hard work." I held him slightly away from me so I could assess his health. He was looking more sickly than usual since his father's death.

"How are you and Cameron managing with the root vegetables?" I asked, smoothing my swollen belly, feeling tinges of guilt. It was a big job for two boys on their own, and they had been working for days.

"Almost done," he said, his eyes bright with his accomplishment.

At that moment, Bertie and Willie tumbled out the door onto the porch. After Bertie had been born, the surprise of Willie's entrance into the world had been told time and again by Joe, "three years of tryin' to have another babe after Cameron, not that it wasn't fun trying," Joe would boast, making women blush and men snigger, "we made up for it by havin' two at one go." I hid my crimson face during each retelling, trying not to think of the real reason why. Many nights Joe had been too drunk to perform.

Shaking off the heavy weight of the past, I beamed at my twins, savouring their auburn curls, rosy cheeks, and perky noses. "Jessie told us not to bother you, Mama," said Bertie.

"Hush, come here, you're not a bother. Here." I opened my large cloak and they snuggled against me and fell quiet as we watched their cousin Hamish skillfully back the wagon close to the woodshed.

"Grandfather," Bertie said loudly. Both twins threw back my cloak and raced on nimble legs across the yard at the sight of Father. Freddie gambolled behind them, and my father was soon surrounded by all his grandchildren. He greeted the boys, then had a word with Hamish.

I struggled to my swollen feet, but Father waved me back. I sank thankfully onto the bench.

A few moments later, as I watched my father crossing our rutted barnyard, I was struck by how completely at home he looked. He wore a wide brimmed, high crowned brown leather hat with a beaten frock coat and leather chaps over work trousers. Despite Mother's pernicious efforts to transform Father into a gentleman, he had remained, instead, a very simple man. At this moment he looked very much like a farmer. "You look well, dear," he said, when he reached the porch.

"I'm fine, Father. There's no need for everyone to fuss."

In one surprisingly swift movement, he leapt onto the porch and sat beside me, grasping my hands. When he leaned in to embrace me, I kissed his cheek and inhaled his familiar smell of pipe tobacco, mingled with the scents of leather and horse. Pulling back, he searched my face.

I beamed at him, struggling to look energetic, knowing fully that I must look drawn and exhausted.

"My darling daughter, I'd do anything to help you. But I need to make certain it is best for you to stay here, that you won't be overwhelmed. Last time—"

"A cow kicked me!" The horrors of my last time rushed in— delivering a dead baby after my belly got in the way of a sharp hoof as it was thrashed out by the mother cow.

"But it might be too much."

"I have to *try*. For my boys, for my sanity. This is the only life they have ever known." I sounded more confident than I felt.

He gripped my hands firmly, then placed them back into my lap. A cold wind rushed under my cloak. I shivered and drew it tight around me.

Father rose, strode down the full length of the porch, the weathered boards groaning under his step. Reaching the end, he turned and walked slowly back to me, considering his words. "It's not going to be easy. Duff said much more at the funeral."

Father dropped back onto the bench beside me. "Take heart. Duff feels a great sense of duty and indebtedness to your sons."

"What do you mean? Joe bought the land?" I straightened my back, fatigue suddenly vanishing.

"He didn't say as much. I'm not sure of his reasons and was afraid I might enrage him if I asked. But he is adamant about two conditions."

"Oh, God."

"They're not so bad. First of all, Hamish must remain until Junior is old enough to take over fully."

"That long? He'd have to be at least sixteen, that's four years. I thought Hamish was temporary. This will not sit well with Junior. Nor does it with me."

"I think you'll need him. Get your back down and hear me out. Duff insists that you continue with Joe's plan for expanding the dairy operation. He's concerned that if you farm barley exclusively, you risk losing everything. He expects the American export market to soon dry up. That's why he insisted Hamish remains for the dairy expansion. He can help you purchase more cows and equipment, negotiate with customers, that sort of thing. You know a woman can't do that on her own. Now, Joe led Duff to believe there were funds set aside for the dairy."

I tried to not bristle at the reference to *Joe's plan*. Nor to worry why Hamish had agreed to stay. Unexpectedly, my exhaustion returned, making me wish I could simply lie down and rest for a while.

"Yes…there was. Joe kept our earnings in a strongbox under our bed," I said, my throat starting to close. "The day Joe died, I discovered our savings were gone. I was furious with him. I've no idea what he did with our money. I…we fought…then he fell, before…"

Father drew me nearer. "You must not blame yourself."

"I left him. I walked away. If only I had stayed, none of this would have happened."

I stared him straight in the eyes. "If you truly want to help me, please, *please*, lend me the money to expand the dairy."

He sat in stony silence, staring off into the distance.

I tugged at his sleeve. "I will return it to you. I promise. Please give me enough for one year. That's all I need. Then I'll repay you. Please give me the chance to do this for my children. And for me."

Father nodded, his eyes steady upon my face. "And what happens to my money if you fail?"

"I will not fail."

***

The next morning, I woke up late and stumbled into the kitchen, fuzzy headed and exhausted. The cottage was empty. Peering out the window in search of everyone, I saw Duff and Hamish coming out of the barn. With a quick splash of water to the face, running fingers through ragged curls, and throwing a shawl over my thin dress, I rushed outside. Holding my huge belly discreetly under the shawl, I tried to walk quickly without waddling like a fat duck.

Seeing my approach, Duff stopped talking and scowled at me. By the time I reached them, I was out of breath. "Duff, good to see you." I said, trying not to pant.

"Aye." His craggy face was red from the cold.

I gestured toward the new barn, not noticing that my shawl slipped, revealing the bulge of my belly. "What do you think?"

Without looking at the barn, he said, "Hamish has done a good enough job of it. But Lass, why's he sleepin' in the barn? What's wrong with ye?"

"Well… it is just… anyway, now he's finished the work he can go home until spring when I'll need his help with the dairy. Thank you. To both of you," I said, beaming at them, receiving blank faces in return.

Looking at my pregnant belly, Duff said, "Don't be daft. He stays. But he'll no be sleepin' in the barn."

I drew my shawl tightly around me. "Fine." I paused for a moment, then summoned my nerve. "May I have a word with you about this land? I—"

"Na. I won't speak with ye about it." Shrugging, he turned, mounted his horse, and rode away.

"Ohhh, he is infuriating," I said, forgetting who stood beside me.

"That he is," Hamish said, smiling at me.

"Why won't he talk to me about this land?"

He shrugged. "You know he's right 'bout me stayin' for the winter?"

Meeting his gaze, I nodded. "I'm sorry, I don't wish to appear ungrateful. We are lucky to have you. It's just…"

He stepped closer. "You are a proud woman."

I tried to laugh. "Probably too much for my own good."

He smiled at me, and I began to wonder if this forced relationship might work somehow. "Why are you really staying here? I'm not able to pay you. Once the dairy is going, of course, I will. But not now."

Leaning in toward me he said, "Let's just say my granda is takin' care of that."

"W-What do you mean?"

He shrugged again—so much like Joe when he avoided my questions, and there was no way I would get an answer.

"Well, if you're staying, you'll have to bunk in with Junior and Freddie. Cameron can move in with the twins. No one will be happy, but we'll have to make the best of it, won't we?"

***

A few days later, I was jolted awake when the kitchen door banged open. I had drifted off to sleep sitting by the woodstove, knitting. I watched Hamish stomp in, wipe his boots, then place Joe's rifle on the gun rack beside the door, hang up his jacket on a peg below it and drop his saddlebag to the floor, looking and acting just like Joe. How will I ever survive the winter with this man living so close?

Noticing me, he strode over, his broad smile expanding. "We shot a young buck. I don't like to take them so young, but we saw nothin' else all day. He'll give us lots of meat."

I smiled back. "Oh, thank you. We'll dry it for winter. Please pull up a chair and warm yourself."

Nodding, he pulled up Joe's favourite chair beside me, sat down and stuck his hands out toward the fire, rubbing them together. "It's a bitter cold day."

Another bang of the door, and Junior came in. Looking over at us, he frowned. "Don't think you can just move in here and take the place of my da," he shouted at Hamish.

Suddenly I realized how we must look, the two of us sitting here, just as Joe and I used to, but that was no excuse. "Junior, please apologize to Hamish."

Junior slammed his rifle into its place on the rack, tore off his jacket, and threw it on a peg. "It's bad enough that he sleeps in my room. Now this?" He ran from the room, his face red and angry.

I looked at Hamish. "I apologize for his behaviour. He's not doing well with his father's death."

"I can see that, but he'll have to get used to me."

"I'll speak to him, but you have to try too. Junior will own this land one day."

He looked away, then rose abruptly. "I best be off. I still have work to do."

I reached out to stop him. "Please stay a moment."

He sat back down and looked at me, his intense eyes searching my face.

"Listen, I've started to plan for the spring." I gestured toward a pile of dairy association journals Father had given me.

Glancing at them he said, "But those won't tell you much."

"It's a place to start. Anyway, I already know how to run a dairy. I just need to learn more about running a much larger operation. I have big plans."

"Do you?"

There was that arrogance again, as if he knew so much more than me. He stood up, grabbed his jacket, and strode out the kitchen door, slamming it behind him.

Chapter 9

It was near the end of the year, and my baby was due. One particularly cold winter day, I sat in the parlour in front of a roaring fire, trying to stay warm. The twins sat at a small table playing with a puzzle, while my other boys helped Hamish and Jessie with the chores.

Working on some mending, I thought about my future. I had Father's commitment to fund the dairy expansion for one year, but he insisted we make a final decision after the baby's birth. Even with Hamish's help, the dairy expansion would be demanding: the new cows and equipment, supplies, another wagon and horses, new fields of hay and other crops to feed the new livestock, expanded pastures, more milkers—and there was bound to be much more.

Could I handle all of this with a small infant suckling at my breast?

As I cradled my bulging belly, I was certain I felt a heartbeat. With a silent prayer to protect this infant, I told myself that there must be a way to do it all. With these unnerving worries filling my head, I was startled by a loud knock at the door. We cautiously opened the door, then threw it open at the sight of my bundled sister shivering on the stoop. "Oh my God, what are you doing here?"

Bringing in the cold in with her, she directed a coachman to leave her valise inside by the door and then leave. Slamming the door against the cold, she turned to me and said, "I am here to help you with your birthing."

Had I not been so grateful to see her, I would have laughed out loud at the notion. Everything in her world was done for Tabitha, she didn't have to lift a finger, and she had no experience whatsoever with childbirth. "I know what you're thinking," she said in an admonishing tone. "But I'm not that squeamish. Now, perhaps instead of scorning me, you might offer me tea? It's freezing out there."

A few moments later we settled in the parlour, while Willie and Bertie left to ask Jessie for tea. "Thank you for coming," I said, reaching for her hand.

We sat on either side of the parlour stove, in chairs so close together that it was easy to grasp each other's hand. She sighed deeply. "I've not slept well since I last saw you. I worried that you thought I was telling you what to do, that I supported Mother. I just want to help. You need someone by your side while you give birth, someone who loves you," she said, her hand fiercely gripping mine. "I can't replace Joe, but at the very least I can hold your hand like I do now, in the hope that it will inspire courage, for both of us."

***

That night, we lay side by side in my tiny bedroom in the pitch black, no moonlight to warm the atmosphere in the frigid room, only the door left open in the hope a little heat from the wood stove would creep in. It was a very long time since my sister and I had shared a bed—years ago when we were little children—and I had been frightened in the night. How wonderful it felt to have her warmth in my bed.

"Are you asleep?" I said, quietly, sure she was not. She must be incredibly uncomfortable on this coarse, hay-stuffed mattress, so unlike the plush down-filled beds of Grandview. But she made no complaint as we crawled into the lumpy bed. Coming here had been an enormous expression of love toward me and I hoped it might be a new beginning for us, that we might become close again.

"No, what is it?" she said, her voice suddenly on alert.

I fumbled under the heavy wool blankets in search of her hand. "I'm fine." The warmth of her hand in mine felt soothing. "I'm looking forward to the day I can sleep on my back again, though." I could hear her laughing softly.

"You *are* enormous. Were you so big each time?"

"Oh yes. And each time, nearing the end, I became convinced I couldn't possibly go on any longer, I had to give birth, or I'd simply burst."

We both laughed. I pulled her hand toward me to lay it on the bulge of the baby. She resisted, but I tugged and placed her hand on my belly. "Can you feel him stretch his little leg? He is ready to come into the world."

Her hand crept cautiously over the mound of the baby. She gave a sharp intake of breath and pressed harder. "I felt it. Oh my, it is truly a miracle." She sounded breathless at the wonder of it.

"I can assure you that when the time comes you might think differently."

"Nonsense. Now, you need rest. I'll hold your hand until you're asleep." Sighing deeply, I pulled her hand against my cheek, and drifted into a dreamless sleep.

***

Later that night, I was jolted awake by a hard pain. "Tabby?" I gently shook her awake. "The baby, it's coming."

"The baby? What, now? But it's the middle of the night."

Despite my sudden anxiety for the coming baby, I let out a long, hard laugh. "The baby doesn't know what time it is."

A flickering light appeared at the doorway. Hearing us, Jessie stood there with a lantern. Taking one look at me, she yelled, "Hamish, fetch the midwife."

There was a great commotion. Freddie and Cameron settled the twins in the parlour as far away from the birthing as possible, and Jessie set water on the woodstove to boil. In a very short time, my pains started coming harder and faster. All the while Tabitha stood against the wall of my bedroom, her eyes darting back and forth as she tried to decide what needed to be done.

By the time midwife Agnes arrived, I was propped up on pillows, ready to push this baby into the world. Tabitha stayed beside me, holding my hand just as she had promised. So far, she had tolerated all the grunting, sweating, and reek, but she was clearly shocked by the animal nature of it.

After Agnes examined me, she looked deeply into my eyes, her brow set in a furrow. "Do not push yet. The baby can't come out. A shoulder is stuck behind your hip bone. Do not push, it will kill the baby."

I looked at my sister gripping my hand, hoping she would reassure me, but she had frozen, her gaze suddenly blank as if she were far away in some happier place.

Agnes spoke urgently, "Tabitha, I will need you to help me save this baby."

My sister's lips were moving in silent prayer, her grip so fierce she could break my wrist.

"Snap out of it or leave the room and send in Jessie," Agnes shouted at Tabitha.

Jolted out of her stupor, Tabitha started to stammer and splutter, "I w...want to stay. Tell me what to do."

"Then, move, woman! Help me turn her across the bed. We must lay her flat. Climb up on the bed by her head. Hold her arms down with your knees." Agnes whipped out words in short barks.

I began to panic when Tabitha pinned my arms roughly under her trembling knees.

"I'm sorry, my darling. I don't mean to hurt you." She looked stricken by her action, but I could sense her growing courage.

Another wave of agonizing pain took me.

"Do not push. Whatever you do, do not push."

I panted through the torturous pain and clawed at Tabby's legs holding me down, until the contraction ebbed away. I lay panting, and tried to speak, searching my sister's eyes. She did not know this could kill me. "If I...if I die—"

"Shush, shush, you will be fine, don't think that," she said, swiping the sweat from my forehead.

"Please, please take care of my boys. Don't let Mother have them, promise me."

Before she could answer, Agnes began to yell, "Tabitha. I need you to pay attention to me. *Now*. Grab her legs. Pull them up and back."

"What? Do what?"

"Get off her. Take her legs, pull them toward her head. Just do as I tell you."

Tabitha climbed off me, struggling awkwardly as she looped her arms around my knees, pulling my legs back.

"Yes, as far back as you can. Now hold onto her legs. No matter what happens, just hold them in place."

Another contraction had overtaken me, pain rocking my body and I fought with all my being—teeth gritted, sweat saturating my face—the overwhelming urge to push.

Reaching between my upended legs, Agnes pressed down hard on my lower belly. I cried out for the first time. "If I could just release the wee one's shoulder," Agnes was saying. She pushed harder on my belly, and I screamed like a banshee.

My sister's face was stark above mine.

"Damn it. Tabitha, hold her still. Don't let her move."

I could not bear it any longer. It had to stop. I struggled to push Tabitha away. "Just let me die." I started thrashing.

Sobbing, my sister struggled to keep me still.

"Tabitha, I need you. Look at me. I need to cut her. Hold her still." Agnes drew close and slapped my face hard. "Stop fighting. Hold still. It'll soon be over. I promise."

Coming to my senses, I laid still. A sharp pain between my legs followed by a warm gush, then tugging and pulling. Agnes must have at least one hand inside me, wrapped around the baby. There was a sickly cracking sound. "Now push, Sarah. With all your might. Push."

Pushing with a strength I no longer thought possible, I felt the baby slipping from my body.

The room fell still, except for our loud panting. Yet, the baby was not crying. Somewhere deep inside me a tiny whiff of relief stirred—another stillborn! So be it. Now I could move on. It would be easier.

I struggled to see, my vision swimming. Agnes grasped a blood-splotched bluish baby by the ankles, hanging it upside down. One limp arm hung longer than the other. Blood dripped slowly from the tiny unmoving body. She slapped the purple bottom sharply. An angry wail pierced the room.

And another, this one from my sister, who was recoiling in shock from seeing a newborn being slapped.

"Tabby?" I reached for her hand, but had no strength.

She grasped mine and held on, her sobs in check as Agnes gently placed my new son upon my chest while she severed the chord.

With tears of joy and overwhelming relief streaming down our faces, I took Tabitha's hand and placed it with mine, upon the wonder of a new life.

***

The morning after, with my tiny baby nestled beside me, his shoulder bandaged where the midwife had broken his collar bone to allow him to be born, I felt on the verge of surrendering to Mother's will. Father had been wise to insist I wait until after the birth. Shaken by almost losing this child, I now wondered about the wisdom of staying on the farm. I tried to convince myself that the boys could adjust to town life, but in my heart, I knew it was impossible. My sons were born to be farmers.

I came back to myself. It was just too high a price to pay. Mother would take over my sons' rearing and make decisions about their lives, while she set about recreating me into the proper lady she thought I should be. She would bully me into conformity and seek a new husband for me, one of her own choosing. I laughed softly to myself, thinking of how impossible her task would be. What sort of gentleman would be interested in a not-so-young widow with six children?

I gave myself an emotional shake. Giving birth had weakened me. Very soon, I would have the strength to carry on. Meanwhile, it was time for me to be honest with myself.

How can I do it all?

Grudgingly, I knew something had to give. Exhausted by such thinking, I slipped into a deep sleep.

***

What seemed like a moment later, Tabitha awoke me by softly saying my name.

"What is it?" I struggled to be fully awake, remembering the little body pressed up against me.

"Sh, don't wake him. You two have been asleep for hours. You need a break. Come to your auntie, little one." She slipped one hand tenderly under his wobbly head. He was moist with the sweat of being against me. She lifted his tiny body securely with her other hand, taking great care not to touch his wrapped shoulder. For a moment she held him close, planting the whisp of a kiss on his brow, then depositing him gently into the cradle. Tabitha had such strong mothering instincts. It was so unfair she had no children.

Watching my sister, an idea began to take shape, an idea that could benefit both of us. "Will you help me into the kitchen? The walk will do me good."

Standing up, I felt a rush of blood fill the thick wad of cloth secured between my legs and winced at the pain. "Really, I am fine," I said, grimacing again, as I tried to walk.

"Please get back to bed. You look absolutely dreadful."

"I can always trust you, dear sister, to speak the truth about my appearance," I said, taking her arm. "Moving around helps." Gingerly, we walked into the kitchen, and I instructed Jessie to attend to the baby.

Once alone, she helped me sit on a chair covered with a cushion Jessie had readied for me. Tabitha pulled over a chair and sat close, leaning her shoulder against mine. We linked our fingers, just like the little girls we once were.

Eyes bright with wonder, she said, "He's a wonderful little baby. I can't get over the way he feels in my arms, so tiny, so perfect. Do all babies smell like that?" I nodded, encouraged by her joy. "Have you decided on his name?"

"Robert. After Grandpapa. What do you think?"

"A marvellous name. The boys were so excited last night. I loved the looks on their faces when they each held their little brother. Oh—" She looked to me, quickly. "You fell asleep so quickly after his birth. The boys were too impatient to wait until you woke. And I so wanted to show him to them. I hope you don't mind."

"Not at all. I'm grateful. I needed the rest."

"And I cradled that little baby for what felt like hours. I just couldn't get enough of him. What a gift you've given me. To know what it is to hold a newborn." She gazed out the window wistfully remembering.

"Where are the boys?"

"They're out with Hamish, trying to find the perfect boughs to decorate the house."

Suddenly, I realized what day it was. "I'd forgotten it was Christmas Eve. You should be home with Albert. What about your festive dinner?"

"Albert agrees that I'm needed here. And Mother took over directing all the preparations. I suspect she's thoroughly loving it." When Tabitha moved to Grandview, the Yuletide festivities became an ostentatious event held in their mansion. Each year, my sister would beg us to attend, but I reluctantly declined her invitations. Joe said we didn't belong. How odd that our first Christmas together in years took place in my shabby little cottage. "Anyway," she continued, "I wouldn't have missed Robert's birth for anything. Terrifying, but absolutely wondrous. I'd no idea he would bring such joy to my heart. I've fallen instantly in love with him."

We sat in silence for a few moments.

"Thank you for being so brave. You helped save my baby's life. It's not usually that bad. I'm sorry for giving you such a difficult time."

"No. You were afraid and struggling against the pain. I was more frightened of Agnes than you."

We both laughed, and I felt a sharp pain. "Ouch, it'll take some time before I can laugh properly again." Tabitha gently caressed my hand, while I collected my thoughts. "Would you have taken my boys? If I had died?"

"You didn't. So, there's nothing to talk about." She shifted, looking at me.

Pulling on her arm, I drew her back to me. "I'm sorry. I can't stop thinking about who would've taken care of my boys if I'd died. With Joe gone ..."

She sat very still, her only movement a gentle tapping on my hand. "I love your boys. And I'll always look after them. But I couldn't possibly take on the six of them to raise at Grandview. Oh, that sounds heartless, but I'm being truthful. I know Albert would never allow it." She was staring across the room, not meeting my gaze.

"No, it's not heartless. I expected as much." I paused for a moment, then touched her chin and turned her face toward me. "Then, would you consider taking one?" My voice sounded small. A piece of my heart broke beneath the weight of what I was offering. I looked deeply into her eyes. "Would you take Robert to raise as your own?"

She was silent, her eyes revealing she was unable to grasp the full meaning of my words. I smiled, giving the slightest of nods.

"Oh! My goodness." She grasped my face in her hands. She was flushed, her breath coming in short jabs. "Take your baby? Take Robert? To raise him?"

"Yes. Maybe at some point in the future, we can consider adoption, if it's best for all of us. Or perhaps, he might come back to me." The hope that one day he would return home was the only possible way I could give him up.

Her face transformed with the full understanding of this gift. Her smile grew enormous, her eyes wide with delight, filling with tears. "But...but how?"

"I'll just give him to you, that's how. You can hire a wet-nurse."

"You don't want to nurse him?"

My vision blurred. "How can I, and then give him up?"

"Then don't. Your grief is getting the better of you."

"No, it's not. I have to stay here. I must try to make this farm work. For my sons, *and* for me. I can do it, but not with an infant to care for. I've decided it would be unfair to little Robert."

"But Jessie would help, surely."

"I already ask too much of her."

"But what will Mother think?"

My jaw clenched. Mother infested everything I did. "I really don't give a damn."

"Oh please. You know Mother won't like it."

"Mother's likes or dislikes are not our concern. We are two grown women, struggling with a decision for the benefit of my new baby—and you—and me. I refuse to let Mother interfere with this."

We stared at each other for a moment. "More important than Mother is whether Albert will agree. He would never take my six children, but would he take one?"

Her face lost colour and her smile sagged. After a few moments of consideration, her smile returned, "Actually, I suspect he will be relieved."

It was such an odd thing to say. When she ignored my quizzical look, I decided it best to not pursue the matter. I suspected I might never learn the truth about her marriage.

Chapter 10

A few days later, Tabitha and little Robert left, with coachman and driver to see them safely home to Grandview. That night the winter bore down heavily upon us, with snow driving against the cottage, mounding up around its windows, swallowing us into its frozen jowls.

Trapped inside the tiny cottage, we struggled to survive over those winter months. After each heavy snowstorm, Hamish and the older boys dug pathways to the barn and sheds, creating a messy web of passages across the barnyard. They spent their days tending our livestock and chopping and hauling in wood to keep the woodstove and parlour stoves burning. Hamish and Junior tried to hunt small game, but most creatures were burrowed, hiding from the harshness of winter, so they seldom came home with fresh meat. Jessie and I eked out the food in the pantry and root cellar, creating smaller and smaller meals as supplies ran out.

When we were about to go hungry, a sleigh unexpectedly arrived from Father—filled with preserved meats, dried fish, cornmeal, and so much more—driven by a servant who could keep his mouth shut about his journey here.

The days were short, so we ate our supper early, then gathered around the stoves in flickering lamplight. The tiny cottage seemed to shrink with all of us crammed within its walls, and the air filled with the smell of wood smoke and poorly washed bodies. Hamish spent most evenings by the woodstove in the kitchen, repairing tools, cleaning saddles and rifles, doing the many maintenance chores long neglected by Joe. I mostly huddled with my sons in the parlour around the stove to feel the heat warming the tiny room, protecting us from the frigid winter outside. Often, I sat at a small table in the dim lamplight, reading dairy journals, and making my plans for the expansion. But I did not share these plans with Hamish—there was nothing to be gained by an argument in front of the others.

I tried to stay hopeful. Still there were too many dark hours with nothing much to do, leaving too much time to ruminate upon my losses and worry about what might lay ahead. And just when I thought the grief might lift, Hamish would walk through the room reminding me of Joe.

Then one morning, I peered out the kitchen window to see brilliant sunshine, and water dripping from the barn's snow-encased roof. The limbs on the nearby dogwood were beginning to flush red, preparing themselves for their new buds, and the snow in the barnyard was melting, exposing the sodden ground beneath. And Father was due for a visit this morning. He had not been here since that day he had agreed to fund the dairy. I was eager to see him. For the first time since Joe's death, I found myself looking forward to the day ahead after this long winter.

A noise drew my attention toward the kitchen door. Junior was shrugging on his winter jersey, preparing to head to the barn. The spring weather must have lightened his mood too. His sad face seemed a little happier. Or it could just be my wishing that he had found a way to let go of his grief and accept that Hamish was not leaving.

"Junior, your grandfather will visit today. It's time to get the dairy expansion started," I said, feeling a flush of pride, thinking about the enterprise we were about to get underway. He nodded with a fleeting smile.

Appearing at the doorway to the bedrooms, Freddie walked, nimble-footed, across the kitchen, looking at me eagerly. "I overheard you, Mother. May I join in?"

"Of course."

He smiled, the first real smile since Joe's death. Over the winter, in the idle hours when the cottage grew dark, he would bury his head in my shoulder and whisper about how much he missed his da. Then he would settle in beside me to read my journals together.

Junior took Freddie's coat from the hanger and threw it at him. "Come on, we've work to do before Grandfather gets here." A blast of cold air rushed in as they left.

I jumped when Cameron piped up from across the room. He had been so quiet I had forgotten he was there. "Not me, Mother. Please. I prefer to study."

I gave him a knowing look. Cameron's interest in the dairy was sporadic, primarily focused on the equipment required. The rest of it bored him. Today, he huddled by the stove for warmth, his nose buried in a science book. The farm life was not in his future. If all my boys were like Cameron, I would have let the dreams for the dairy die with Joe.

"No, of course not, concentrate on your studies. Just watch the twins for me while the rest of us talk."

"Yes, Mother," he replied in a bored voice and buried his nose back in his book.

Hearing their names spoken, the twins raced into the kitchen, skidding to a stop in front of me. "May we play outside, Mama?" they asked eagerly. Over the winter, their auburn hair had grown into long ringlet-curls—Joe would have said it made them look like silly girls—but I loved their curls and had taken to combing them back and tying them with little strings of rawhide.

"Yes, of course, my darlings," I said, and impulsively touched the softness of their young cheeks. Unbidden, the regret of giving Robert to Tabitha tugged at my heart. With no babe to suckle, my milk had quickly dried up and my body had returned to itself. All that was left was a dull ache deep inside me. With a sad smile, I shooed the twins out the door to play.

***

An hour later, I heard sleigh bells, a merry announcement of Father's arrival. Soon, Junior and Freddie came stomping into the cottage, the two of them dragging the many sacks their grandfather had brought. Father walked in, the twins beside him. His cheeks were bright red from the cold, his eyes watering. "Sarah, my darling. How are you?"

I rushed to him, and we embraced. "So much better for seeing you, Father." I inhaled the comforting smell of his pipe tobacco on his coat.

Pulling back, I said, "Please warm yourself by the stove, then sit. Jessie has prepared lunch."

Soon, all of us were seated at the pine table. The lonely pot of stew sat in the middle with a loaf of stale rye bread beside it. Father reached into one of his sacks and dropped a large round of cheddar cheese onto the table with a thud. "I thought this might set the tone for our new dairy venture," he said, laughing as he brought out three loaves of fresh bread and a pot of butter. We were sworn into secrecy about the food he had bought us and the money he was about to give me. For if Mother ever learned of these gifts, she would realize how tenuous my life was and swoop back to the farm, forcing my return to town.

Just then, Hamish strolled into the kitchen, tucking his jersey into his pants, his face damp after shaving. Father looked at him, then turned to me with a look of astonishment. I almost laughed. He leaned in and whispered, "What's going on?"

"Nothing! Duff insisted Hamish sleep in the cottage," I whispered in his ear. "He bunks in with Junior and Freddie."

Hamish sat down in Joe's chair and stared at me with his blue eyes, and we both smiled warmly at each other. I was getting used to him living here.

After we finished eating, I asked Cameron to take the twins into the other room, so the rest of us could discuss the dairy expansion.

"Before we begin," I said, keeping my voice strong, "I'd like to propose a name for this land and the dairy farm we'll build here. I will call this place *Edenwae*. This land was my *Eden* with Joe, where we raised our sons and dreamed of what we would become. Now I endure the sorrow, the *wae*, of his loss."

"A perfect name. To Edenwae." Hamish held his cup high, looking around the table as if this were his family.

Not letting his presumptive attitude throw me, I continued, "I've studied the success of large dairy farms in America and England. Their breeding practices are innovative. The cows' mating times are staggered throughout the year, eliminating the winter stoppages in milk production. It's a novel idea I plan to try. By next winter, we will produce milk year-round." I went on to detail my plans, all the while trying to ignore Hamish's skeptical look from the other end of the table. At least he had the courtesy to keep his opinions to himself. For now.

***

Later that day, I walked beside my father toward the barnyard. "Thank you, Father," I said, as we approached his sleigh. The horses were snorting, eager to move.

Heaving his satchel in, he turned to me. "You've such courage. I am very proud of you."

"That means so much," I said, leaning into him, savouring his encouraging words. "I wish Mother felt the same way."

"I do, too. It would certainly make my life a great deal easier."

"Do you think she suspects anything?" My voice quavered at the thought.

"No. I don't." He squeezed my hands in reassurance "Anyway, she's completely distracted these days by Tabitha, while she's furious at her."

"For what?"

"Oh, perhaps I shouldn't say anything."

"Please, tell me. I thought I was the only daughter who could make Mother furious."

"Oh darling. She's still livid with your sister for taking your baby. Add in the fact that she wasn't consulted. I don't think you realize just how affronted she felt in not being asked to be involved in such a matter."

"But why would she *care*?"

"You forget how much she wants you in town."

"How awful a mother who would wish her child to fail."

"She'll discover in time how strong her daughters are. Perhaps, who knows, she may even learn to rejoice in them."

"Miracles do happen. Well, she was right in one thing. I gave Robert to Tabitha for that very reason, to help keep me strong for the work ahead."

Father's brows drew together. "You don't allow for the depths of your mother's feelings. She accuses Tabitha of aligning with you, the two of you conspiring to undermine her wishes. She views it as a profound act of disloyalty, bordering on treachery. And I must say, Sarah, given her reaction to Tabitha's helping you, I suspect your mother would draw and quarter me if she found out what I'm doing here." He chuckled, pulling himself onto the sleigh.

But I found no humour in his words. I felt somewhat ill at the thought of the fury Mother would unleash upon Father should she find out about his help. As he left that day, I swore to myself that I would make Edenwae a success, no matter what it took. I hoped I could do that before my mother rooted out the truth.

Chapter 11

"**Y**ou can't go in there," Hamish said, trying to bar my way. I pushed past him into one of the livestock pens, picking my way around mounds of dung, breathing through my mouth to avoid the foul smell. Farmers' heads turned, with squinting eyes exploring me as I moved amongst the cows examining ears, mouths, eyes, and hooves, looking for signs of disease. The hem of my skirt became caked in mud. My unruly hair refused to stay captured within Junior's borrowed cap, and tendrils hung out, making me acutely aware that I was the only woman present. Men elbowed each other and pointed their chins, laughing.

Hamish followed, muttering protests in my ear. "At least, let me do the bidding—"

"Only if you do as I say," I hissed back at him. After staring him down for a moment, I returned to the cows. "This one, that, and there, that one too." Hamish added each number to his list, and we proceeded toward the auctioneer, just as he was about to begin. "Stay back here." I kept us at the back of the small gathering of men, but it did not stop them from staring at me in disbelief.

When the first cow on our list came up, I nodded at Hamish each time the bid went higher, and he upped the bid. At the next round, he suddenly refused, shaking me off. "It's too much for that cow." Everyone had turned toward us, trying to assess who was in charge. I looked down at the muddy ground, shrugging my shoulders.

Once attention was drawn elsewhere, I pulled him out of earshot. "Do as I say."

"But you don't know what you're doing. Let me do the bidding without you interferin'. You can't be seen as the boss."

Women did not run large dairy operations. Farm wives used to manage their small dairies by themselves, but once their husbands heard of the lucrative, reliable income possible by expansion, they took the dairies over, believing that only men were capable of running larger scale dairy production to supply the cheese factories. Should these factories learn that Edenwae was *managed* by a woman, they would refuse to buy our milk.

"Very well, but I'm keeping the money. I'll give it to you when it's time to pay." I retreated to the shade of a nearby tree to contemplate how to maneuver through this world run by men. If farmers were already put off by my presence at this auction, I might need to take a leap of faith and trust Hamish to conduct all my negotiations without me being present. By summer, I hoped to add another twenty-five cows. It was ambitious, but I needed a fast return to pay off Father's loan before Mother found out.

***

A few days later, on a warm spring morning, we stood in the corral looking at the new cows that had just arrived the day before. The milking last night had not gone well. Hamish, Junior, and I had each tried to take charge and give orders. The cows, confused by their new home and agitated by our quarrels, were uncooperative and gave little milk. Today, the three of us needed to do better. "Junior, fetch our old cows and milk them by the shed. Keep them quiet. Hamish and I will decide what to do with the new ones."

Junior scowled, then nodded and ran to the pasture to round up our old brown cows—they had been too intimidated by the new Guernsey cows to enter the milking station.

The new cows eyed Hamish and me suspiciously, as we stood in the muck of the corral. The reek of dung was overwhelming. Looking to Hamish, I said, "You get set up inside and I'll bring in the first one."

Winking at me, he strolled into the milking room located within the foundation of the barn.

Picking the least anxious looking cow, I rubbed the length of her nose and smoothed my hand down her side, "There you are, girl. You'll like it

87

here. I promise. Now come with me, you'll soon feel better." Lowing loudly, she let me push her gently into the entry door. Making sure she was all the way in, I left her to Hamish, then returned to the corral to choose another cow for me to milk. I took my time, getting to know my new beauties, thinking of the wonderful milk we would produce as I rubbed their bodies. Finally, I selected one and gently nudged her toward the door.

Suddenly, I heard Hamish yelling, "I'm not surprised she picked you. You're as stubborn as she is." I rushed into the barn and saw him on a stool yanking on the poor cow's teats so hard she was bellowing in pain. The animal shoved her fat side against Hamish, knocking him off his stool. Within the second, he was on his feet and punching the cow violently with one hand. When the other was about to strike, I shouted at him.

"Hamish, stop it, stop it. What's the matter with you?"

With his fist in mid-air he stopped and looked at me, making me gasp at the fury I saw in his eyes. "These cows are bad, Sarah. I tried to tell you at the auction, but you never listen."

Approaching him carefully as if he were rabid dog, I said, "Leave her to me." He lowered his fist, and I started rubbing my hands over the cow's injured flanks, turning away from his fury. "The fence needs to be inspected before we release these cows into the pastures. Could you ride the line to check? Junior can help me with the milking. Freddie too." I had taught Junior and Freddie how to milk, how to be gentle and kind, relaxing the cows with soothing words, even singing to them. Both my sons had become expert milkers, easily filling their buckets with delicious milk.

Hamish scowled, reminding me of Junior scowling at me earlier. I would have laughed if I had not been shocked by his sudden rage. He made a face at the cow and stomped out.

***

A few hours later, after we finished the milking, the boys and I returned to the cottage for lunch. I changed into a clean work dress, grabbed the pouch I used for collections, and headed back to the barn. Once a week, I accompanied Hamish on the milk deliveries to collect the money owed, making certain the amounts were correctly calculated.

Walking slowly across the barnyard, I fought off the haunting image of Joe falling from the barn's roof. To distract myself, I marvelled at the brilliant design of the dairy barn. The high fieldstone foundation could only be seen at the side of the barn where the land sloped down to the pasture below. The location was chosen specifically because of that downward slope; it allowed the foundation to be built right into the hillside, the full length embedded within the earth, providing protection against the frigid north winds. The land embraced the barn, keeping its roots sheltered, safe and warm. On the buried side, the stone foundation was hardly visible beneath the towering barn, with the ground banked high to create a ramp into wide doors. Our hay and dairy wagons were hauled up the ramp by work horses, allowing easy loading and unloading. The corral lay on the far side with two doors set into the foundation: one for the cows to enter for milking, and one for them to exit, keeping the process running smoothly. In winter, during harsh storms, the cows could be sheltered safely within the stone walls, the warmth of their bodies providing heat for them, as well as for the wooden barn above.

I climbed the ramp and walked through the open doors, expecting to find Hamish, returned from the fence line and working on the milk delivery. He was not there. Looking up, I enjoyed the soaring rafters reaching so high it felt like gazing into the ceiling of a cathedral. I inhaled the pungent odour of manure and animals, the exhilarating smells of my new enterprise. The barn was quiet with the cows out to pasture. One of the wagons was filled with milk cans, waiting for the horses to be harnessed. The sight of it, filled with raw milk, made me proud of what I had accomplished.

The rear doors of the barn were thrown open to the fresh spring day, providing a glorious view of Edenwae's lush pastures and hayfields. Walking toward the back of the barn to enjoy the vista, I glanced into the storage room and saw Hamish. With the warmer weather, he now chose to sleep in a solidly built bunk in the barn rather than be crammed in with the boys. He was turned away and had not noticed my approach. He wore only his trousers and suspenders with his jersey thrown off in the warmth. Unintended, my gaze lingered upon his muscled back, so much like Joe's. Were I to stroke it gently, would this man turn around and, by some miracle, become my husband?

Shaking my head, I let out a breath, returning to a true sense of time and space. "Hello, Hamish. I'm ready to go when you are."

At the sound of my voice, he quickly scrambled to pull his jersey back on. "Be right with you."

I retreated to the barn, waiting for him by the stalls. When he joined me, his blue eyes caused me to wonder, for the thousandth time, if I would ever be comfortable around him.

Not smiling, he eyed my collections bag and sauntered away to fetch the horses.

***

A short time later, we headed down the laneway and out onto the road toward our first stop. We swayed back and forth, sitting side by side on the bouncing seat. I intended to use this time together to review the milking practices, unhappy with Hamish's behaviour earlier. "About this morning. With the new cow—"

He opened his mouth to respond just as the wagon hit a deep hole in the road, causing us to lurch against each other. "Hold on," he said, pulling back on the reins and throwing an arm around me.

Suddenly, I felt like a small child yearning to be protected. Just as quickly, the feeling left me and I became furious with myself for yielding to this unbidden desire. Holding fast to the edge of the seat, I shook off his arm and stared at the towering wall of pine forest passing by on the side of the road.

"As I was saying, I wasn't pleased with your treatment of that cow this morning. It will affect milk production."

He kept looking straight ahead. "The problem is the cows. And I find your remarks surprisin'. I milk the way my granda taught me. Are you tellin' me my granda doesn't know how to milk a cow?"

"That is ridiculous. I've said nothing of the sort. And you'll not be convincing Duff that I'm critical of him. He would never teach you to be so rough. You're just making an excuse."

We fell into a troubled silence, not speaking until we reached the first cheese factory. There, we spoke long enough for me to give him instructions about how much the factory owed us. I stayed with the wagon, waiting for him to return with the cash and then discreetly counted the money before we moved on.

Bouncing along the road toward the next stop, I resumed our discussion, "Please respect my standards about how milk is produced at Edenwae."

"It's not about respect, it's simply a different approach. And I am insulted you think it's about standards."

"But it is. I believe it's important to feed my cows well and to treat them with respect and kindness. It results in delicious tasting milk. You've seen it for yourself, the cheese factories value Edenwae milk above all the other farms."

"Are you sayin' your milk is better than my granda's?"

"Will you please stop being so difficult? And stop putting words in my mouth."

While we continued down the uneven road, I clutched furiously to the seat. After a few more minutes of angry silence, I rounded on him again, "And another thing, the milking station isn't clean enough. Make sure you work harder at cleaning out the manure and washing down the floors."

"Oh, for God's sake, Sarah. We had no contaminated milk. Why are you goin' on at me for? What have I done?"

I should have known better than to criticize a Drury—it never ended well. Thinking of the many times I had remained silent with Joe just to keep the peace, a furious lump formed in my throat.

By now, we had arrived at our second stop. Before he jumped off the wagon, I reached for his arm. He looked at my hand on his shirt, then raised his blue eyes to mine, anger broiling within them. "Can we please get along. It would make running the dairy so much easier. Is there any way we can call a truce?" I said, pulling my hand away.

His face suddenly softened, his eyes dancing in the sunshine. He leaned in close to me, his breath sweet on my face. "There is. You'll just have to trust me." He turned and leapt off the wagon. Strolling toward the factory, his hips swayed with that slight Drury swagger.

When he returned, I counted the money without a word spoken, simply nodding at him to indicate we could move on. I felt his tension return, no doubt it did not sit well with him that I counted the money as though not trusting him.

I toned down my voice. "As you know, we've more cows arriving next week. Have you thought more about who we could hire as milkers? We can't possibly handle all the additional milking ourselves."

"What about Cameron?"

I burst out laughing. "Not likely."

He, too, laughed at the notion. "Well, perhaps I can hire a few hands. But I don't like strangers about the place."

I glanced at him. He was a stranger who looked like my dead husband, but acted nothing like him. I hated to admit that Hamish was a much harder worker than Joe. I should trust him, but for some reason I could not. There was something about the authority that slipped into his voice that sounded much too proprietary. "Perhaps one of your many relatives could help?"

"I do have a young cousin about Cameron's age, who doesn't have his head buried in a book. I could ask him."

"Just make certain they can churn butter for the days we can't get the milk to market. Perhaps, one or two young girls would be better."

"Oh, I don't like the idea of young girls around Junior and Freddie, you never know what might happen. And where would girls sleep?"

He was laughing at me now.

I decided to forego any further attempt at resolving our differences and remained silent for the rest of the journey home.

***

Shortly after arriving back at Edenwae, I heard the dogs barking and the clatter of a carriage coming down our laneway. Rushing out the front door, I saw Mother's carriage come to a halt, a coachman leaping down to offer his hand. I furtively looked toward the barn to see if the new cows were hidden in the pasture behind it. "Mother, what a surprise," I said, pasting a polite smile on my face.

The coachman struggled to keep Mother upright, while she rudely swatted his hand away. "Let us not bother with pleasantries, Sarah," she said. The dogs were now sniffing at her skirts and barking. "And get these filthy beasts away from me! Take me inside out of the dust and get me some tea."

I commanded the dogs to leave. Lifting her skirts, Mother waddled up the path and into my house. Fearing the worst, I rushed in behind her, calling to Jessie for tea.

It took a few minutes to remove her cape and settle by the warmth seeping from the parlour stove before Mother spoke. "I'm here to take Cameron," she said, her head held high as if she were issuing a royal command.

I felt a strange sense of relief that my mother had not come to threaten Edenwae, then bristled that she was here to take one of my children. "Take him where?"

"To live with me, of course, in town. He can attend the Academy, with the hope that one day he will be a well-educated young gentleman. He is the only one of your brood with such potential." While she waited for a response, she scrutinized me: the dusty work dress, the mat of unpinned hair, and my chipped nails rimmed with dirt.

Offended by her interference in my life again, I was just about to demand she leave, when I heard Cameron's voice. "Mother, please, may I go?" He stood at the entrance to the parlour, his eyes bright with hope.

"Did you know about this?"

Before I could vent anger at my mutinous child, Mother snapped at me. "Oh Sarah, if you paid attention to your children instead of pretending you're a farmer, you might realize that Cameron is not happy here. When you refused to move back into town, he asked your father if he could live with us and attend the Academy."

My boy was now looking panic stricken, his eyes darting back and forth between his grandmother and me. "It wasn't actually like that," he said. "I mean...well...the other day, I told Grandfather I hoped to attend the Academy, perhaps go on further too. That's all, I said. And I know I was eavesdropping just now, but when I heard what Grandmama offered, I had to speak up. I'm sorry, Mother, but I'd really like to go."

"But why didn't you talk to me?" I asked him.

"Oh, for God's sake, don't be so hard on the boy," Mother said coldly. "Perhaps I misrepresented how this happened. But you clearly can't see what's best for him. It's so unfair to keep such a smart boy *here*," she ended, glancing around my cramped parlour.

Something gave way inside of me. Mother was right. I went to Cameron, grasping his shoulders, and returning his sharp penetrating stare. He stood rigidly, his determination to leave this place breaking my heart. "This is what you truly want, Cameron?"

He nodded.

"Then, yes, you may go."

His attractive young face came alive with excitement. "Oh, Mother, thank you. I'll come back to visit often, I promise."

As I drew him to me, I saw the gloating look of utter satisfaction on Mother's face.

Chapter 12

One hot hazy summer day, Father and I sat upon our horses, high atop the hill in the shade of the maples. The air stank of horse sweat. Looking down, I saw our fat cows laying beneath trees at a pasture's border, sheltering themselves from the heat of the sun. Huddled in a tight circle, their mouths chewing cud, they looked as if they were having a chat. Perhaps they were gossiping about the bull eyeing them from the confines of his corral. In the background, the barn, with "Edenwae" painted in white letters across its gable end, towered high into the sky, obliterating any view of my humble cottage. I felt sweat rolling down the middle of my back. I reached for my canteen to take a big gulp of water, offering it to my father first. It was an extremely hot day, so hot that the birds refused to sing. The only sound was the ceaseless buzz of insects.

Father took the offered canteen and drank deeply before he spoke. "What a marvellous sight, Sarah, look what you have done." Sitting a little higher in my saddle, I basked in my father's praise. His horse started pawing the ground, but he held firmly to the reins. "You have gone way beyond my wildest expectations."

I grinned, taking back the canteen and drinking deeply. It had turned out to be an ideal time to buy dairy cows. Farmers who had stubbornly stuck to one crop, refusing to diversify into dairy were now in dire straits as wheat prices fell, forcing them to sell off their livestock. There was a glut of high-quality Guernsey cows at auction, I had even managed to buy a very healthy bull at a bargain price. Benefiting from the misfortune of others bothered me slightly, but how could I have resisted?

The expansion of our dairy was timed perfectly; the local cheese factories' sharp-tasting wheels of cheddar had become popular in England, which meant there was a constant demand for the raw milk needed to make their cheese. With my herd now numbering upwards of thirty cows, Edenwae had become a major supplier. I was considering building another dairy barn since many of my cows would be ready to calve over the next few months.

Surveying all that I had accomplished in such a short time, a tiny snake of anxiety crept into my belly—Edenwae had become overextended. I was thinking of asking Father for an extension on his loan, even asking to increase the loan to include the cost of a new barn. I turned to Father, wondering if this might be a good time to ask. "But I couldn't have done it without you, dear Father."

"My faith in you has paid off, my dear. But I must ask you something." He started to fidget with the reins, making his horse jittery. "It is just. . .well dear, Edenwae appears to be doing so well. . .do you think you are in a position to repay my loan—starting immediately?"

My jaw clenched reflexively. Mother must be behind this request. Unintended, I pulled back on my horse's reins, and he started to move sideways. Needing to stall for time, I said, "We need to get these horses out of the heat and watered. May we talk later?"

He nodded, his eyes avoiding mine as we headed slowly down the hill.

***

After the sun set, the heat eased. Father and I sat alone on the kitchen porch in the pitch black of night. The stars hid behind a blanket of dense clouds. Crickets, frogs, and all manner of night creatures were exuberant in a cacophony of chirps, croaks, and soaring trills. "I hope you'll be comfortable on Junior's cot. I am happy to give you my bed," I said.

"No, of course not. I look forward to sleeping with the boys, it will be an adventure for us."

"What's going on? Is it Mother?"

"No. It's not that. . ."

It was too dark to see his face and read his thoughts. "Then why ask for repayment now? Didn't we agree to one year? That's next spring, isn't it?"

96

I heard him sigh heavily. "Yes… I was just hoping you could begin paying me now."

"But why? Does Mother know?"

"No. She's suspicious and keeps asking me how you could possibly be surviving on this farm. But I haven't told her anything."

"Why, then?" The space around us filled with the persistent chirps of crickets. When he did not answer, I plunged into the defence prepared in haste this afternoon. "These are the early days. Your investment covered the purchase of the herd, but I bought the bull, another wagon and work horses. I hired more workers. And we needed more equipment and supplies than I first anticipated. All the earnings, which are impressive, help with these additional costs. By spring, with winter milking, I hope to make a profit."

"What if it is a heavy snow year?"

I sighed. "If the roads are impassable, we'll churn butter… but we may have to throw away milk. Everything is new, so we're bound to have problems. Surely, you know that?"

He remained silent. Not being able to see his face made his silence feel much more ominous. "Would you like to see the books? It's been a few months since you last reviewed them."

Finally, he spoke, "No need. If I understand you correctly, you are telling me you don't have the money." He struck a match across his boot, his face illuminated in the flare. Sucking the flame into the bowl of his pipe, cheeks drawn in and lips puckered, he looked like a very old man, wrinkled and sad.

"Father, what is it?"

"Nothing, nothing…I was just hoping…" He broke off for a moment, puffing on his pipe, its sweet smell now surrounding us, before saying, "Very well then, we'll wait until spring. But no longer."

***

The next morning when Father rode away, I watched the dust his horse kicked up disappear into the air. I felt Edenwae teetering on the verge of following that dust, simply disappearing into thin air if Father insisted on the loan repayment in the spring. I had lied to him, I needed the full spring, and likely well into next summer before there was profit. I made the decision to not tell him the truth, planning to ask for an extension next spring. Deceiving my father did not sit well with me after all he had done, but he was not honest with me either, and that bothered me more. Why could he not carry this loan for a few seasons longer? The amount must be such a small portion of his fortune. None of this made sense.

Chapter 13

Autumn transformed the countryside into a striking tapestry rioting with reds, oranges, and yellows intermingled with the green of pines. On a clear cool day, I rode among the hilltop maples, now a brilliant shade of red. Dismounting, I sat down on a flat boulder. It was one year ago today that I had sat on this very rock, furious with Joe. On such a sorrowful anniversary, I felt a compulsion to visit this spot and be alone with my memories of that day.

Perhaps, I hoped to chase away the question Joe would never be able to answer. *What happened to our savings?* If only I could find that money, Father's debt could be paid. It was a faint hope, but it was all I had. The debt was always on my mind. If he insisted on repayment, I would be forced to sell my herd. If that happened, there would never be enough money to buy this land, and Duff would be sure to give up on me and my sons. There had been no sign of him since that day he refused to talk about this land. Hamish was undoubtedly keeping my father-in-law well informed, and I thought often about what he might be saying and whether it might eventually cause Duff to withdraw his support.

Frustrated by my inability to solve this problem, I remounted and headed home. Emerging from the trees I was stopped by the thought that through some strange alchemy of time and space I might see Joe on the barn roof. Instead, a startling question presented itself: if Joe were still alive, would this situation exist? He would have refused any money from my father. We might have finished the barn, but without the savings we could not have purchased the cows and equipment. It was so much better to have gotten this far, to see Edenwae before my eyes, even if it might be snatched away from me at any moment. Although my heart still ached for Joe, his death had made all of this possible.

Feeling the need to outrun my thoughts, I urged my horse into a full gallop and raced downhill into the barnyard.

Freddie ran straight into my path, and it took all my strength to pull up the reins fast enough to miss him. "What is it?" I called out, a shiver sweeping up my spine. "What's happened?" I slid off my horse to hug Freddie. "You need to be more careful around horses," I said, my voice shaking.

He buried his head into my bosom. "Sorry, Ma." His muffled voice made him sound like a toddler. Looking over his head, I noticed Junior leaving the barn, throwing his cap to the ground in frustration. Seeing me, he stomped over, his face looking like thunder. Making certain Freddie remained at a safe distance, I tied my horse to a hitching rail, then braced myself for news of Hamish's latest offence.

"Ma, you have to talk to Hamish. The barn is simply not clean enough. He's gone off to the cottage and left it in a mess. For God's sake, I could run the dairy better—"

I cut him off. "All in good time. You know it will be a few more years before you can take over. We don't own the land yet."

"But I can run the dairy, and so much better than he does. I understand what you expect. He fights you all the time. Wouldn't you rather have me run things?" Even though his voice was deeper these days, he was starting to sound whiney. The sun highlighted the shadowy beginnings of facial hair, and his arms and legs were becoming lanky. "Of course, I would, but I've no choice. Your granda wants Hamish here. Anyway, he's been a big help."

He turned to go, muttering, "It's just not fair."

It felt wrong to crush his ambition, but a boy could not possibly negotiate with men. I knew all too well the frustration of being dismissed. Grabbing him by the arm, I pulled him back to me. "I know, my love. But there's no need to rush. We've just got started." I reached up to muss his hair, but he pulled away.

Linking an arm though Freddie's skinny arm I tried to link my other into Junior's, but he was having none of it and stormed off back to the barn. In need of solace, I snuggled in close to Freddie, pressing my strength into his frail body.

"It's one year ago today, isn't it?" he said.

I should not be surprised. Freddie still felt the loss of his father. "Yes, my love. I didn't wish to remind you."

He stopped abruptly, turning toward me. "Every single day I feel that Da is with me, but today the feeling is incredibly strong. That's why I rushed to greet you. I think he's here with us. I can feel his spirit, Ma."

Thankfully, his older brother was out of earshot. Junior was not kind to Freddie about the boy's belief that his father was still with us in spirit, hovering over our every day. "You know I think you may be right, Freddie. I have the same sense."

We arrived at our cottage, and I gave him one more squeeze before releasing him.

When I stepped over the threshold, Cameron bolted toward me. He was home for a weekend visit, anxious to speak with me, but I had put him off, needing my time alone amongst the maples. "Mother, I have just the thing to increase our production." He waived a journal in my face. I struggled to see what he had. "Look at this. It's a milking machine. Faster and higher-yield milking." He stopped waiving the journal around and held it still for me.

I looked at the drawing in a worn copy of *Scientific American*. Pictured under an alarmed cow, was a bulbous glass contraption with long tubes attached to the teats. "Well, that's wonderful. Does it really work? Are other dairies recommending it?"

"Yes, it's being used all over America. Read what it says here. It's the newest and best thing for large dairies."

Hamish appeared behind Cameron. "I told him it won't work. The cows will be injured, and the milk spoilt. It'd be better if he joined us in milking." He nudged Cameron in a manner that was not playful.

"Don't listen to Hamish. This model is different. Those issues were fixed," he added resentfully, in a tone that grew into condescension towards Hamish. His studies at the Academy were giving him a surer sense of himself.

"It's a very bad idea. We won't do it," Hamish said.

Ignoring Hamish, I spoke to Cameron, "May I look at that more closely, please?"

Cameron handed me the journal and we looked at it together. "Here's everything you need to know. You can set several of them up at once, milking many cows at the same time. It's ingenious."

After a study of the page and illustration, I looked at Hamish. "Actually, I think this could be a very good idea. And it just might allow us to survive the winter without paying for hired help."

"But it'll cost a great deal to buy these machines? Why would we take such a risk?" Hamish said, his anger now directed toward me.

"I could make most of the machine myself," Cameron asserted. "We'd just need to buy the parts. I know I could do it." His face was so full of determination, he reminded me of myself.

"It's worth a try. You put a list together, then make us one."

"You're havin' him on, Sarah," said Hamish. "Stop feedin' his ridiculous ideas."

"Everyone thought my ideas were ridiculous too, didn't they?" I replied, staring him down. "It costs little to explore an idea."

Suddenly the dogs started barking, and we heard a horse canter into the barnyard. Peering out the window we saw Duff yanking hard on his poor horse's reins.

Hamish hurried outside to greet him. Junior and I followed, staying behind, watching as Duff slid off his saddle, his eyes riveted to the spot where Joe had died. He lifted his hat as though standing before an altar, then straightened, putting his hat back on as Hamish went up to him and touched his shoulder. Undoubtedly, he remembered this day a year ago too. He brushed off Hamish's hand and looked at him sternly. "I've come to see what ye have been up to." He turned to me. "How are ye, lass?" His piercing eyes scanned my body as if looking for weakness.

"Fine, thank you, Duff. I'll be happy to show you around."

His eyes darted to Hamish. "He will do it."

"No. I will," I said, but he was already walking into the barn, Hamish beside him. I followed with Junior alongside me.

Once inside, Duff looked around, taking in the long line of milk cans waiting to be loaded for delivery, then he turned to Hamish. "The milkin' station is below?"

"Yes, granda, let me show you." Junior jumped in, eager to take Duff to the ladder leading to the bottom level. I decided to stay put, expecting Duff to watch me critically as I struggled with my skirts on the ladder.

After the three of them returned, and Duff had examined the gear and supplies in the storeroom, he looked to Hamish. "Ye have been workin' hard. Well done, lad."

"Thank you." Hamish rubbed his hands down the length of his suspenders, straightening his shoulders.

Junior stood defiantly before his grandfather. "We have all worked hard. And Ma—"

Duff cut him off, "I know that." He strode over to the open back doors to look at the corral. "I see you've a bull. And some of yer cows are ready to calve. Are ye plannin' winter milkin'?"

"Yes, we are," I said. He turned to me, his hard eyes wide with surprise. His silent stare unnerved me. "I know it's a risk."

"Aye, that it is. Hamish didn't tell me 'bout it." He looked at his grandson with a hard glare.

"It was Sarah's idea," Hamish said, with a sideways grin that could have been pride but was more likely passing the blame on. Before I could decide which, Duff turned on me.

"Was it, then?" Duff examined my face, his angry stare disquieting me. "I have been hearin' 'bout all the Guernsey ye bought. It's a big herd."

"We have enough contracts to sell all the milk," I said.

"Do ye now?"

"There's plenty of demand for raw milk. Room for all of us."

"I know. . . I have no issue with ye." He cast his eyes around my dairy and out to the pastures.

A pause, and then I asked, "Please tell me the amount owed to you for this land?"

"I will not discuss that with ye."

"But you must. I plan to pay out the rest soon, in Junior's name. I need to know what's owed."

He turned toward me and said nothing. I stood straight, my son alongside me. Junior squared his shoulders under the fierce stare of his granda. With a grunt of disapproval, Duff looked to Hamish. "Walk with me to my horse."

Junior and I were left alone in the barn, burning with impatience and frustration at his dismissal of us. Why won't he tell me the truth about this land?

Chapter 14

For the remainder of the fall and into the winter days before Christmas, my dairy thrived. With no harsh winter storms yet, we had been delivering our milk daily, and I hoped this was a sign that the winter would be mild. Hamish built an addition onto the cottage with two connected rooms, one with a bed for him, and another with two cots crammed in for the lads he had hired as milkers. All appeared to be going well. Still, if it turned into a stormy winter and the horses could not pull the sleighs through the deep snow, I might sink under the weight of undeliverable milk.

On Christmas Eve, Father surprised us with his first visit since that hot summer day when he had asked for repayment of the loan. He stood just inside our front door, hat pulled down over his ears and a wool scarf encircled his neck, the collar of a frock coat pulled up high. Father's face was more drawn and wrinkled, looking almost ghostly pale. Junior and Freddie stomped in the door behind him, burdened with packages and gifts.

After the boys returned to their chores, Father and I settled in front of the parlour stove, with tea steeping on the nearby table. He handed me a letter. "From your sister."

Nodding, I placed it in my skirt pocket. "How is she? Her letters are always vague."

"You know, the road runs both ways."

I fidgeted with my skirt. "I can't take the time away from the dairy."

He searched my face. "I'd hoped you would come to town with good news. Cameron told me of his milking machine. If it works, you could save costs."

"Maybe... he just got it up and running last weekend. It is still an experiment, and we've had problems." I fell silent for a moment, then asked, "How is Mother?"

"She still has no idea about my help to you. If that's what you mean?"

I knelt to add more wood to the parlour stove. "I've not seen her since she took Cameron away. And he says very little about either of you on his weekends here." I looked up at Father and saw his drawn face, eyes riveted on the flames. "How are you, Father?" I slammed the door of the stove shut.

"If you could only give me a small payment, it could make all the difference."

Drawing close to him I took his hand. "Forgive me, but it makes no sense to me that you'd need my money. Is the foundry not doing well? Please tell me your problems."

He heaved a sigh so great it was as if his entire body exhaled. "I've been worrying for some time now about what would happen when the railway moved further west. I might lose contracts. There are foundries all along the new route, much closer to the new construction. It's not just the rail companies I worry about. Local business is declining as well. That is why...". He lowered his head in silence.

"What is it?"

Looking up, he said, "Never mind. Just pay me in the spring please, and all will be well." He gripped my hand firmly. "Now tell me, why haven't you visited your sister?"

I paused for a moment, considering how much to reveal. "When Tabitha took my baby, I was certain we'd visit each other often. Both of us were comfortable with the arrangement. But I can't bring myself to go to Grandview now, and she's never asked me to." I bit down hard on my lip to quiet a quiver.

"I suspected as much." He squeezed my hand. "Robert is a wonderful little baby. You can be proud of him."

"Do you see him often? Has Mother——?" My voice choked on her name.

He stared into the fire for a moment before answering. "She visits him often. Even more, now, after we learned of Albert's plan to adopt him."

"Adopt him?"

"Oh dear, I assumed Tabitha had told you in her letters."

"She never writes about anything important, just nonsense. Oh, I should've known she was up to something." My mouth felt suddenly dry.

"But was that not the intention all along?"

"I'd just hoped that once the dairy was up and running, I could. . ." I trailed off, then went to the small tea table, poured two cups, handed Father one and took a gulp from mine, burning my tongue.

"Do you really think that's fair to your sister and her husband?"

I shrugged, holding back a scream about what was fair to *me*.

We subsided into an uneasy silence before he continued. "Sarah, I brought a goose for your Christmas dinner and some other supplies, I also have gifts for all of you. After tea, I'll head back to town. The skies look like a storm might be on the way."

***

That night a dense blizzard blew in. Great drifts of snow banked up against the dairy barn. On Christmas morning, we dug our way out the kitchen door to reach the barn and milk the cows. Later that day, while the snow kept falling outside, we gathered around the long pine table laden with food. The smells of the roasting goose, yams, potatoes, turnips, onions, and baking mincemeat pies had permeated the cramped cottage, and we were eager to tuck in. Hamish and the hired hands had planned to visit their families for Christmas day, but with the storm raging they were trapped here with the rest of us.

I held up a cup of wine. "Cheers everyone, Merry Christmas." I felt the intensity of Hamish's eyes. When I looked at him, his eyes held mine. Heat rushed to my cheeks.

After plates were cleaned, and fingers were licked, we pushed back from the table. I turned to Junior. "Would you like to read *A Christmas Carol* this year?" Every Christmas, Joe would read this story to us. By the way my son smiled and nodded, I could see that his grief had been set aside for a moment, replaced by the pride he felt at stepping into his father's shoes in such a small way. What would he feel when Edenwae was finally his?

We soon gathered around the parlour stove, with the twins nestled around me, and the boys and the hired lads scattered on the rug near the heat. Jessie sat nearby on a stool and Hamish stood behind me. After the reading, the children ran to the kitchen to play with checkers and other games given to them by Father. Jessie left to tidy up.

Hamish dragged a chair close and sat down beside me. He had a small bottle of whisky in one hand. Pointing to it, he said, "Would you like a sip?" He pulled out two small cups from a pocket, filled them, handed me one, and set the bottle down on the floor. He looked at me and leaned in. "To your health."

I downed the whisky and enjoyed the warmth of it spreading down my throat. I looked at him, smiling. "Thank you for everything you've done to help me."

"It's been my pleasure," he said, leaning closer.

Meeting his gaze, I said, "What will you do after you leave here?"

He drew nearer. "Do you really want me gone?"

The look in his eyes and his breath on my face caused me to pull back.

"Hamish," Jessie called from the kitchen, "Can you fetch more wood?"

Still looking at me, he yelled back, "Be right there." Then he left me alone to wonder what would have happened next if Jessie had not called out.

***

Two days later, the snow finally stopped. That morning, Junior, Freddie, and I struggled through the deep snow. We could hear the cows complaining loudly; they had been confined within the lower level of the barn for days and were clearly fed up. The wide barn doors had yet to be cleared of the deep drifts piled up against them, a chore that must be done to allow the wagons out for deliveries. Following the dug path down the hill to the rear of the barn, we found the hired lads pouring more milk out into the large frozen pond of undeliverable milk. The sight of it caused my heart to sink—all that lost income. The lads had been useless at churning the milk into butter, and there was too much for Jessie and me to churn on our own.

Entering the barn, we dodged cows as they pushed for the door, eager to be released from captivity. The air inside reeked of dung and sour milk. In the murky darkness, Hamish sat on a milking stool, yanking on teats. Seeing us, he smiled and indicated towards the cows waiting impatiently for their turn, their loud moos making it difficult to hear as he yelled, "Watch your teeth."

Stroking the side of one of the agitated cows, I pulled up a stool and started milking, yelling over my shoulder, "Junior, get that milking contraption going. See if Cameron's experiment can help us milk these cows faster."

Soon I started up our favourite milking song:
> *"Cows of my beloved Colin*
> *Iain's cows, my dear —*
> *Cows that would fill up the milking bucket…"*

Everyone joined in, our voices blending into a surprisingly beautiful choir. Since the beginning of the cold weather, this has become our daily ritual. Glancing at Hamish, I caught him smiling at me, a pleasant look in his eye, so unlike the fury I had seen when he punched the cow that day.

After the cows were milked, Hamish and I stood in the corral outside the dairy watching the liberated cows plough through the belly-high snow. The lads were using large wooden shovels to clear the drift from the barn doors, and Junior and Freddie were making sure the snow runners were securely attached to the wagon.

"More storms like that and we'll have a terrible winter indeed," I said.

"You knew the risk."

I stared at the cows, refusing to look at him. "I made a mistake. Is that what you want me to say?"

He sighed. "I didn't mean that. So far, we've done well. I can see the value in producin' all year."

"You were quick to blame me when you thought your granda was criticizing the decision," I snapped.

"What? That wasn't it. I was givin' you credit." He touched my arm. "It'll be fine. Everythin' will work out. I promise."

I turned to him and searched his face. "Why are you here?"

His face took a serious turn, and he drew close "To help you. And I—"

Junior suddenly appeared behind us. "That milking contraption of Cameron's has damaged the cow's teats."

Turning away from Hamish, I glanced upward to see ominous black clouds obliterating the sun.

Chapter 15

For the rest of the winter, we had too many crippling storms to count. While the winds raged outside, we hunkered down inside our cramped cottage, then dug our way out to milk the cows and throw away the undeliverable milk. The likelihood of paying my father in the spring drained away each time we threw out that milk, and I was not looking forward to the day he would come to collect my debt. Like last winter, we spent the long dark evenings with Hamish and Jessie sitting around the kitchen table and me in the parlour with my boys. This year, the milking lads were there too. Every so often, Hamish would appear at the parlour door, smile at me, then come in to sit nearby and suggest an idea he had for the dairy, or explain a problem he had solved. We were never alone, leaving me to wonder what he had meant to say to me that day in the barn.

Finally, spring arrived. The trees dripped with melting snow and great sheets of ice crashed down from the dairy barn roof. On one exceptionally warm day, Father rode up our laneway and I could no longer avoid facing my reckoning.

We spent a few pleasant moments in the parlour with the boys, before I sent them away. Father and I settled by the parlour stove, and I stared at him, struggling to find the words to tell him there was no money.

He reached into his breast pocket and handed me an envelope. I recognized it immediately as Mother's stationery.

"What's this?" Opening the envelope and unfolding the thick notepaper inside, I caught a whiff of lavender. After reading the note, I shrugged my shoulders. "What in God's name is she up to? I haven't set foot in your home for years, why is she now inviting me to tea?"

"Your Mother insists you attend." He stared into the fire, remaining silent. The sounds of the ticking clock and the roaring of the fire filled the space between us. With every passing minute the lump in my chest grew larger.

"Does Mother know about your loan to me?" I reached over to touch his hand, noticing the fire hadn't yet warmed it, the bony feel of it still icy cold.

He met my gaze with the hint of a smile nudging the edges of his pale lips. "Actually, your mother has found a gentleman she'd like you to meet."

Ripples of laughter pealed from my mouth. "Oh, I'm sorry. I-I can't help it. What a fool's errand that is. No gentleman would be interested in a widow with five boys. Oh really, she can't be serious?"

Affected by my laughter, Father chuckled. "You know how she is. She's determined to find you a match."

"But, *why?*"

Father dropped his head slightly and peered at me through unruly eyebrows. "Because she believes you can still elevate your circumstances through marriage."

"That's ridiculous. I don't need a man to make my way in this world."

Grasping my hand, he searched my face. "Are you so certain of that, Sarah? You would not have survived without help from me. And from Duff. And from Hamish."

I dropped his hand and turned toward the fire, struggling to remain calm. "I'm well aware of that. But with your support, why would I need a husband? And you know your help is only temporary. I'll repay you... soon."

Father heaved a great sigh. "You know perfectly well your mother abhors your circumstances. She insists upon making you an honest woman and she loathes the gossip around town about you and Hamish."

"And is that the way you feel too? That there is truth to the rumours?" His expression reminded me of the look I received when he learned of my first pregnancy.

"I've noticed the way Hamish looks at you."

"Oh, Father, you don't think——?"

"Of course not. I know you loved Joe, and it was your way of getting what you wanted. I don't believe you are given to impulsive behaviours." His forehead compressed into a maze of deep wrinkles. "However, it is just...well.... I'd feel better about your future if you had a husband. This is a cruel world for a woman on her own, there will be a day when I'm not here to help and protect you."

I knelt beside him and grasped his arm. "Father...." My vision blurred. "Are you ill?"

"Hush, please. I'm fine. It's my concern for you, that's all. It would relieve me of a great burden if you were to marry."

I rose and walked slowly across the parlour on shaking legs, turning my back so he could not see the impact of his words: *a great burden*. Had he stopped believing in me?

After a moment, I turned to confront him. "But what about Edenwae? You see for yourself that I'm succeeding. I just need more time."

"That is another matter entirely, my dear. We'll not speak of it now." He stared into the fire.

Striding back to his side, I knelt beside him and pulled on his arm until he looked at me. "You're not making sense. Is it Mother? Does she know about your loan to me?"

His eyes hardened, and then he turned back toward the fire. "I'm not prepared to discuss that today."

"Please tell me what's going on."

"I wish it was as simple as your mother trying to get her way. There are other reasons that I'll not share with you," he said, his eyes fixed upon the flickering flames.

Not knowing what else to do, I sat in my chair and rocked gently, soon joining my father in staring blankly into the fire. I jumped when he spoke after a long silence. "Before I leave, you must accept the invitation to your mother's tea party. I cannot face her should you refuse. You owe me this."

Heat flushed my cheeks. "Yes, of course I'll attend."

"Wonderful." He was acting as if there had not just been great tension between us, smiling warmly at me and patting my hand before he stood up. "You are to arrive in town two days in advance to shop for appropriate attire. The boys aren't invited." And with that, he said his farewells and left.

***

Later that night, alone in my bed, I fumed over father's visit. I was completely at the mercy of men—all their infernal secrets—and me, powerless to learn the truth. They could do whatever they liked, and not answer to me, a mere woman. Would I ever be able to forge my own path in this world ruled by men. Making it even more infuriating was that my parents believed the best way forward was for me to marry again. *There must be another way!*

Chapter 16

The day before Mother's tea party, I rode toward my parents' home. The sun had finally made an appearance, chasing away the grey skies, and its warmth on my face lightened my mood, hopefully enough to help me endure whatever pretentious event my mother had planned. Fourteen years ago, I rode away and never returned, swearing to Joe that if he was not welcome in my parents' home, I would never again ride this street. Now Joe was gone, yet I still resisted coming here, fearing I might become trapped by one of Mother's plots.

Turning onto the laneway leading to my parents' home, I was surprised by new filigrees and ornamentations on the gables, and an extensive addition built on the south side. Following the laneway around the back, I found a large stable housing a collection of carriages. Looking around, I wondered why on earth Father needed money. By all appearances, he possessed a great deal of wealth. A stable boy appeared and took my horse. Following his directions, I made my way toward a grand entranceway within the new addition.

Suddenly, the door flew open, and Mother waddled out. "Really, I was expecting you here yesterday."

"So nice to see you, too," I said, trying to not sound sarcastic, "Didn't Father tell you I couldn't leave my farm for that long? There's too much work to just leave for several days."

"He did. But you really should have come yesterday, that is a ridiculous reason. Now, we've so much to do with too little time. We must leave immediately. I have an appointment with my dressmaker." Noticing my appearance, she abruptly stopped talking. "Oh, for God's sake, Sarah. You look like a peasant." I wore men's work trousers with leather chaps and a long frock coat, with my hair stuffed into a wide brimmed hat. "Go inside immediately and clean yourself up. You reek of horse. Oh Lord, save me. Humphreys!" A servant appeared magically behind Mother. "Have the maids fill a bath for my daughter. Immediately!"

***

Several hours later, cleaned and dressed up, and taken clothes shopping, I fled to my childhood bedroom, claiming the need for rest. Not bothering to shed the ill-fitting gown borrowed from Mother, I sank into the softness of my old bed. I could not think of the last time I had the luxury of laying down in the middle of the day.

There was a quiet tap at my door. "Mother, it's me, Cameron. May I come in?"

I rushed to open the door and pulled him inside. "Oh, my love, I've missed you. How are you?"

After a long hug he gently pulled away from me. My third-born son wore a young gentleman's attire: crisp woollen trousers, brand new boots and a satin vest with a school jacket and tie. His dark curls were trimmed close to his head and looked freshly washed. It suited him, to wear such fine clothes and to be freshly scrubbed. Holding up one of his hands, I saw his nails were clean and clipped short. In only a few months, Cameron had been completely transformed from a farm boy into an academy student. "I'm fine. School is incredible."

"And what about living here?"

"Come, I'll show you my rooms." I followed him down a passageway to the new addition, through an oak door into a large room lined with bookshelves. At the centre of the room were desks and comfortable chairs. "This is where I study. And wait until you see my room." Cameron opened one of several doors leading off the main room to reveal a well-appointed bedroom with deep blue patterned bed linen and a large wardrobe. "This is my room and there are four more just like it. I had my pick. And there's a whole room dedicated to bathing, and it even has a toilet chair. No more running to the outhouse. I can have a hot bath every day if I like."

"What wonderful rooms, my love. But who else lives here?"

"No one yet, but Grandmama says my brothers can live here any time."

I shivered as Mother's plan for my sons became clear.

***

The next day, after hours spent with maids styling my hair and fussing over my face and hands, I was transformed. Mother chose a pale blue silk tea gown for me with a fitted bodice, discreetly cut to provide a glimpse of breast. Standing in front of a full-length mirror, I appreciated the slim fit of the skirt and how it swirled sensuously about me. It had been such a long time since I felt pretty.

Walking carefully downstairs, I entered the formal parlour at the front of my parents' house. The wallpaper was festooned with swirling patterns from tall baseboards running right up to the sculpted plaster cornice. The large windows were flanked by heavy drapes of another flamboyant pattern and topped by great valances of gathered material. The finely carved furnishings were decorated with crocheted doilies and swathes of tasselled covers, apparently designed to protect the furniture's modesty. Even the grand piano had its legs covered. The large tea table was set with china, crystal, and silver I had not seen before, and servants stood at the ready to serve.

My attention was drawn to a very large portrait of a woman hung on the wall behind the tea table. It took me a moment to recognize the woman as Mother. She was portrayed as a much younger and slimmer woman, posed in a manner that was reminiscent of the Queen, holding a bible in her lap. The artist had done a masterful job of capturing Mother's stern expression of disapproval with her mouth turned down in a slight frown. Walking past it, I had the distinct sensation that the eyes in the portrait were following me. Distracted by the portrait, it took a moment to realize that my mother's guest had already arrived.

She rushed over to me, looking like an overstuffed doll in her embroidered tea gown. "There you are my darling Sarah." After making a great show of kissing me on both cheeks, she took my hand and led me over to the fireplace where Father stood with a young gentleman.

"Allow me to introduce you to my charming daughter. Sarah, this is Mr. Charles Bulmore," Father said, as my mother placed my hand into the man's outstretched fingers.

He touched my fingertips and bowed graciously to brush my hand with his lips. A well-practiced greeting from a perfect gentleman. I had expected a wizened old man who hoped his money and position might entice a poor widow into his bed. Instead, Charles was a vibrant young man with well-tamed hair and sideburns in a riot of brown, red and blond, a sharp nose and jawline, and hazel eyes dancing with flecks of green.

"Pleased to meet you, Mr. Bulmore," I said, suddenly grateful for my mother's insistence on an attractive presentation. When he smiled, I noticed his lips were finely sculpted—there was something about the pleasing curve of them that made me feel comfortable in his presence.

"My pleasure. May I call you Sarah?" He spoke with a refined English accent.

I almost laughed at the thought of the alternative, addressing me as Mrs. Drury in my parents' parlour. But it might have been worth it to see the expression on Mother's face. Smiling broadly, I met his gaze. "Yes, of course, and may I call you Charles?" I heard a loud tut, tut from Mother. I had forgotten it was impertinent for a lady to respond in such a bold way. However, Charles appeared to neither notice Mother's reprimand, nor did he seem to mind my direct manner. In fact, given the gleam in his eye, I suspect he quite liked it.

Mother motioned to her servants while she addressed us. "Please, let us be seated." The four of us sat down at the large tea table, Charles sat to my left, Father to my right and Mother across from me. A parade of serving plates filled with tiny sandwiches cut into precise squares, rectangles, and spirals were offered to each of us by a servant while another poured tea, brandy, and sherry into our cups. Once the first service was finished, the staff withdrew discreetly, and Mother held court.

"I am so delighted you could join us for tea, Charles. You know that our Sarah was widowed after the untimely death of her husband, and she's moving back to town." With eyes gauging every minute exchange between Charles and myself, she kept smiling, as if indicating that we should start courting this instant.

Smiling politely, Charles nodded toward my mother, then looked at me with a sudden recognition. "Actually, I believe I've heard a great many things about your daughter." I gulped my tea and stared at him.

Mother coughed loudly. "Well, Charles, you surprise me. I did not think you would listen to gossip." She drew out the last word as if it were something she would never consider herself.

Smiling, Charles kept his keen eyes on me. "You live on some of the finest farmland in this area, do you not?" There was an edge to this man that seemed slightly inappropriate for a gentleman.

I leaned closer, cleared my throat and avoided looking at Mother. "Well, yes I do. The land has been owned by my late husband's family for three generations."

"That would make the Drurys one of the first settlers in the area, would it not?" At the mention of the Drury name, Mother snorted, almost expelling her sherry out her nose.

Resisting the urge to laugh, I spoke soberly to Charles. "Yes, that's true. They own much of the land running north and as far west as the next township."

Mother interrupted. "We must not speak of the past. Charles, may I interest you in the sweets course?" Snapping her fingers, the servants appeared but looked confused as to what they should do, since our plates remained full of sandwiches.

Fortunately, Father intervened. "Please pour us more drinks."

Before Mother could speak, Charles turned back to me. "I hear that you have a large-scale dairy on your land?"

"Why… yes," I replied, wondering again who this man really was. "My late husband was in the midst of expanding my small farm dairy when he had his accident. After he died, his family helped to complete our plans." My voice choked off. It felt wrong not mentioning Father's support. But how could I, with Mother looking at me?

"Yes, Charles, it is a thriving enterprise," Father said, reaching for my hand.

"And are your sons involved in the dairy?"

"One of my grandsons is attending the Academy and living here with us." Mother interrupted again, clearly determined to hide the aspects of my life she deemed unattractive or irrelevant.

"Really, that is marvellous. And the others?"

"My two eldest boys are very involved in the dairy, but the twins are too young."

"It is time for the sweets," Mother said, as she snapped her fingers once again for her servants. While they served, she whispered to Father, who then began a lengthy discussion with Charles about the railway industry.

About an hour later, with the plates cleared, the men pushed back from the table. Mother looked to Father. "Now, Bertrand, will you accompany me to our quarters, I may have had a little too much sherry, I must lie down."

"Now? I was just about to invite Charles for a smoke in my study?" Father had his pipe in his hand and was rooting around in his pocket for the tobacco pouch. But Mother was rising, holding out her hand for Father's support. "See to the needs of our guest," she said to the servant standing nearby. "Charles, it was a pleasure. Stay as long as you like. Sarah, I assume you will entertain our guest. Come, Bertrand."

Charles sprang to his feet, "Thank you for your hospitality. It has been a wonderful evening. Bertie, I hope to see you soon, perhaps I could tour your foundry one day?"

Nodding, Father shook his hand and followed Mother out the door.

Turning to our guest, I said, "I'm so sorry. Mother can be rather overbearing."

He gave a reassuring smile. "I don't mind, really. I was hoping we could resume our earlier conversation."

"Of course." I dismissed the servants and invited him to sit on the comfortable wingback chairs on either side of the fireplace across the room, far away from Mother's portrait. The warmth of the fire, combined with the soothing effects of the sherry, made me feel relaxed and comfortable.

"Please tell me more about your dairy." Charles looked at me with intelligent, inquisitive eyes.

I told him all about Edenwae. There was an undercurrent in his manner, something that was not easy to identify. He was so unlike any gentleman I had met. He was well educated and sophisticated, but there was a sharpness to his manner. His interest in my dairy was flattering but seemed slightly too solicitous. After he left, I realized I had learned absolutely nothing about him.

***

The following day, I joined my parents in the morning room for breakfast. The servants had arranged a selection of grilled sausages, breads, and a soufflé on the buffet cabinet. After helping myself to food, I sat down and secretly fingered the underside of the chair to find my name carved years ago. Looking at my mother sitting across from me it felt as if I were sixteen again. "Who exactly is this Charles Bulmore, Mother?"

"Apparently, he arrived from London several years ago, but we only recently made his acquaintance through Albert." The saggy skin under her chin trembled as she spoke. "Such an English gentleman. Did you see his impeccable dress? He is residing at the Arlington Hotel, in a suite." Her eyes rounded as she emphasized the last word.

"Is he a railway man?"

"Probably. Most gentlemen are involved in the rail business in some way. He certainly could carry on a lengthy conversation with your father about it. What does it matter anyway? His reputation is… well, good enough."

"What does that mean?"

Ignoring my question, she continued her lecture. "Stop talking about yourself, and that farm. Have you forgotten everything I taught you?" There was a noise at the window, two blue jays were pecking at dead seeds caught on the outside of the frame. "Blasted jays," Mother said, flapping her napkin uselessly in the direction of the window. At that very moment, Father strode into the room. "Bertrand, I want all the birds dealt with. They have become an intolerable nuisance."

Looking confused, he nodded and sat down at the head of the table. He said nothing to me, nor would he look in my direction. After being served with tea, Father asked the servants to leave.

Suddenly, the atmosphere in the room became tense and my instincts told me to flee. I rose. "Well, I'd best be packing my bag to return home. Mission accomplished Mother, Charles Bulmore has met me. And he'll visit me at month's end. I assume I am free to leave now?"

"Not yet, young lady." Her tone reminded me of when I was younger and under her control. I sat back down with an audible thud, my lower lip forming a reflexive pout. She stared across the table at Father sitting to attention. He was about to speak, when she snapped at him, "Never mind, Bertrand, I will take care of this matter." She turned her determined eyes toward me, while I focused on the baggy skin that drooped beneath them, hoping to avoid the intensity of her stare. "I decided not to discuss this matter until after you met Charles, just in case it affected your mood. I've learned that your father has loaned you money," she said, casting him such a shredding look that he appeared to shrink in size. "It is now time to repay your debt."

I stared at her, speechless.

"Not all of it at once, Alice, surely," said Father, tentatively.

"*That* is what I said, Bertrand. *All of it.* I would not have given her a penny if I had known. It is absolutely ridiculous. And it is indecent for her to live on that farm with that *Hamish* person. I don't understand why you are helping her. If she has any hope of regaining her reputation, she must move back here and court Charles Bulmore. Besides, where do you think this investment will lead?" Mother enunciated each word with anger.

Father flushed. "Sarah plans to buy Edenwae." He straightened up in his chair.

"*Edenwae!* You have actually named that hovel you live in? Really, Sarah, and you think I am pretentious."

"Stop it, Mother. I've had enough." Somehow, I found myself on my feet, even though my knees were trembling. "Yes, I gave Edenwae its name because I am certain of its success for my sons. That's all I've ever wanted." My voice started to break, and I gestured toward my father as he rose to his feet. "Father lent me money to start the dairy because he believes in me. I wish you would too." On the verge of tears, I went to Father's side and, grasping his hand, turned to face Mother. "I will not tolerate you tearing him down for helping me. I have no idea how, but I will pay Father back. I just need more time. Besides, what's the rush? You don't need it." I gestured out the window at the stables and new addition that were clearly visible.

Mother struggled to her feet. Her eyes surveyed us, father and daughter, hand in hand, in defiance against her. "You really have no idea what you are talking about. Your father needs his money back. Now. And Bertrand, you have brought all of this upon yourself. There's so much more I could tell your precious daughter—"

Father stiffened at my side, raising his arms as if he would strike Mother. "Alice! Do *not* say another word! I forbid it. I remain your husband and I command your silence."

Mother clamped her mouth shut dramatically and stormed out of the room, her hand smacking at the jays in the window, almost shattering the leaded glass.

Father and I stood motionless for a moment. Then I turned to face him and saw how crumpled, wrinkled, and weary he looked. "What is going on?"

"I can't say. . ." His eyes looked sunken into his face. "Please go back to Edenwae and pay back my loan as fast as you can. I implore you. If not, you will have to sell the herd. There is no other choice."

***

It felt like a plague of secrets! Nothing was making sense. Why could my parents not wait for their money? Now I was desperate to repay that debt before it was too late. Tabitha might help if I confess my messy and impossible circumstances, and beg her. At the very least, she might know about the threat to Father.

After bidding a hasty goodbye to my father, reassuring him that I would find a solution, I headed toward Grandview. Riding through town I suddenly remembered that a visit to my sister's home would mean seeing little Robert, and I almost turned away. But I kept riding. If I were to fail now, giving him up would have been for nothing.

Once inside the magnificent front hall, I straightened my dusty riding clothes and remembered the feelings of ill-ease that accompanied my visits to this mansion. It felt more like a museum than a home, with its grand central stairway and long hallways sprouting in all directions.

Suddenly Tabitha's voice spilled down from the hall above. "Darling, Auntie Sarah has come to visit. Isn't this a wonderful surprise?"

The babbling sound of Robert's approach made me shrink. I, his mother, stood in dusty farmer's clothes, to beg my sister for help, with my sacrificed child at her side. I turned and ran toward the front door with tears welling in my eyes.

"Sarah, where are you going? I'm so thrilled to see you, what a lovely surprise." Tabitha's voice was warm and welcoming.

I swiped at my cheeks, speaking over my shoulder. "I left something in my saddlebag." My voice sounded weak and shaky.

"I'll send someone to fetch it. Look, here's Robert come to see you."

Forcing a smile, I turned around. Tabitha and Robert stood at the top of the staircase. His tiny hand was enclosed in hers and his fat baby cheeks dimpled as he smiled broadly and looked down the stairs at me. The

Drury blue eyes shone brightly as he struggled to stay upright on his chubby legs. Dressed in a toddler's frock with a deep-set sailor collar, matching stockings, and miniature boots, he looked the perfect portrait of the son of a prosperous gentleman. If he had remained with me, he would have been wearing sack-cloth clothes passed down from his older brothers, toddling barefoot in the dirt.

His hand held firmly by my sister, he crept down each stair tread, enabling his tiny legs to handle the challenge. Her face was bright with pride when they finally reached the marble floor. "Good boy. Now, walk to your Auntie, darling. Sarah, he's just learned to walk." His little feet secure in baby boots, Robert stumbled forward. He looked certain to tumble onto his padded bottom at any moment. A beaming Tabitha trailed behind by a step, close enough to rescue him if he should topple.

Falling to my knees, I held out my arms, willing him to make it all the way to me. With bright eyes, so alive with the sheer joy of movement, fixed upon me, he smiled.

"You're almost here, my darling boy, come to me," I said, my voice trembling. As they neared, Tabitha released her finger, and he ran headlong into my arms. "Oh, my beautiful boy." My vision blurred as I clung to him, remembering the feel of his tiny newborn body pressed to me. But he struggled to be free, and I had to let him go, my lower lip trembling as he plopped with a tiny thud onto the floor and laughed at the surprise of suddenly being seated.

Tabitha knelt down and embraced me. "I'm sorry, I shouldn't have brought him down to see you." She called to the nanny, who must have been lurking in a hallway, and Robert happily went off with her. I felt queasy at the thought that the nanny spent more time with my baby than me. Or Tabitha, for that matter, I suspected.

"No, it's not your fault. I can see what a wonderful mother you are, just as I knew you would be. But, oh Tabitha, I must speak with you urgently. I need your help."

A short while later, we sat in Tabitha's private parlour. I perched upon an elegant chaise longue, unsure of where to position my dirty riding boots. Tabitha sat on the edge of a small wingback chair, her eyes wide.

"Tabby, I didn't mean to cry. It's just. . .well, I've just left Mother and Father. I am completely devastated."

"Whatever is going on? Are they ill?"

"It's nothing like that. So much has happened since I last saw you."

Tabitha's eyes were now compressed with her brow furrowed.

"Father loaned me money to expand my dairy, but kept it from Mother," I said, deciding at the last minute to not tell her about the missing savings. Tabitha's look of complete disapproval reminded me so much of Mother that it seemed as if I had just confessed to *her*, instead of my sister.

"Oh, no," was all she said.

"He has every right to help me without Mother's agreement."

"I suppose so, but you know how Mother is." My sister heaved a great sigh as we both contemplated the omnipotent nature of our mother.

"But now she knows. . ." I went on to tell her about the confrontation with Mother, and Father's last words to me. Then, I gulped in air, making my words sound like hiccups. "I don't have the money to pay him back. . .I am failing my children."

"Why can't you pay?" she said, her voice sounding critical.

"I can, just not right now. Probably in a year, maybe less. But they can't wait. There's something they're keeping from me, a reason they need money urgently." As I told her about Mother's threat to Father and his reaction, her eyes darkened, and a crease appeared between her eyebrows.

When I asked her if she knew of any reason they were in urgent need of funds, the crease deepened. "I've no idea. Last I heard the foundry was prosperous. And their household keeps expanding."

I shook my head. "I think they are on the verge of disaster, and I can't stop it. And I'm afraid that their problem, whatever it is, will cause me to fail too."

"I think that's unfair. Surely it wouldn't be all their fault?"

I paused for a moment. "Yes, it would. I may have made a mistake or two, but nothing that would force me to sell my entire herd. Will you speak to them? Please try to learn what is happening. Ask them to wait." My words caught in my throat.

Tabitha darted her eyes to the window. "No. Absolutely not. Mother remains furious with me about Robert. I will only make it worse."

"Why would she care?"

"Because she thinks I've given up trying to have my own baby, now that I have Robert."

"Have you?"

Tabitha ignored my question, then brightened. "Of course, if Albert were to adopt Robert, Mother would quickly change her tune. You know how she adores Albert." I felt like snatching up Robert and running home, but instead, sat numbly while she continued. "He desperately wants a son. There's enormous pressure from his family in England, and Robert could be Albert's only option."

"Why?" I immediately regretted trying to push my sister for an answer she clearly did not want to give.

Tabitha simply bowed her head, refusing to look at me, her secrets pushing us apart.

Grasping her hand, I said, "Listen, could you possibly lend me the money to pay back Father? I hate to ask, but I really have no other choice."

Keeping her head bowed, she whispered, "I've no funds of my own. Albert won't allow it."

"None?" It was customary for ladies to be given a small allowance. I heard that a few had amassed a small fortune that way, squirrelled away in a secret hiding place, just in case. But, to have none? Tabitha shook her head, still looking away from me.

"Well," I said, loudly, "We'll just have to take Albert into our confidence then and ask him to help."

She quickly looked up, "Oh no, I couldn't do that. You ask him. This is your problem, not mine." Looking away again, she said, "It's almost time for our luncheon. You can ask him, then."

"Fine, I will," I said, stiffening my spine.

Visibly relieved, she rummaged through her wardrobe to find something for me to wear. "Why were you even at their house in the first place? You haven't visited them for years, ever since—"

I cut her off before she could say *ever since you left there with Joe*. "I attended a tea party." I said, relieved to talk about something else for a moment. "Believe it or not, Mother has tracked down a prospect for me."

"Really, who is he?"

"Charles Bulmore. I believe Albert knows him, in fact Mother claims Albert introduced him to her."

"Ah yes, Charles. Mother met him at our Christmas feast. She was gushing for days afterwards about how he'd be absolutely perfect for you. I had no idea she'd pursued it further, and frankly I'm surprised Charles was interested in meeting you."

I gaped at her. "Do you really believe I'm such a dreadful woman?"

"No, of course not." She smiled at me and softened her eyes. "You are beautiful. Any man would be pleased to have you on his arm. What I meant was that he has a reputation as a confirmed bachelor."

"Is he a womanizer?"

"Not at all. Albert has told me that Charles is so absorbed in his business affairs he has no time for the fairer sex. Perhaps, he has changed his mind and is looking for a wife?"

"I've no idea. He will be coming for a visit by month's end. I am not certain of his intentions. In truth, his prime interest seems to be Edenwae."

"Now, that sounds more like Charles."

***

Shortly afterwards, I sat in the spacious family dining room at the rear of Grandview, with its lovely view of the river and lake below. I had changed into a gown borrowed from my sister, to appear reasonably presentable when begging my brother-in-law for money. It had been several years since I last saw Albert, and I was a little surprised by how quickly he had aged. His wolf-like appearance was more accentuated by the greying of his hair, and it seemed as if his nose had grown longer. The three of us sat at one end of a long table: Albert at the head, my sister and I across from each other. We had just settled into our first course, when he suddenly spoke loudly, making me jump. "Well, dear sister, you must tell me. What brings you to Grandview, it has been some time since your last visit?" He drained his wine glass and a servant promptly refilled it. He was slurring his words. Why was he drinking so much this early in the day?

"Actually, I've been at my parents' home for several days."

"Really, I say, do tell. Are you and your mother still fighting?" There was glee in his voice and his effeminate manner grated on my nerves. Albert was always keen to hear gossip and sniff out conspiracy.

"Not at all. She invited me to tea, so I could be introduced to a friend of yours, actually. Charles Bulmore."

"Oh, I thought she might. I could tell by the way she was fussing over him at Christmas. Your mother has a knack for sniffing out blue blood." He grinned and took another long drink of wine and waved at a servant to replenish his glass.

"What can you tell me about Charles?"

Albert became serious. "Oh, I could not possibly say. But if he is interested, I would encourage you to take him seriously. He would be an enormous step up from that scoundrel you married." He was staring at me with such intensity that I took in a quick breath. Albert's mood could turn so quickly; one minute he was jovial and gay, the next, he could lash out viciously. I reminded myself to tread lightly.

Bowing in acquiescence, I smiled sweetly. "Albert, I have a favour to ask of you."

"Really?" he said, his good humour restored, "I will most certainly oblige if I can."

Glancing across the table at my sister, I noticed she had lowered her head into a supplicant posture, looking down at her lap. "I have a business proposition of sorts," I blurted out, wishing Tabitha would show support.

"You have?" His sharp eyes were wide with exaggerated interest. "Oh my dear, I am all ears."

"I'd like to offer you a small share in my dairy in return for an immediate loan of funds to pay off a debt."

Albert tilted his head backward, staring at me down the full length of his nose. "Why ever would I do that?"

"Because it's a good investment. I'll give you a fair rate of return and repay it within a year."

"Why is it a good investment?"

My throat was closing, and words evaporated as I searched for the best arguments to sway him. "Well. . .ah. . .the dairy business is doing very well. . . daily deliveries to several cheese factories. And. . .we're considered the best supplier of raw milk in the area."

"So why are you in debt?"

Suddenly, I realized that I had now adopted a similar supplicant posture to Tabitha, we must look like nuns in prayer. The harshness of his inquisition was excruciating, as if I had committed some heinous crime. His eyes darkened with each question, waiting for my reply, giving me the distinct impression that he already knew the answers. "Sarah, why are you hunched over, do you have anything to be ashamed of?"

I straightened my spine and locked eyes with him, hoping to stare him down. But his gaze was too penetrating, causing me to break off first. "I'm ashamed of nothing!"

"Oh well, I couldn't possibly agree unless I knew the truth of it." He paused for a moment, inclining his head toward me. When no answer came, he drained his glass and rose to leave.

Shocked to lose so quickly, I leapt out of my chair trying to stop him. "No, Albert, please consider my request."

He hesitated at the door and turned back to face me. "I know why you borrowed from your father and why your mother wants the money back. In fact, I know much more about your parents' affairs than you do."

I grasped his sleeve. "Then tell me, please, what do you know?"

"I am afraid I am not at liberty to say." He stared at me, then brushed my hand off and left.

Chapter 17

Defeated, I retreated to Edenwae, welcoming the sight of Willie and
Bertie scrambling out of the cottage door to greet me. I gathered
their slight bodies into my arms and inhaled deeply. "Oh, my boys, I'm so
happy to be home." Just then I heard a shout and turned to see Junior and
Freddie running toward me from the barn. Behind them, Hamish leant
against the barn doors and smiled broadly at me.

I was soon surrounded, and my sons tried to talk all at once.

"Ma, we've a new calf. I helped birth him." Junior was grinning from
ear to ear.

"I helped too," Freddie piped in.

"We helped Jessie with the seedlings," Bertie said, clinging to one
hand, while Willie grinned silently at his side. Listening to my children
babble on, the weight of my failure felt as if it might crush me.

***

Much later that night, I collapsed upon the kitchen porch bench. Leaning
my head against the cold stone of the cottage wall, I gazed up into the
brilliant stars filling the sky and covered myself with a blanket. What on
earth could Father have *brought upon himself?* And why would he confide
in Albert instead of me? And forcing me to sell the herd, now when I
have just begun, knowing it would ruin everything. My lips trembled, then
tears leaked down my face, the brilliant sky above dissolving into a bleary
smear of light.

"Can I help, Sarah?"

I straightened at the sound of Hamish's voice. He came toward me
out of the dark, with a burning torch held high above his head.

"Hamish, you startled me. Were you spying on me?" I rubbed my
cheeks.

"I thought I heard a commotion around the chicken coop. I was checkin' to see if it was that damn fox. Then I heard you... sounding so upset. Are you all right?"

He drew uncomfortably close to me. The torch's wavering flame sent ripples of light and dark across his face, making him appear unworldly and ominous. "Please put that torch out. It hurts my eyes."

He stuffed it into a pile of dirt by the kitchen door. When it was smothered, everything turned black. Waiting for my eyes to adjust, I felt the bench move as he settled beside me and gently took my hand. I had no idea why I did not snatch it back.

"What has upset you?"

Words choked in my throat when I tried to speak, and I started to cry, hating myself for being weak. Before I could take in what was happening, his arms were around me, and I buried my nose in his jersey. For a few moments, I pretended it was Joe holding me, murmuring into my ear with a soft Scottish lilt that *everythin' will be fine.*

Suddenly, I pushed him away. We sat looking at each other, a hand's reach away, unsure of what might happen next, the air between us alive with uncertainty. I stuck my hands under my blanket to stop them from reaching out for him. "I am so sorry. That was wrong."

"You can unburden yourself on me. Trust me. What's the matter?"

I might as well tell him the truth. "My father lent me the capital to start the dairy."

"I know that."

"You do?"

"Well, I was fairly certain Joe left you with nothin', so you must be gettin' money from somewhere."

Why would he think that? That Joe left me penniless?

"Yes, of course..." My voice started to tremble. "But it might all be for nothing."

"Why's that?"

I told him everything, the force of the telling lifting me.

"Why will he not give you more time?"

"I don't know." I decided not to tell him about my mother's accusation of Father.

His voice softened. "And if you sell the herd, you fear my granda will take back his land and make you leave?"

"Yes," was all I could manage to say.

"Well, I agree. That's very likely. And he'd be none too pleased with me neither. So, I guess I can't let that happen."

"What can we do?"

"Oh Sarah, I'll take care of you. You can have Edenwae. I promise."

In the dim light, I watched Hamish reach toward me. I moved further away, making it clear that he should keep his distance, even though a part of me wanted to feel the heat of his hand. "Please, tell me what you mean?"

"Your tears have given me the courage to finally say what I've wanted to for some time now. Helpin' you build Edenwae has changed my life. Working alongside you I've learnt a great deal and I've grown to appreciate what a fine woman you are." Hamish suddenly knelt down in front of me. "May I please hold your hand?"

"No, you may not!" I realized that by kneeling in front of me, he had blocked my only escape. "Please, just leave me alone." I drew the blanket tight around me.

He did not move. "Please hear me out," he said, moving closer to me, the sweet smell of his breath on my face. "Watching you take Joe's dream and turn it into Edenwae. You are a marvel to behold. Sarah, I… I love you. I want you to marry me." He grasped my face between his hands and kissed me. It was long and passionate, and I too kissed him that way.

Then it began to feel wrong. I struggled to push him away. He was slow to release me, but eventually, he did. "Please, Hamish, don't presume that I've agreed to your proposal."

"Well, you seemed to be enjoyin' kissin' me, just now."

"You caught me by surprise, that's all. Please sit back down, while I think. This is so sudden."

Feeling a little confused, struggling to sort through my emotions, I knew I should get away from him. It was the pull of his body and the heat of his kiss that distracted me. But I must not let attraction cloud my judgement again. Especially with another Drury.

He sat back down on the bench, closer to me. "But I insist on holdin' your hand."

Reluctantly, I went along with him, allowing his large hands to swallow mine while I considered whether his marriage proposal provided any hope for me. In an instant, I could see the messy challenges I would face with my sons, in particular Junior, not to mention the scandal my family would be forced to endure. "I confess it's too difficult to think of your proposal while my dairy hangs in the balance."

"But don't you see? If you marry me, I'll pay off your debt and buy the land too."

I pulled him to me. "What? You would do that? You *can* do that?"

He paused for a moment, then, "Well…I don't have the money right now, but I could borrow it."

"From Duff? And do you know how much is owed on the land?"

"No, he doesn't take kindly to lendin' his money."

"Then where? Where would you get it?" Suddenly, I saw it and pulled back. "Do you own this land? That is the only way a bank would lend money to you. Tell me, Hamish, is that why you stay? Because you own this land?"

He put his arm around my shoulders. "Don't be daft. Do you think I would sleep in that tiny room if I owned this place? With you so lonely in that bed of yours?" He tried to kiss me again.

I shoved him away. God, another Drury with big promises and not a penny to back it up. I snatched my hand out of his grasp.

He took my hand back and gripped it tightly. "Wait. I still have an idea. I can get money without ownin' this land. Trust me, I know how to get it."

"And why should I trust you?"

He leaned in close, his breath on my face. "Because I'm the only hope you have and I'm certain you'll marry me to save Edenwae."

He rose and disappeared back into the night, just as suddenly as he had appeared.

Chapter 18

One week later, Hamish had yet to secure the needed money. Just as well, for I needed time to sort through my feelings. A part of me wished we would find a way to marry, to pay off the debt and to live happily ever after. But, by marrying him, I would lose all authority over myself, my sons, my money, and my dairy. The future land purchase would be in his name and my sons' legacy might disappear forever. He might even disown them. Still. Should my sons' rights be protected, it might work out for the best.

All this uncertainty would have to be put aside for today as I faced a further complication—Charles was due to visit. Before he arrived, Hamish must be convinced to behave properly. Nothing should get back to my parents that might inflame Mother's worry about him. Not until I got what I wanted.

The morning was humid, with vapour rising off the land after a heavy downpour in the night, creating a dense mist over the pastures. The sun was burning away the fog and the day was warming. Peering into the barn from the threshold of the wide doors, I saw Hamish in the loft, stabbing hay with a pitchfork and heaving it below. "Hello, Hamish," I said, much louder than was necessary.

He turned to greet me with a broad smile. "How are you this morning?"

"I'm well, thank you. And you?" I smoothed my long skirt, shaking mud off the hem.

Moving to the edge of the hayloft, he thrust out his chest, placing hand on hip, the other on his pitchfork. "I'm fit, as you can well see, my darlin'." He looked down at me with a gleam in his eyes.

I looked over my shoulder. Junior was nearby. "Shush, be quiet, you're being indiscreet."

He hurried down the ladder, after taking in my furrowed brow and agitated hands. "You look upset. What is it?" he said.

"I'm just so worried that I'll lose everything and be forced back to town."

Hamish's cockiness disappeared. "Don't you think I know that. I've been workin' very hard to secure the funds we need. Soon you'll be my wife."

"Shush. You need to be quiet about that. I hope you haven't told anyone about your plan."

He averted his gaze for a moment, then said, "No, I haven't told a soul."

"And nothing happens until you secure that money." He nodded. "And you know we must act as if nothing has been spoken between us, around the boys, around my father, around anyone who comes to Edenwae."

"I know how to behave." He winked at me.

Glancing over my shoulder, I saw Junior heading our way. "A gentleman is coming to visit me today," I whispered urgently to Hamish.

He took a step toward me, his eyes pleading. "Tell me you'll marry me. That you feel the same way." His voice was low and resonant, his eyes filled with desire.

"Stop. Do not come closer." I glanced outside and was relieved to see Junior had almost reached us. "I have to go now, do not say a word. I swear you to secrecy or you might ruin any chance we have. Swear it. Promise me." By then Junior was standing beside me, looking quizzically at the two of us, wondering if he had missed something important.

Hamish gave me a quick nod. It would have to do.

***

Next, I gathered my sons together to prepare them for the upcoming visit from Charles. They were scattered around the kitchen, impatiently waiting. "Boys." I clapped my hands. "I'm expecting a gentleman caller soon and I'd like you to clean up."

Junior huffed. "For God's sake, Ma. It's bad enough with Hamish. Now there's another man?"

I turned to my angry boy. "There's nothing to worry about. I met him at your grandparents during my visit there. He's just interested in seeing the dairy."

"Why? Is he after it too? Why did you invite him here?"

"Enough! I don't have to explain my reasons to you. Now, all of you, scrub your faces and hands, and wipe the dust from your clothes. I expect all of you to behave properly. Shake his hand if offered. Come to the parlour shortly after he arrives."

Retreating to my room, I washed my hands and splashed water over my face, then scraped a brush through my ratty curls. Struggling to make myself more presentable, anger bubbled up. It was difficult enough trying to understand Hamish and his interest in Edenwae. Now there was Charles—another threat to my home? Oh, how I wished I could rid my life of men!

Flinging off my worn work dress, I pulled on leather riding trousers and a clean blouse with an embroidered gusset. Giving up on my hair, I jammed it into my wide-brimmed hat. There was little resemblance to the well-groomed lady Charles met a week ago, and I could not care less. I would have placated my parents a little while longer, and I hoped this gentleman would rush back to town having lost all interest in me and Edenwae.

***

"I was concerned the weather might put you off coming here today," I said to Charles as we walked toward my cottage a short while later.

"It was rather difficult to see when I first headed out. Reminded me of a London fog, actually. Should prove to be a marvellous day after all." He stopped to lean down and ruffle the dogs' ears as they sniffed at his boots. Glancing up at me, he took a long appraising look. "My, my, you appear to be a completely different woman. How absolutely delightful you look." His comment stunned me into silence for a moment, giving me an opportunity to take in *his* very different appearance as he straightened and stared. The normal riding attire for a town gentleman was tailcoat and cravat, often with a top hat, but Charles wore leather trousers under his black frock coat and a wide brimmed hat, making him look more daring than the gentlemen I knew.

Standing on my broken pathway he looked around. "So, this is Edenwae." I reddened watching this stranger survey my tiny cottage, ramshackle sheds, chicken coop, and outbuildings. Only the barn stood proud.

"Yes. As I mentioned at my parents' home, I've only just begun. I thought we'd tour the dairy barn and then ride the pastures and fields for a bit. It's the best way for you to understand the full potential. But first, you must refresh yourself after the journey from town. Please, come in."

Once inside, I hung his damp coat in the hall and led him into the parlour. Coffee and cake had been laid out on my small tea table, so tiny compared to the great table around which Charles and I had first met. "Would you enjoy a cup of coffee? I could get tea if you prefer?" Mother would be mortified to hear Charles had been offered coffee. Such an American beverage, she would say, the worst insult of all.

"That would be delightful, actually."

I raised my eyebrows in surprise. "You must feel out of place here, I imagine." I poured his coffee into my only un-chipped cup.

"Actually, I find it rather invigorating. I've spent many a day riding these hills, having no idea you lived here. I'm delighted to visit. Thank you very much for the invitation." Grasping his cup, he sipped tentatively.

"Did you visit my father's foundry?"

"Yes, I did. Very inspiring. I can see where you get your entrepreneurial spirit from. Your father's enterprise is a great success. Built it from nothing really. Just proves what one can achieve in this new country."

There was a commotion at the parlour doors, and I turned to see my children standing there. "These are my sons." I noted with satisfaction that they had scrubbed most of the dirt off their hands and faces, but had forgotten to swipe the dust from their clothes. Charles stood up to greet them. With a nod to Junior, I indicated they should enter. "This is Joseph Junior, my eldest."

Junior stood straight-backed and shook the hand of our visitor. "Pleased to meet you, Sir."

Holding onto my son's hand, Charles leaned toward him. "Tell me, young man, what do you make of the dairy your mother has built?"

"It is a great success, Sir. And I will own all of this one day. And—"

"Yes, perhaps you will," I was quick to interrupt him, lest he lapse into rudeness. I turned to Charles. "I hope one day my son, all of my sons, will own Edenwae."

Charles's eyes darkened for a moment, then he returned to his affable manner. "And who is this?"

"This is Freddie." When my next born stuck out his hand, it was trembling and the palm looked sweaty. "Pl...Pleased to meet you, Sir," he gasped shyly.

Grasping his slim hand within both of his, Charles seemed to sense Freddie's anxiety. "It is a pleasure to meet you, young man. I can see that you work hard around here."

Cameron, who has been visiting for the weekend, appeared beside Freddie and touched his brother's arm. "And this is Cameron," I said.

As he shook Charles's hand, Cameron said, "Pleased to see you again, Sir. I didn't know it was you coming to visit."

"Cameron, a weekend off from your studies?"

"Not, really, Sir. I created a milking machine. We had some problems, but I'm confident I can make it work."

"That's marvellous, I would be interested in seeing your design."

Cameron smiled broadly at the encouragement.

My twins peered out from either side of Junior, holding onto their eldest brother's trousers. "And these are my twins, Bertie and Willie."

"Oh my, you two are completely identical. Which one is Bertie?" Thank goodness he chose Bertie. Willie would have been speechless.

"That would be me... Sir."

"May I shake your hand?" With Junior's gentle encouragement, Bertie took Willie by the hand and they both moved closer. Charles laid his hands out flat toward each of the twins and smiled warmly. They both stared at him, wide-eyed. Gingerly, they each placed a hand into his. "It is delightful to meet the two of you." Willie and Bertie broke out into their most adorable smiles. Gently dropping their hands, Charles turned to me. "You have fine young men." For a moment, his manner resembled that of a man Father had once introduced to me—stating, rather disparagingly afterwards, that the sly gentleman could sell anything to anyone.

Recovering from this unexpected compliment, I said, "Thank you. I think so too." Turning to my children, I smiled at them. "Now boys, please return to your chores."

As they filed out of the room, Junior stared angrily at me. I smiled at him, then turned to my guest, hoping he had not noticed that stare. "Shall we begin our tour?"

***

We walked through the wide barn doors just as Hamish jumped down with a great thud from the hayloft, startling us. He blocked our path. "Charles, this is Hamish, my right-hand man. Hamish, may I introduce you to my visitor, Mr. Charles Bulmore."

Hamish smiled cockily at our visitor. "Hello, Charles, I had no idea it was you comin' for a visit."

Towering over him, Hamish shook his hand. Charles winced as Hamish gripped hard and the two men locked eyes, reminding me of two bucks squaring off, ready to fight over a doe. When Charles's gaze darkened, Hamish released his grip and backed away.

"Ah yes, Hamish..." Charles did not seem at all surprised to see Hamish here. Turning his back on him, Charles gazed upward. "Look at this barn, I have never seen anything like it. Please show me around, Sarah."

Behind Charles's back, Hamish gave me a wary look and sauntered outside, shaking his head as he went.

Guiding Charles through the barn, I explained the fine details about running a modern dairy. His keen interest and pleasant manner encouraged me, and I felt completely at ease and free to be myself. When I reached the top of the ladder leading down to the dairy station, I grasped a railing with one hand and glanced at him. "Ready to see where we milk the cows?" I liked the way his eyes crinkled at the edges at my suggestiveness.

A short while later, after inspecting the milking stations, Charles and I were on our horses walking out into the pastures. "Want to gallop?" I said, pulling down my hat securely. He nodded, and I spurred my horse to a fast gallop. We rode easily together, exploring the many acres of Edenwae, coming to a rest in the shade of the maples on top of the hill. Dismounting, we tied our horses to a tree and walked together amongst the gently swaying trees, the breeze causing the newly born leaves to make a soft rustling sound. The air was filled with the earthy smell of freshly sown fields. "I hope to build a manor house here one day."

"It would be a lovely spot, but…" He looked down the hill toward the dairy barn, "I thought, and forgive me, for I'm afraid I don't know much about such things, but I heard that farm manors were generally built adjacent to barns so that the owners were never far from their livelihood. It made sense to me when I heard it."

I had never questioned the location of the manor. It was Joe's idea and I assumed he knew the best place to build. Thinking back on the day I stood here with Joe, I wondered if he suggested this location expecting I would find it all the more exciting and romantic to have our home high on a hill, surrounded by maples. "Thank you for that observation." I waited for a moment before continuing. "What exactly *do* you do, Charles?"

He took off his hat, ran smooth long fingers through his curly hair, and looked out over the hills. "I have many business interests."

"Such as?"

He continued to stare at the view, as if I had offended him. His eyes had darkened, just as they had in the barn when he stared down Hamish. "Some of my interests are in other countries. England, a few in Ireland, even one in Australia, and many here, of course."

He turned to face me. "I have a question to ask you. Your mother has been adamant about your imminent return to town, yet you don't act as if that's the case. You speak earnestly about your plans for the dairy, as do your sons. Just now, you spoke of building a manor house. I'm rather confused. Are you staying at Edenwae or moving to town?"

Breaking away from his curious stare, I looked down at the barn. "I loathed the genteel life imposed on me by my mother when I was a girl. That's why I married a farmer and moved here. And I don't plan to leave if I can possibly help it." My voice faltered towards the end, and he moved closer to me, lightly touching the small of my back, causing me to turn to him.

"I have upset you. I apologize, I do tend to be too direct sometimes." His hazel eyes, flashing with specks of green, held my gaze. "I hope you stay. You come alive on this land. What you have accomplished in such a short time, and this land—remarkable."

I saw my face reflected in his eyes and wondered what sort of man he really was. He could have any young lady in town—without the complications of children—why such an interest in me? "I do not give up easily." My voice was strong again.

A smile crept across his handsome face, with a cunningness that suggested a deeper understanding. "Splendid. In that case, I'll visit next week?"

Chapter 19

The next morning turned hot and humid. I was down on my hands and knees, weeding the kitchen garden. The creak of the garden gate opening surprised me. Looking up through my sweaty brows and wiping my eyes, I saw Hamish walking toward me. "Good day, Sarah." He walked carelessly across the expansive rows of carrots and parsnips, his big boots crushing my fragile plants.

"Watch where you plant your feet, for God's sake." He had been quiet and sullen ever since Charles's visit, and I was avoiding him. "What do you want?"

He stood, one foot resting on the low picket fence built to keep rabbits and squirrels out, his hat lowered over his brow. "We need to talk about that Charles comin' here. It's not right."

"Really? Why's that?" I said, stuffing a trowel into the earth.

Lowering his foot, he reached down, took my hands and pulled me up to him. "He's courtin' my future wife. That's why."

"I haven't promised you that," I said, hastily gathering my skirts, walking past him and out of the garden to the water pump.

He followed. "Have you thought about us, then?"

"No. I'm sorry, I told you already. Finding the money is filling my head."

"I don't see your father comin' here to get it. Why was Charles Bulmore here? Is it Edenwae he wants, or you? You don't need the likes of him when you have me. I promise to find the money we need. Now come here." He took hold of my arms, pulling me against him. The force of him made me gasp, and I struggled uselessly to break free.

It was the sound of a horse racing up the laneway that dampened his ardor and he let me go. "That better not be that damn Charles. I've had enough of him." He thundered out to the barnyard. I ran after him, pulling on his sleeve.

Coming around the corner of the cottage, I saw my father reining in his horse. Hamish stopped at the sight of him and smiled at me, "Well, perhaps it's time I had a word with your father."

"No. Please. Not now," I whispered, "Let me handle this."

Father dismounted. "Sarah, I must speak with you urgently." Glancing quickly at Hamish, he handed over the reins. Looking annoyed that he was being treated as a stable boy, Hamish started to say something, then stopped at the shake of my head and yanked my father's horse in the direction of the corral.

Once inside the cottage, Father closed the doors behind him. His face looked younger, softer, the worry-crease across his forehead had virtually disappeared.

"What is it?" I guided him toward a chair.

He refused to sit, instead he held me at arm's length while he spoke. "I have the most wonderful news. I cannot tell you the details, but suffice to say you don't need to repay your loan."

I had difficulty understanding what Father had just said "What? Did you just say the loan is forgiven?"

His smile widened. "Consider it a gift, my dear girl."

"A gift? Why? What's happened?" It felt as if my mind had ceased to function.

"Let's just say my fortunes have turned for the better. An investment is finally paying off."

"Tell me more. Why were you so desperate?"

His face closed in. "Nothing to worry about now. To tell you the truth, I'm a little embarrassed I put so much pressure on you." He pulled me closer, embracing me warmly.

I pulled back to look at him. "I've been very worried...about you...about losing Edenwae. Can't you tell me why you were so burdened earlier?"

He bowed his head and the fatigue of the past few months returned to his face. "Please…it was just a rough patch. I am fine now."

I pulled him back into a hug, hoping to restore his good mood. "Thank you, Father."

His smile returned. "Now, let's sit down. There is one condition, however." As we settled around the unlit parlour stove, a lump of anxiety formed in my throat. "Please don't look so stricken. Your mother simply insists that you continue to court Charles."

"Oh, for God's sake. Does Mother think that Charles will marry me and force my return to town? Is that her new plan? Really, she can't be serious."

Father set his brow and met my gaze. "Listen. Charles has become a frequent guest at our home. Your mother is convinced that he's very interested in you, and she insists that you continue to receive Charles at Edenwae."

I held back my impulse to laugh at Mother's pretentiousness, making Edenwae sound as if it were a royal castle. "I'd prefer not to marry again."

He reached for my hand. "Please, your mother has your best interests at heart. If she sees potential in your relationship with Charles, please don't fight it."

"As you well know, Mother and I differ greatly on what is best for me, and for my sons. Edenwae is all I need, and I don't want the problems a husband would cause. If I married him, the land would be in Charles's name and my boys could end up with nothing. So now that I no longer have the debt hanging over my head, I'm free to save for whatever is left owing on the land. Then put it in Junior's name. Why would I compromise that?"

He tightened his grip on my hand, staring at me with his soft grey eyes. The furrow in his brow had returned. "Please don't make this difficult for me. Your mother and I would both feel better about your situation if you were married."

Suddenly, I regretted my arrogant attitude toward my father. "I'm sorry to sound unappreciative. I'm delighted that your fortunes have turned around. And that I have benefited. Maybe one day, you'll tell me the whole story." He glanced away, and I pulled on his hand. "Father, if it makes you happy, I'll see Charles."

With visible relief, he smiled at me. "Should Charles propose, I'm certain there would be room for negotiation. I will step in on your behalf to make certain the boys' rights are protected. If he truly wants you as his wife, he'll agree to it, I imagine."

"Thank you, Father, but I think I'd rather do my own negotiating."

***

That night I could not stop thinking about Charles. He certainly had his attractions, but he remained such a mystery and had not hinted about a proposal. This was ridiculous! He would never propose so quickly. It's just Mother's wishful thinking, and the idea had seeped into my thoughts. Yet. If he did propose, why would he do that? What was he up to?

Then, there was Hamish. Without the debt hanging over my head, I suddenly felt no desire for him. Would I really have married him just to save my dairy? Falling in love with him to justify it? A tiny quiver of nausea twinged my stomach as I realized I probably would have. No more; love had not served me well! I want something better with Charles.

***

The next morning, I strode toward the barn, determined to tell Hamish my feelings, and to avoid further confusions, insist he pack his things and leave. I would go to Duff, tell him I no longer needed Hamish, and demand he tell me what was owed on this land. Stomping through muddy puddles left behind after a cloudburst last night, I prepared myself for the ugly confrontation, oddly gaining strength from each squelch of mud under my boots.

As I reached the barn, Junior came storming out, not even bothering to greet me. Freddie came rushing out behind his brother, his face etched with concern. "He's had another argument with Hamish. I'll go after him." Freddie was gone before I could reply. How happy my boys would be to learn Hamish was leaving.

Returning my attention to the task at hand, I looked for Hamish. I found him in one of the stalls, hidden by the massive bulk of one of the workhorses. Bent over, with his side against the horse's flank, he had its front left hoof lifted, prying off an old shoe. I strode into the stall and stood behind him. "We need to talk," I said loudly, the tone of my voice signalling that I had serious business to discuss.

He finished removing the shoe, dropped the horse's hoof, and turned to face me. "Sarah, no pleasantries? Has something happened?" He moved toward me, making me step back.

Suddenly, I wished Junior or Freddie had stayed. "Well, I—"

"What is it?" He kept advancing, and I retreated further, the heel of my boot hitting the boards at the back of the stall.

"Hamish, I... I am sorry, but I have to refuse your offer of marriage."

His face stiffened. "Why's that? Is it your father that demands it? Have you given up on Edenwae too? Are you sellin' the herd?"

"No, no...I..." He was too close—the smell of horse and barn and him, it was all too close—how could I tell him the truth when trapped in this stall?

"We can't lose the herd. My granda is sure to take the land back. I can't have that."

I stared at him. "So, it's really Edenwae you care about? More than me?" All of my suspicions flared within me. "Was that your plan? The truth of why you're here? What sort of deal do you have with Duff?"

"You don't seem as broken up as I would've thought to lose Edenwae." His blue eyes darkened, and his lips twisted. "It's that scoundrel Charles. You plan to marry him instead of me. Him and all his money." His nostrils flared, his hands tightening into fists.

I looked for escape, but he, and the horse, blocked me.

He rushed forward and forced his chest against me. "I will prove my love to you. I'll make you mine. You want me too. I can feel it." He grasped my face roughly, then crushed my mouth with his snarling lips. His body pushed me against the rough boards, his hands roaming eagerly over my breasts.

Fighting him I managed to yank my mouth free. "Stop it," I protested, but my voice merely whimpered against the pressure of his body

His hips ground into me and his breathing grew harsh and frantic in my ear. He raised my skirt and tore at my undergarment. I felt his skin against mine. I tried to break away, beating at his arms, his back, but I could not shift the weight of him pressing me to the wall.

"What the hell are you doing?" *Junior!*

At Junior's shout, Hamish froze but did not free me. I could not see my son, nor could I shout with my face smothered by my attacker's chest.

"This is no concern of yours. Your mother will soon wed me. Now, leave us be."

"Mother?" Junior's voice was broken and shaky.

Hamish clamped his hand over my mouth and hissed in my ear, "Make him go away. You don't want to see what I'll do to him." The rage in his eyes confirmed his threat. I nodded tightly, and Hamish took his hand away from my mouth.

Gasping for air, horrified by what my son must be seeing, I stammered "Just leave, Junior. Leave!"

As he ran away, I heard my son yell back at me, "I hate you."

Hamish chuckled at my boy's words. "That's better. Now we can enjoy ourselves." He moved against me with renewed force, squeezing my breasts and buttocks painfully as his intention strengthened. He reared up and forced my face into his chest as he brutally entered me.

I clenched my teeth against the pain and uselessly beat my fists against his back. I twisted away from his ugly face, my eyes meeting the terrified gaze of the horse trapped beside us in the stall. The animal yanked her head back and forth trying to be free from the tether, her powerful legs stomping backward.

Mercifully, Hamish finished quickly, then moved away from me and buttoned his fly. He grinned. "There. I made the choice for you. We'll wed as soon as we can."

Shoving down my skirt, I swallowed the bile rising in my throat. I would never give him the satisfaction of seeing me throw up and tremble before him. Instead, I spat on the ground. "I'm not some innocent girl you've just ruined, with no choice but to marry you."

"That's what Joe did. How else could he win such a bride?"

"You're a fool. I planned that. So Joe and I could marry."

"Hah! Duff was right. You trapped Joe into marrying you."

"No, for God's sake! Get out of my way. I'll tell Duff what you've done." I tried to shove him out of the way, but he stood solid as a rock, blocking my escape.

"And who do you think he'll believe?"

I tried to stare him down, but he grasped my arm, his grip tight and hard. "Let me go." I shouted. "I have to find Junior."

"Not so fast. You may have my child in you now."

"If I did, I'd find a way to get rid of it." I lashed out and scratched his face.

He raised his hand to strike me back, his eyes dark and furious, when suddenly the panicked horse heaved her bulk against him. He defended himself by throwing his weight at the beast's side. With the whites of her eyes showing, the horse slammed to the opposite wall. The dogs were now barking behind us. With one final toss of her head, the horse shrieked, broke the tether, and bolted out of the stall.

I darted past Hamish, then stopped in my tracks when I saw one of the dogs whining at a pile of rags on the floor. I screamed. It was Freddie. He lay in a heap, his head bloodied and his eyes closed. I fell to my knees and tried to rouse him. His chest was still moving.

"What was he doin' there?" Hamish said, reaching for my broken boy.

"Stay away from him." Gathering Freddie with a strength I did not know I still possessed, I rose to my feet and ran. "Jessie, Jessie. Help!"

Hamish ran alongside me. "Let me carry him. Let me help you."

"Then fetch the doctor. And my father," I roared at him, the urge to kill him only held back by the boy in my arms.

Jessie ran to me, and together we got Freddie inside the cottage. We laid him on my bed. I patted at his face, calling his name. "We must do something. What can we do?" I pleaded. Jessie tore up a sheet and wrapped his bleeding head. I pressed my hand against it, willing the doctor to magically appear.

***

I've no idea how long it took Father and the doctor to get here. When they did, I mumbled about the horse trampling him. The doctor gently unwrapped blood-soaked sheet from Freddie's head. "The bleeding has stopped, but we must get him into town to treat the wound properly."

"Why is he not waking up?" I looked at the doctor, then at Father, panic rising in my throat.

"You must go with him," Father said, putting his arm around me.

The doctor lifted my boy and took him outside to a makeshift bed in the back of his wagon. I jumped inside the wagon and cradled Freddie's head in my lap.

Father leaned in and said, "The twins will ride with me in the carriage."

"Where's Junior?"

"I don't know. He was gone before I got here. Hamish said he rode away." When he saw my face tighten, he added, "Junior knows where you'll be. He will come to you."

We followed the doctor to his house and around the back to his examining room. Once Freddie was safely inside, the doctor asked us to wait in the carriage. I slumped against my father; the twins stared at us.

After what felt like an entire day, the doctor finally waved us in. We crowded into the small room, only to see Freddie much as he was before—the only difference was a clean bandage—his eyes shut and his lips slightly parted.

"Why is he not awake?" I rushed to my son and called his name, shaking him gently.

"There is only so much I can do," said the doctor. "We can treat the visible wound, but we cannot say what has been damaged inside his head. We have to wait and see. The important thing now is to heal what we can. And keep him quiet while his body heals the rest."

I felt Father at my side. The twins crept in between us. "Come, we'll take him home," my father said, and lifted Freddie gently.

Arriving at my parents' home, Mother and Cameron took charge of the twins, while Father took Freddie to my old bedroom, placing him gently on the bed. Then I laid down beside him.

***

The next morning, it was the sound of the door creaking open that awoke me with a start. Father stood at the door. I looked towards Freddie. He remained the same. I checked the rise and fall of his chest, then kissed his soft cheek and willed him to open his eyes.

I turned to Father.

"No difference?" he asked. I shook my head and quietly stood up. He pulled me away from the bed into a far corner with two huddled chairs. He grasped my hand.

Fighting back the urge to cry, I looked down at the floor. "I'm trying to cope. But it is all so horrible…" I wanted to tell my father everything, but I found it impossible to look at him. If I told him Hamish raped me, he would feel compelled to act. And nothing would be gained. It would be my word against Hamish's, and no woman had ever won that battle. "It's just…well…you see, I must speak with Junior."

I started to get up. Father reached out to stop me. "He's not here."

The knot of anxiety in my chest from yesterday, returned. "Is he at Edenwae?" Oh God, Hamish might still harm him.

Father lifted my chin. I noticed the deep groove on his forehead had returned, a sure sign that something was terribly wrong. "No one knows where Junior went. And he hasn't shown up here."

"Where could he be?"

"Was there a disagreement? With Hamish? With you?"

I could not look at him and tried to find some truths that might make my lie sound true. "There was a fight…Hamish and I were…Junior heard. I didn't know Freddie was there too. Oh God, maybe Junior thought he should have saved Freddie."

Father looked at me intently. "None of that seems like a good reason to run away."

The truth, unspoken, hung in the air between us: Junior believed I had betrayed him; Hamish would take Joe's place, and the promise I made to my son, that he would one day own Edenwae, had been cruelly broken by my selfish needs. Junior would never come home to that.

"I must find Junior," I gasped.

"Of course. I'll report him missing. And I can hire men to search for him. We will find him."

There was a knock on the door. "Mother, may I come in, please?" The sound of Cameron's voice was a sharp reminder that I had other children who needed me.

Father let Cameron in and began to leave. "Please stay Father."

Cameron rushed to me, and I stood to hug him. Then, we both moved toward Freddie. Cameron laid his hand tenderly on his brother's arm. "Freddie? It's me. Can you hear me?" When there was no response, he turned to me, his face sad. He raised a book in his hand. "May I read to him? I brought one of his favourites."

"I'm sure he would love that." A pause, then. "How are Willie and Bertie?"

"They have the bedroom next to mine. You need not worry, if they awaken, I'm right there. Grandmama had toys and books brought in. And they had a wonderful time in the bathtub last evening." I smiled weakly at him.

"While Cameron is here with Freddie, let's go downstairs. You need something to eat," Father said, then led me down to the parlour, ordering tea and sandwiches on the way.

I slumped down onto a settee. "Oh Father." I hung my head down, but refused to let myself cry.

He sat down and put his arm around me. "You must stay here until Freddie is better. I will oversee Edenwae in the meantime."

"I can't think about anything until Freddie recovers. Oh God, the cost has been too high." The words gasped from me as I felt the enormity of my mistakes. "Giving up Robert... and now... Freddie lying up there, Junior gone... and Cameron *here*. What is the point of Edenwae any more?"

We sat in silence for such a long time that I forgot Father was beside me, until he spoke. "You believed staying on the farm was best for your sons. I helped you build your dairy because I believed it too. Your boys were born to be farmers."

I nodded. "But without Junior.... Even if Freddie recovers fully, he will never be strong enough. And what if he never recovers? What then?" He started to disagree, but I cut him off. "No. Mother has been right all along. We should have moved to town after Joe died. If I'd listened to her, none of this would have happened."

Suddenly, Mother walked in as if she had been eavesdropping. "How is our Freddie?" She sat on the other side of me, the weight of her causing me to fall against her, and I wished she would hold me. Instead, she patted my hand. "You know, my dear, even though he is small, your Freddie is a tough little boy. I knew it the minute I saw him." I leaned into her. "Now, we will get through this together. As a family. Stay here for the rest of the year. I'm certain Freddie will be better by then. Let the twins experience the town school. Cameron has settled in nicely. I'm sure they will too. Junior might even like it here. I know he is a farm boy, but your father could teach him how to forge iron. He might like that."

I dropped my head to her shoulder, saying softly, "I think I will try. . .I will try."

She patted my hand softly. "Wonderful. I'll take care of everything."

***

During the days that followed, I stayed at Freddie's bedside, washing him, massaging his arms and legs, trickling water through his parted lips, doing everything the doctor told me would help. Cameron read to him every day, giving me a chance to splash water on my face and grab something to eat. Then I returned, sleeping in the bed beside Freddie, or dozing in a chair, waking often to check the rise of his chest. My parents visited, but mostly I was alone, with regret and fear as my only companions. Every time Father walked in, I hoped he would have news of Junior, but at my expectant look, he would only shake his head.

On the third morning, I was jolted out of an exhausted slumber by the sound of someone saying, "Mother?" I looked to the door thinking it was Cameron or the twins, or by some miracle, Junior.

No one stood there. Turning to the bed I saw Freddie's blue eyes staring up at me.

Rising slowly, I touched his face. "Hello, my darling." With shaking hands, I tipped a glass to his lips and poured a little water down his throat.

Swallowing eagerly, he started to choke. When his spluttering had stopped, he said, "Where am I?"

"At your grandparents' house."

"Why?" He reached up and touched his bandaged head. "What?"

"You were trampled by a workhorse. Do you remember anything?"

He looked puzzled. "No, not a thing."

"How do you feel?"

"My head hurts."

I kissed him tenderly, trying to not let my tears fall upon his face. "I'll send for the doctor. He'll have something to make you feel better." I rushed to the door and yelled, "Come quickly, everyone."

Before I could return to the bed, my family started pouring in. Father, then Cameron and the twins, then Mother, who gasped, "Oh my word."

Cameron fell onto the bed beside his brother and grinned at him. "You really had me worried, you know." The twins stood by the bed unsure of what to do, with Father and Mother behind them on either side of me.

Freddie looked at the group of us, shiny eyed and grinning. "Why is everyone looking at me that way?"

***

Later that day, after the doctor visited, assuring us the worst was now behind us, yet warning that it would take many weeks for a full recovery, I settled in the bed beside Freddie, and sighed. For the first time, I felt like sleeping. I was just about gone when he said, "Where's Junior?"

Turning to him, pushing his long curls off his brow, I tried to steady my voice. "He ran away. When. . ."

His eyes grew round, and I knew he remembered. "Why was Hamish. . .?"

"Hush, we don't need to talk about it now. Let's rest." I tried to hug him to me, but he pulled away and stared at me.

"But I want to know. Hamish was—"

"He forced me." I sighed and turned my red face away.

"Why did Junior run away? We could've saved you."

Difficult as it was, I met my frightened boy's gaze. "I told him to leave. Hamish threatened to hurt him if I didn't. Junior thinks I plan to marry Hamish. You didn't hear?"

"No, I came running when I heard shouting. Junior stormed past me in a rage, yelling 'I hate you.' I thought I had done something and ran to find you. Then I saw you fighting Hamish, and. . . both of you yelling. . . and. . . I don't remember anything else. . ."

I pulled his trembling body to me. "Hush, let's not talk about it anymore."

He drew back. "But Junior. . ."

Seeing his fright, I quickly added, "Your grandfather is looking for him. He will be found."

Freddie tried to sit up. "I can help. . ." Then he fell back into my arms. "Just as soon as I'm better. I'll make sure he knows the truth."

I touched his face. "Thank you, my love. For now, promise me you'll never tell anyone about what happened."

He nodded and trembled again, sending a sharp stab through me for asking my son to keep such a secret. Here I was, surrounded by secrets, and breeding more. But I saw no other way.

Drawing him close, I calmed my voice. "Lay back, my darling. I'll read you a story until you fall asleep."

Chapter 20

"No, Sarah. Wrong again." Mother's voice was shrill with her frustration at my pathetic needlework. No matter how agreeable I tried to be, Mother found fault in everything I did: my needlework was a disaster, my knitting was even worse, and my table manners were atrocious. As we did on most days, we sat in the family parlour, surrounded by Mother's many treasures, while she tutored me on how to become a perfect gentlewoman.

I sucked on my pierced finger and stabbed the embroidery needle back into the stretched frame, hoping to not add blood to my messy work. "I'm sorry. I hardly slept last night worrying about Junior." It was near the end of the year and there was still no word from him. The nights were long and lonely with thoughts of my son's last words haunting me. Did he really hate me?

"He will come home when he is ready. It is best to think about the good things that have happened. Like, Freddie's full recovery, and his attendance at the Academy with his brother." I smiled at her weakly, deciding not to tell her how Freddie complained every day about the arrogant town boys. "And you really must see Charles. He was here again today. Asking for you."

I shook my head and returned to my embroidery, jabbing the needle in my finger again. Seeing Charles would only confuse things. Deciding whether to return to Edenwae had now become my main concern. Yet, there was no clear way back with Hamish there. I had become lonely and bored, with nothing to occupy my mind except regret and anger. This burden was too heavy to carry on my own.

"I need to see to this." I displayed my bleeding finger. "Anyway, I am going to Grandview soon. Tabitha is decorating her tree, and the boys want to see it."

"Very well. Make sure you are home by the afternoon. I have a woman coming to work on your shabby hands. And please consider seeing Charles."

Rushing out the door, I pushed aside my unspoken reason for avoiding Charles; how could I trust any man again after everything that had happened?

***

A short while later, Tabitha and I reclined on a comfortable settee in the ballroom at Grandview in front of a roaring fire set in one of its many fireplaces. The air was infused with the smells of pine, beeswax candles, and burning firewood. We lounged in comfort while servants erected a twelve-foot Christmas tree and hung ornaments upon it. "No, please over to the left just a little further," Tabitha said, directing the placement of each decoration. "That's it. Thank you, that's just perfect." Tabitha's face beamed with joy at this small accomplishment.

I forced a tepid smile for my sister's sake. Watching Tabitha supervise the servants, I began to realize what irked me most about genteel life—none of it mattered, the work was meaningless and trivial, the primary activity being the ordering around of poorly paid servants. A lady had nothing interesting to do. Smouldering embers of love for Edenwae lingered under the ashes of my sad and boring life.

Unbidden, memories of last Christmas pricked me; my boys so happy and excited for our life ahead. Then, I had been fooled into thinking Hamish might be my friend. Or more…

Tabitha turned toward me and saw the tears in the corners of my eyes. "Oh, my darling, is it too hard? I'm being thoughtless." She reached for my hand, pressing her elegantly embroidered handkerchief into it. "Should we retire to my dressing room, away from all of this?"

Dabbing at my eyes, I smelled a pleasant whiff of lavender perfume embedded in her handkerchief. The familiar scent was comforting. "No, I'm fine. The boys will want to see your beautiful tree. I am determined that they'll have a joyful Christmas even though we all miss Junior so." The twins were playing with Robert in the nursery. Just yesterday, Albert announced he had adopted Robert, sending me further into a spiral of regret. In my bleary attempts to find a way forward after Freddie's accident, I had foolishly hoped that living in town might allow the return of Robert to me. But Albert's decision, had ended once and for all, the faint hope to which I had uselessly been clinging. Above all, now that I spent so much time at Grandview, I saw the strong bond between my sister and my baby. He knew only her as his mother, and she loved him dearly. How wrong it would be for me to change that for my own selfish need. "But I'd like to speak privately with you before the children join us. You always make me feel better."

"Of course." She dismissed the servants, then moved a little closer to hold my hand.

"I was remembering last Christmas. I wish I knew where Junior was, where he'll spend the Yuletide. The thought that he could be suffering somewhere, all alone and frightened keeps me awake at night. Every day I look down the road hoping to see him riding toward me. And I worry that he'll never return, not as long as I live in town. Why would he? All he's ever wanted to be was a farmer."

Tabitha looked a little baffled for a moment. Then she intertwined her fingers with mine. "I thought you had given up on Edenwae?"

"I've been in such a confused state since Freddie's accident and since Junior left. . . honestly, I don't know what I want any more. Edenwae has cost me so much . . ." I trailed off. Despite spending much more time together, my sister and I had not repaired the divide between us. The closely held secrets we kept from each other still stood between us. We had become used to living with our lies, the burden of the truth too heavy and timeworn to reveal to each other. I had to change that.

"Some days I convince myself that I'd been a selfish fool to pursue my dreams and to have believed in Joe. When I feel that way, I accept that giving up Edenwae would be best for my sons. But, at other times, I believe that if I were to quit now, it would all have been for nothing. And the only chance for Junior's return would be if we lived at the farm. Freddie and the twins are not happy here, bullied by the town boys for being stupid farmers who can't keep up with their lessons. Almost every day they ask if we can go home."

Trying to compose myself, I picked up a silver ornament resting by my hand and looked at it. I saw my face reflected by the shiny surface and I did not recognize myself sitting in this grand place. Unexpectedly, I knew what I wanted. "I feel as if I am mourning the loss of Edenwae. Not as much as I suffer for Junior of course, but I feel bereft without my dream. The promise I saw in Edenwae gave me strength and purpose. Now, I doubt I will ever be happy again, not if I stay in this town."

"Then go back." She made it sound so simple.

"I can't." I stammered, my voice catching. "I'm afraid."

Her eyes rounded. "Why?"

I hesitated, then said, "Because of Hamish."

Her eyes narrowed and her mouth drew into a thin line. "What did he do?"

My lips trembling, I told her about Hamish. Tears sprang to her eyes when I told her about the brutal rape and his threatening of Junior to get his way. "My God, how horrible."

"The worst part is that he hurt my boys."

"Freddie is fine now."

"But Junior. . ." I looked at her helplessly.

"That's why he stays away. I never really understood before. Did you tell Father?"

"How could I? He would think it was his fault for letting me stay there. For threatening the dairy's future by needing his money back, forcing me to solicit Hamish's help, putting myself in further jeopardy. How could I do that to Father?"

"There must be a way to make Hamish pay for what he did. To get rid of him."

"No one would believe me." I stared down at our intertwined hands.

She gently pulled my chin up to look directly into my eyes. "I do."

My burden lifted slightly as I stared at my sister. "Thank you, my darling... but that's not enough." Fresh tears wetted my eyes as I forced out my next words. "Half the town believes I'm bedding Hamish already, and the rest will think I'm trying to bring a good man down, just to get rid of him. There is no way I can win."

I sat in silence for a moment reflecting upon my powerlessness, then let the unfairness of it fuel a new anger. "I can't let Hamish win this way. I must find a way to go home."

At that very moment, our sons scrambled boisterously into the ballroom, eyes agog at the enormous tree. My twins were on either side of Robert, each holding a hand. In an unsynchronized tapping of small boots, the three of them started to run across the room. "Walk please, gentlemen," said the nanny rather harshly, striding in a few steps behind them. Noticing us on the settee, she softened her voice. "Sorry, Madame, am I too soon? You had requested I bring them down at this time."

"No, it is perfect timing. Exactly what we need." Tabitha beamed at me, and we welcomed our little boys into our arms.

Chapter 21

On Christmas Eve, as a special treat, my children were invited to join Mother and Father for tea in their formal parlour. Having lived with my parents for some time now, Cameron understood how to please his grandmother, behaving like a perfect gentleman at the table. Freddie sat beside him trying to imitate his brother's behaviour, looking overwhelmed by the complexity of it all. Unfortunately, the twins resisted learning better manners, and, over the course of the tea, they were frequently corrected by Mother. They were eager to be excused. Thank goodness she was distracted by Cameron, or she might have caught them giggling at her looming portrait hanging on the wall immediately behind her.

I tried to keep a serious face while scolding them with a stern look, but I too felt like giggling. When I saw a bursting smile on Freddie's face, the giggle escaped; the contrast between the diminutive smiling gentlewoman in the portrait and the rotund humourless grandmother sitting beneath it was just too funny. Noticing that I was not terribly annoyed, the twins began fidgeting, barely able to control themselves, eager to leave for my sister's house. It would be the first time we attended the holiday festivities at Grandview and everyone was looking forward to it.

Mother looked around the table and clapped her hands loudly to stop our laughter, "Everyone. Off to your rooms to dress for the evening." Cameron graciously helped his grandmother out of her chair and led her out of the room on his arm. Willie and Bertie scampered behind them, having been warned by me not to push past their grandmother.

Freddie rose to escort me. "Go on ahead. I'll be with you shortly," I said, smiling at him. I caught my father's eye. "Father, could I have a moment of your time, please?"

"Of course." He closed the door and looked at me quizzically.

"I'd like to discuss Edenwae."

"Right now? Couldn't it wait?" He looked down at his hands, pretending to pick at an errant cuticle.

I took a step toward him, but he refused to look up. "It'll just take a moment. I wanted to thank you for taking care of the dairy. Please, tell me. How is business? We must be making a profit by now."

Without glancing up, he walked over to the window and looked out at the snow-covered courtyard behind the house. The snow, that had been falling for two days, had finally stopped, the setting sun was now casting shadows from the tall trees across the yard. The long black fingers against the fresh white snow looked beautiful, yet felt ominous. Continuing to look out the window, he said, "Everything is running smoothly."

His evasive manner put me on edge. "I'm concerned that Duff may have withdrawn his support. Have you spoken with him recently? With me living in town, I'm worried he has changed his mind about selling the land to my sons."

He continued to stare out the window. "You worry too much. It will all work out."

I moved over to stand near him, clasping my hands together so he wouldn't see them shaking. "But if I were at Edenwae, I'd be well on my way to buying the land. But because of… I need to know what's going on."

He finally turned toward me, meeting my gaze. "Sounds like you want to return to Edenwae. I'm pleased to hear that. Now, I really must get dressed. Let us talk further tomorrow." With that said, he left me.

I was too stunned to pursue him and beg for the truth.

***

An hour later, I was in my bedroom preparing for the evening ahead. Outside my window, the evening was clear and cold, the sun had set and the lamps were lit, casting pools of warm light upon the crisp fallen snow. It reminded me of a picture-perfect Christmas Eve, right out of a Dickens tale. I sat at my vanity table, fastening a modest green velvet ribbon around my throat. There was a knock at the door, and Mother burst in, as usual, not waiting for my permission. "Let me look at you."

I stood up for her inspection. The grand festivities tonight presented an opportunity to fully embrace Mother's wish that I become a perfect lady. Once I stopped resisting her, Mother and I had become much more amicable. When she suggested a trip to her dressmaker for a new ballgown I graciously accepted her offer. The result of our expedition had been a deep green velvet gown with a revealing neckline, cinched waist, and long sleeves. She was thrilled at the choice, while I wondered if I would ever feel such joy over a gown.

As she spun me around to view my own reflection in the standing mirror beside the vanity, I looked at myself. Tonight, I would be happy for the others, no matter what my heart felt. I planned to observe my sister more carefully and learn how to acquiesce graciously in this world ruled by men—smile and be pretty and never, ever, have an opinion or speak out of turn.

"You look absolutely exquisite. It has taken us some time to restore your beauty, but here you are. My beautiful Sarah, once again. And just in time—" she said, cutting herself off as if she had just said too much.

"Mother, are you planning on introducing me to another gentleman tonight?" I hoped not; I must deal with Charles first. Any ambition with him had been obscured by that awful day in the barn and everything that happened since.

Yet I had spoken rather playfully to mother, no longer using the confrontational tone of my past, finally accepting that it was impossible to stop her from matchmaking. I now viewed her obsession differently. After Junior's disappearance and Freddie's accident, I had developed irrational fears about my children. Every time one of them was out of my sight, I worried he might be in danger and wondered whether this awful feeling was how my mother had felt after my brother William died. Was that why she tried to control us? Perhaps my mother's obsession with social climbing had been much more complex than I had originally thought, maybe it was her belief that a good marriage to a wealthy gentleman was the best way to protect us. All this time, I thought my mother did not love me, but now I began to understand that love, in some form, might have been involved after all.

Picking at a piece of fluff on my gown, she averted her gaze. "Of course not. I just meant that this will be the first time you have attended a Christmas Eve at Grandview. Everyone who is anyone will be in attendance, a perfect opportunity for town society to see the beautiful lady you have become."

Moving closer, I took her hand in mine. "Thank you for the new gown. It is truly beautiful."

She sniffed a little, lifting her chin up so her nose was high in the air. "Well, I just wanted you to be pretty tonight."

I leaned down to embrace her. She stood stiffly in my arms, patting my back briefly before she withdrew. "Shall we go?" she said, turning abruptly to leave.

***

Later that evening, standing in the front entrance hall at Grandview, I told the twins to join the other children in the nursery for games. Cameron and Freddie stood at my side looking handsome in their new waist coats and vests. In the crowded entrance, I noticed a pretty girl about Cameron's age sneaking sideway glances at them. "I believe the young people are gathering in the front parlour. Please, go and join them."

"Thank you, Mother," Cameron said, then "Come on Freddie." As they walked down the hallway, I noted the young girl following them, accompanied by several of her friends. My sons would be kept busy tonight.

Mother and Father joined me, and we walked into the great ballroom. The tree was breathtaking, hundreds of lit candles, popcorn garlands and tiny packages filled with treats for the children. The room was decorated with laurels and wreaths. Tabitha had outdone herself. I stumbled as all eyes in the room seemed to turn toward me at once. There were familiar faces from my youth, silly girls who were now fine ladies, turning up their noses at me. "Oh Bertrand, look there are the Gilberts. Please excuse us." Father glanced back at me and smiled as he led Mother on his arm across the ballroom.

Feeling the need to shrink into a corner, I was about to flee to a quiet place, when I saw Tabitha gliding across the expanse of hardwood flooring toward me. "Sarah, you look so lovely in that dress. Absolutely glorious." She kissed me on each cheek. "And look who is here?" She tilted her head in the direction of the north fireplace behind me. I glanced in the indicated direction and was surprised by the sight of Charles politely listening to Albert pontificate.

I blushed. How handsome he looked in his formal attire, his lanky frame coiled into a wingback chair. Suddenly unsure, I grasped Tabitha's hand and pulled her out of sight behind a pillar.

"I'm not ready. Not after. . ."

"You haven't spoken to him, at all?"

"No. I couldn't. . ."

"He's been asking about you and is looking forward to seeing you tonight."

She pulled at my arm to force me into action. We walked toward Albert and Charles, arm in arm, heads held at a respectable angle, not too high, not too low, just the correct posture for ladies. I felt unsteady on my feet and wished the floor would swallow me up.

The men were engrossed in their conversation and did not notice our approach. Albert posed by the fireplace, his elbow perfectly placed on the mantle for effect. "And that, old chap, is why Crossen Car produces the highest quality for my money."

But Charles was not looking at Albert any longer. His eyes were fixed upon me, the flickering of the fire causing flashes of gold and green to appear in them. My blush deepened under the intensity of his attention.

"Ah, my dears." Judging by the clipped manner of his voice, Albert was clearly annoyed at the interruption. "Charles, you remember my sister-in-law, Sarah."

"Charmed to see you again." Charles rose with an easy grace to grasp my outstretched hand. Without dropping his gaze, he drew my hand up to his mouth and kissed it. A shiver ran down my spine, but I could not sort out whether it was excitement or the shock of a man's touch again.

Charles complemented Tabitha on her tree, which promptly set her off into a monologue of minutiae about the decorations. I glanced at Albert, noticing his agitation grow. "Tabitha, dear, no one loves that tree like you do," he said sharply. She tensed at my side.

Just then, little Robert skidded to a stop in front of the man he knew as "Father." Standing to attention, barely able to contain his excitement, Robert waited for his father to speak. His short pants ended above pudgy knees, and I could see tremors running through them, like a puppy being restrained from its natural instinct to bound about the room. I smiled at Robert and wondered if I would feel so sad whenever I saw him.

Albert's expression softened as he bent over his adopted son. "Good evening, young Robert. Shall we get a closer look at the Christmas tree?" He swept the boy onto his shoulders and walked away. Tabitha and I exchanged looks of astonishment before she hurriedly followed them.

"Your brother-in-law seems to have been infected by the Christmas spirit." Charles smiled at me warmly and drew me close to him by the fire. "I am so sorry about the terrible accident."

"Thank you. I'm sorry that I refused to see you. I was . . ." My voice broke.

"Freddie is fully recovered now?" He handed me his handkerchief when my eyes blurred.

I fiddled with the handkerchief, not knowing what to do with my hands. "Junior is gone."

"Yes, I heard."

I gazed across the ballroom while an uncomfortable silence settled between us. I felt his eyes upon me. "Sarah, I hoped we might speak privately. I have respected your wishes and stayed away. Could we find somewhere to be alone?"

Charles extended his arm, and I led him to the library, my apprehension trailing behind us. "We should be alone in here," I said.

He closed the door and started pacing the room, while I sat on the edge of a wingback chair. There was a look of such confidence on his face that I felt off balance. I still held his handkerchief, and it was becoming a mangled mess. He stopped his pacing to stand immediately in front of me. "I have bought Edenwae."

The room whirled around me. "You what?" I knew in my bones that something was going on, that decisions were being made without any consideration for me, nor my sons. But Charles? "How did that happen?" I said through clenched teeth.

His eyes met mine, and I shivered at their intensity. "It started when Hamish approached me for a loan."

I could feel my heart thump as the pieces started falling into place. "So that's why you two knew each other that day…" The heat rose in my face.

"He claimed he wanted to pay a debt you owed your father, then buy the land. He asked me for a loan."

"Why would he ask you?" I felt slightly sickened speaking of Hamish and wondered what else he may have told Charles.

Charles looked away as he spoke. "I lend money out. On occasion." He started pacing the room again and kept talking. "I refused him the loan, of course. I prefer to deal with gentlemen."

"You went to Father?" I gasped and shot out of my chair.

Nodding, he kept striding through the room, refusing to look at me, making me all that more furious. "You are the 'investment that suddenly paid off,'" I said, as everything became clear.

He stopped his pacing abruptly and grasped me by the arms, making me cringe. "Then I bought the land from Duff."

I struggled out of his grasp, my breath coming in short gasps. "I suspected you were interested in Edenwae," I said angrily, "but how could you... you knew how much it meant to me?" I could hardly believe this man was flaunting his victory in my face.

He reached for me again, another man who thought he could take what he wanted. When I raised my hand to slap him, he pulled back. I was trembling. "Please Sarah, I don't wish to harm you. I want to marry you."

I stood breathless for a moment, starring at him, wondering if we were both mad.

He kept his distance and gestured toward a chair. "You misunderstand me. Please sit down. I can explain."

Rigid with anger, I remained standing. "You have Edenwae, why do you need me?"

He smiled and looked at me through furrowed brows. "I paid off the debt to your father on the condition he kept the matter confidential until I was certain."

"Of what?" I demanded.

"Certain that you would say yes."

"And what makes you certain now?" My voice trembled with anger.

"In truth, I was certain right after my visit, and I planned to return and ask you, but with the accident... I respected your wishes to give you time. I simply need to *own* Edenwae. The dairy is your passion, and under your management it will grow and prosper. I will fund whatever you need and help you in any way I can."

"Why ever would you do that?"

He smiled with that cunningness I noticed the day of his visit. "Because it leaves me to take care of... well, shall we say, my own affairs. This will be a matrimonial relationship and a business relationship. And..." He scanned my body with sharp eyes, "...I need a wife. We'll be a married couple, and I sincerely hope we will have children of our own. I enjoy your calculated approach to life, and I believe we would make ideal partners."

Feeling as if I was watching myself speak from far away, I said, "Why do you *need* a wife?"

That sly smile reappeared. "Let us just say it gives me a certain...respectability. And having children will make my father very happy. Carrying on the family line and all that..."

"What will happen to my sons?"

He nodded. "Your father warned me that you wouldn't agree easily without getting something for your children."

"So, that's why my parents have been acting so strangely. They knew. Why wouldn't Father tell me?"

"I asked him not to." He gently took my hand. "As to your sons, what do you want?"

Hitting my stride for the first time, I shot back, "Adopt them and make them heirs to Edenwae."

He considered that, then nodded.

"And help me to find Junior. Promise him a section of land right now if he comes home."

"I can't guarantee he'll be found."

The ways his eyes shifted and his smile disappeared made me start. "What do you know?"

"Nothing." He averted his eyes again. This man knew something important to me. I would need to gain his trust to find out more.

He paused for a moment, and I stayed silent. Then he continued, "But there is one stipulation, only one condition you must agree to. You must never ask me about my business affairs. Ever. It is all I ask of you, and I will give you everything you want in return. What do you say?"

"No words of love to entice me?" I mocked, relieved that he hadn't tried to woo me.

He smiled broadly. "I knew such words would never sway you. I believe you and I are cut from the same cloth, shall we say."

Even though he remained a shadowy stranger, I knew I would marry him. It was the only way back to Edenwae.

1878

Chapter 22

On a hot summer's day in July, I cooled my face with an ivory fan and sat down in one of the cushioned wicker chairs on the wide terrace adorning the new manor at Edenwae. It has been two years since Junior left and my heart still ached for him. Where was he? This question bored into my mind so often it would surely drive me mad. How could he have believed I would betray him like that? On my worst nights, the thought that he was dead haunted me.

Charles hired private investigators to find him, and we posted personal messages in the newspapers. We sent a sealed letter with the searchers to give to Junior should they find him. It contained the promise from Charles that he had bequeathed Edenwae to Junior and his brothers, along with my plea that he return home, and the assurance that my marriage to Charles protected his legacy. It had been difficult to write the letter without revealing to my husband why Junior ran away when he did.

Leaning back into the comfort of the chair, I contemplated my new life with Charles. He was a man of his word—adopting my sons, willing Edenwae to them, mounting a search for Junior, and funding my dairy, leaving me to manage it on my own. The new manor was completed shortly before our wedding day, and we had lived here for over a year. The two-storey house was designed with a high watch tower at its centre, large bay windows, and steep roof lines with ornate filigree gable ends. On the main floor, there was a formal parlour and dining room, a family parlour, and Charles's study. Behind the main living quarters, were the servants' wing and kitchen.

Having spent most of the day in the dairy barns, I was hot and clammy. I pulled at my mat of sweaty hair and loosened the embroidered shirt tucked into my tailored work trousers. The fine cotton fabric was wet with perspiration, and it felt good to fan the skin beneath. The air was filled with the smell of pink peonies that bordered the terrace. A glass of lemonade sat on a small table beside me, beads of water running down the cut-glass as if it were sweating too.

The sound of the dogs barking alerted me, and I saw three riders approaching. Charles and his two men, Roy, and Sam. I stood and waved.

Reining in his horse and looking up to me, Charles took off his black hat and smiled, shouting, "So good to see you, dear. I will be with you shortly." When he smiled that way, I felt drawn to him, and wished I knew more about this man I had married out of necessity.

I watched them tie up their horses outside the private entrance to Charles's study and head to the door. He was returning from another of his mysterious trips, leaving for days, reminding me of how Joe did the same. There was no way to ask him about it either. I had sworn never to question his business affairs when I accepted his marriage proposal. How could I not agree to that one stipulation when he offered me so much in return? At the time it appeared easy, but now his secrecy nagged at me.

And those men, looking more like outlaws than hard workers, each with a rifle in its saddle scabbard. Only once had I met them, when Charles invited me to his study in the early days after my return to Edenwae, to introduce them so I knew they were not trespassers. Roy was large and brawny, with slick brown hair, dark eyes, squashed nose, and stringy mustache. Sam was small and wiry, little eyes always darting, his hands in constant motion. When Charles rode with them they reminded me of a gang about to rob a bank. They would be in Charles's study for several hours now. Then they would leave.

And why was Charles's study always locked? The key resided in his pocket, so like Joe and his key to the strongbox.

All of this—the mysterious trips, the strange men at his side, the locked study—made me worry about my husband's affairs; that they might be immoral, or even illegal. If they were not, why the need for such secrecy? I should have waited to accept his proposal, but everything had been arranged and it felt safe.

After Charles disappeared through the study door, I flopped in the chair again, resting my head against its back, and took another long drink of lemonade, frustrated by secrets disrupting my life again.

***

At the dinner table that evening, Charles sat at the head with me at his side, Willie on my left and Freddie and Bertie opposite us. "I forgot to mention that my parents are coming for a visit tomorrow, Cameron too," I announced.

"Wonderful," said Charles. "I would like to hear how his college application is progressing." When he was adopted by Charles, Cameron had been eager to change his name to *Bulmore*. I felt a tug of sorrow that he so quickly gave up his father's name, but Charles's name would serve my ambitious son much better than *Drury* would. With Charles's encouragement, Cameron was hoping to be accepted into Victoria College, with aspirations beyond that to attend an American university, perhaps Harvard.

"Freddie, how are your mathematics studies?" Charles asked. My new husband had identified early on that the boy had a gift for numbers, and had encouraged his studies in mathematics, hiring a special tutor and spending many evenings reviewing Freddie's work himself. Now, at the age of fifteen, Freddie kept the dairy's books and hoped one day to be involved in Charles's business. Given my worries, I was not sure how I felt about that.

"Very well, Father. I just started on the Pythagorean theorem and the various proofs, geometric and algebraic. May we discuss it later?" Right after we married and moved back to Edenwae the boys had started calling Charles *Father*. It felt right from the beginning—maybe because they had called Joe *Da*—and I should be grateful to Charles for setting a strong example of a good man. If only I could be sure he was.

"I look forward to that. Always one of my favourites. Willie, Bertie, how are your horses?" Charles had purchased gentle mares for them, but I expected they would be riding stallions by their teenage years. They had been delighted to return to Edenwae and leave the town school behind. Charles hired a private teacher who visited three times a week to provide lessons and review homework, but my nine-year-old twins would rather ride the trails on their new horses than do their studies.

While Charles and my sons continued to catch up, I sat back, half-listening, and gazed at my husband's handsome profile and thought that it was not just me. My sons were also forming strong attachments to him.

***

Later that night, Charles and I settled into our down-filled bed and extinguished the bedside lamps. He pulled me into a tender embrace, and I buried my face into his neck, smelling the sweet lemon scent of his shaving soap. "Are you in the mood to try again tonight?" I could not understand why it had taken so long. Maybe I was spent, like an old hen.

"Always," I said, reaching for him. He kissed me deeply, running his hands down my neck, caressing my breasts. I smiled as he kissed his way down my breasts and belly, then drew me on top of him. As we fell into a sensual rhythm, I smiled again, remembering my wedding-night expectation of an uninspired performance in bed, devoid of all passion without the drive of true love. How ridiculous that seemed now, as I threw back my head with pleasure and gasped.

Later, we lay entwined within each other's arms.

"I must be pregnant after that!" I giggled. There was only a muffled sleepy reply. I snuggled against him, enjoying the pungent scent of our lovemaking. "What happens if I don't give you a child?"

When he didn't reply I shook him gently and repeated my question.

"Oh darling, I guess my family will have to be content with step-sons."

"Ah. I see. It was my sons you were after all along," I teased, pushing playfully at him.

More fully awake now, he pulled me to him. "Nonsense. You were just proven breeding stock, producing high quality boys." He dodged my playful slap, then grabbed me around the waist, and pressed his bare belly into mine, kissing me to quiet any further banter.

After the kiss, I drew back and asked soberly, "Why is it so important for us to have a child? My sons are legally yours. Won't that do?"

He fell onto his back and starred at the ceiling. "In truth, it's likely more important to me than my father. It's just that my older brother, George—well, I told you about him—he inherits everything. But he still hasn't produced a child, causing a bit of a stir."

"Just like Tabitha," I blurted out.

He became lost in his own thoughts for a moment, then said, "Yes, I suppose."

"Anyway, I can't guarantee it will be a boy."

He pulled me against him again. "You've worn me out. Let's sleep." He was starting to mumble again. I brought his hand to my lips and kissed his smooth skin, while he drifted off to sleep. Shifting quietly in the bed, I turned to face my sleeping husband. The moonlight streamed in through the window, casting a soft light across his elegant and refined nose, bushy hair, and those well-sculpted lips that drew me to him.

I had finally won Edenwae at a great cost to my heart and I would not let anything ever threaten it.

***

The next day, I spent the early part of the morning in the dairy barns. A second, much larger barn had been added and our herd now stood at ninety cows. We had hired more workers, built a large bunkhouse to house them, and we were even embracing the use of the milking machine Cameron had designed and now perfected.

Hamish had been replaced by Malcolm, a right-hand man who did not have the last name of Drury. All I knew of Hamish was that he had disappeared after Charles fired him. Without knowing his whereabouts, my stomach still lurched whenever an unexpected rider appeared in our laneway. And, crossing the barnyard this morning, my stomach did just that at the sound of horse's hooves.

Then I saw him. A lone rider with his brim pulled down and the horse gently swaying as he rode toward me through the shimmering heat of the day. I thought instantly of Joe.

At the sight of me, he took off his hat and waved. I would know those curls anywhere. *Junior!*

My feet barely touched the ground as I ran to him, the dogs hot on my heels. He reined in his horse and leapt off. We fell into each other's arms.

Hugging and touching him, hardly believing that he was truly here, my face was wet with tears and my heart was bursting at the sight of him. "Are you hurt?" I cried. Patting him all over, then looking more closely, I saw the changes—tall as his father, with broad shoulders, deep chest, and muscled arms, whiskers on his attractive face—my boy was now a man. "Where have you been?"

Junior pulled away from me, his eyes wet too. "I'm fine. I was working on the railway out west… I thought you no longer wanted me…I'm sorry, Mother. I feel awful—"

I interrupted him. "You are home now. Nothing else matters." The dogs leapt at him with a mad frenzy, and he reached down to ruffle their ears.

Suddenly, Charles stood beside us. "Welcome home," he said, holding out his hand.

Junior stepped forward to grasp the extended hand, looking Charles squarely in the eyes. "Thank you, Sir, for everything. If it hadn't been for the letters—"

"I thought there was only one?" I said, looking at Charles.

"Freddie sent his own personal appeal, making me swear to not open it," Charles said, rubbing a reassuring hand down my back.

"That's true, Sir, but it was your promises that made me realize my future was here. I'm so grateful to you. And Roy was very convincing too."

"Roy? Your Roy?" I said.

He nodded. "Once I was certain where Junior was, I sent someone I could trust to make sure he came home."

He grasped my son's shoulder. "Please, call me Charles. And you should know that this was all because of your mother. We have much to discuss about your future."

I linked arms with Junior and the three of us headed toward the manor. The front door flung open, and Freddie raced toward us with the twins close behind. Freddie hugged his brother, then beamed at me. "I told you we would find him."

While the twins took their turns hugging their eldest brother, I eased back and took my husband aside. "Why did you keep this from me?"

"I had to be sure he would come home. I didn't want to raise your hopes."

"Would you have told me if you'd found him, and he had refused to come home?" I immediately regretted asking the question.

"Of course, I would. And I was fully prepared to travel west with you if that's what it would have taken to convince him."

"Really? You would do that?"

When he nodded and smiled at me with such tenderness, I told myself to stop worrying about his business affairs and be content.

Rejoining my sons, I said, "Come on everyone, let's get Junior settled before your grandparents and Cameron arrive."

"I can't wait to see Cameron's face when he sees you," blurted Freddie, bumping affectionately against his brother.

***

Later that morning, I left Junior to settle into his new bedroom in the north end of the second floor. The boys' suite of rooms contained many bedrooms, one for each of them including one that had stood vacant awaiting Junior's return, a library, a games room, and a large bathing room.

Walking away down the hallway, I planned to freshen up before my parents arrived. I entered the bedroom suite I shared with Charles: the master bedroom, a dressing room for each of us, a bathing room complete with the latest in indoor plumbing, and a smaller room we hoped would one day be our nursery. I stripped off my trousers and shirt. No longer the poor daughter who made bad choices, I now liked to look my best whenever Mother visited, and today would be a very special celebration. I bathed, then changed into a form-fitting day dress, the gorgeous light blue silk complementing my dark skin. I brushed my unruly curls, leaving them loosely falling over the shoulder. Finally, I donned new shoes from London, the very height of fashion, and checked my appearance in the standing mirror. Mother would undoubtedly admire the attire before descending into a flurry of criticism about my unfashionable sun-darkened skin and unpinned hair. I was content that Mother's sharp words could no longer hurt me.

Satisfied at my appearance I went to find Junior. I needed to clear the air between us. Reaching the boys' rooms, I asked the others for a few moments alone with my eldest son. He was bathed and dressed in a clean shirt and trousers given to him by Charles. He was freshly shaved, and his long curls still wet. For a moment I wondered if he was truly standing here—maybe my imagination was playing tricks on me—but when he spoke, with his voice so low, my heart jumped with delight. After two years of worrying and wishing for his return, it was fantastical.

"May I speak to you about that day?" I asked. I drew him closer. "We must. I don't wish for anything to ever stand between us again."

"It won't. Freddie told me in his letter what Hamish did... I should have protected you."

I touched his arm. "He would have killed you. You weren't the man you are now."

He stared intensely at me. "Where is he?"

"He will never bother us again. Not with Charles and his men here."

"If I ever see that bastard—"

"Hush." I placed my finger on his shuddering lips.

Brushing it away, he said, "And if I had stayed, Freddie wouldn't have been hurt."

"He's fine. You are home, that's all that matters." I pulled him into an embrace, enjoying the feel of my grown boy.

He drew back. "Please. I need to talk too. I was so angry after Da died. That day... he was so drunk he could hardly stand up. I heard him fighting with Granda about his drinking, about owing money to someone. There was something else, Granda said, but I couldn't hear it... something about what Da was doing in town. Da was in a state after that, he just sat and drank... muttering that we'd be better off if he were dead. I tried to talk to him, but he roared at me, so I let him be. I will always regret that." His shoulders slumped and his eyes glistened, but he refused to let me embrace him. "We all thought he went somewhere to sleep it off, but then I heard Granda yelling at him to get off the roof. I saw him too... he was stupidly staggering around up there, then I saw he was looking at you and I yelled for him to get down. Then—"

"It wasn't your fault."

He starred at me with red-rimmed eyes, wide and frightened. "I think he fell on purpose."

"I know." I said, pulling him into me. It was the first time I admitted, even to myself, that Joe had killed himself, taking the cowardly way out rather than face what he had done.

Junior pulled back. "I was so angry at him, at you, at Hamish, at Granda, at myself. I believed Hamish. I was sure you'd let me down just like Da had." His eyes brimmed with tears, and he bowed his head.

I tilted his chin up. "You were hurting, my love. I made mistakes too. I should've found a way to appease Duff and send Hamish away. But there was a part of me that trusted Hamish. And I feel a fool for having done that."

"But that's not all. When I heard you married Charles instead of Hamish, I decided to never come home, thinking you'd abandoned me. If it hadn't been for Roy finding me, I would have never known what you did for me."

"I'm so happy you're back. Let's forget that horrible day. And please promise me you'll never tell Charles or anyone else about what Hamish did. It is my story to tell, no one else's."

"You seem so happy with him. I'd never do anything to upset that."

I smiled at him. "Yes, I suppose I am."

Just then we heard the clatter of my parents' carriage and the yipping of the dogs. "Sounds like we'd better get downstairs."

When we emerged from the house, Cameron was stepping out of the carriage, greeting the dogs, Freddie and the twins were already waiting for our guests. We all cried out when Cameron looked up and saw his long-lost brother standing beside me. His face exploding with excitement, he raced to embrace Junior, then pulled back. "Where the hell have you been?"

"It's a long story."

Looking past them, I saw Mother struggling out of the carriage with the help of Father, while Bertie and Willie kept the dogs away. When she landed safely on the ground, Mother saw Junior and yelled, "Come here, boy. Let me look at you." When Junior ran to her, she shouted, "My God, you look just like him."

Junior laughed and reached down to hug her.

She tapped him lightly on the back before pushing away. "Now, young man, how dare you make us worry so." Not a true scolding, for joy lurked around the edges of her face.

Now it was my father's turn. "Oh… my boy." Father gripped Junior fiercely. He looked so frail against my strong boy—starkly thin, his hair now completely grey. Father used to stand perfectly erect, looking strong and invincible, but now even as he reached up to Junior, he was stooped over and fragile looking. Was there something much graver transforming his appearance than the mere passage of time?

While the two of them talked earnestly to each other, I approached Mother.

"Just delighted that he is home. I am so happy for you," she said, "Now, I need to freshen up after the journey."

"Yes, of course. Did the new carriage cushion the bumps on the road?" Apparently two carriages had not been enough.

"As you know, I hate the journey to see you. I do not know why I do it. The new carriage has much better springs, all the latest you know."

"The guest cottage is ready for you. Boys, help me with the luggage." Charles and I had refurbished the old settler cottage into a guest house. Two spacious master suites had been created out of the mishmash of small rooms that had once housed my life with Joe. Combined with a new kitchen and servant's quarters, it provided comfortable accommodation for my visiting family. I took great satisfaction in forcing Mother to stay there whenever she visited. It kept the visits down to a minimum.

Mother scowled and snorted. "I loathe that place. Why can't we stay in the main house?"

"But you know there is simply no room there." In truth, there was plenty of space, but I preferred to have her stay in the guest cottage, far away from me, with a cook and a maid to see to her needs for most of the day until dinner time. That way, Father and I could ride the fields or check on the dairy operation without having to answer to her. My father had maintained his enthusiasm for the dairy, and he was generous with his praise about my accomplishments. Our time together was the highlight of their visits.

"Freddie, you and the twins take the valises directly to the guest cottage now. Then take the packages to the manor please." Undoubtedly, Mother had brought all sorts of useless presents for us again. On her last visit, she presented me with a full tea service for twenty, although she knew we would never use it. Taking Mother's arm, I guided her down the pathway to the guest cottage.

"The problem is that Charles insisted upon an American architect. If you had chosen a British man, he would have designed a proper London house like ours, with ample room to accommodate guests. And forcing me to walk all this way. Why do you continue to torture me so? You have always been the impossible one."

Forcing a contrite smile, I said, "It is always so lovely to see you, Mother."

***

That evening, we sat at the large walnut table in our dining room. Charles had commissioned a local craftsman to build the table from a giant tree he found at the northern border of Edenwae. The design was distinctively sturdy and plain, unlike the more ornate style popular in Europe and coveted by Mother. "Do you think I might at least have a cushion for my chair? This rustic approach to your furniture is so uncomfortable." Mother moved theatrically on the hard chair, wincing to emphasize her point. She sat to Charles's left and directly across from me. Father held the end seat facing my husband, and the boys were arrayed between us.

"Alice, I regret that you find our approach to furnishings does not suit your comfort," Charles said, as he waved to Jessie, who happened to be passing in the hallway. "Please fetch a cushion for Madame." Our household staff were minimal compared to Mother's. Jessie was now our main housekeeper, supervising two housemaids, two cooks, and a groundskeeper.

Dutifully, Jessie bobbed her head, and departed in search of the required padding. "I do not know why you keep that woman," Mother said, in a loud whisper that was sure to be heard down the hallway. "She is so common. And Irish! I could find you a proper housekeeper."

I was about to respond when my father snapped at her. "Alice, stop it for once, please." Mother snorted, causing the twins to erupt into barely suppressed giggles, Cameron shushed them, while Freddie and Junior tried not to laugh.

"Please pass the potatoes, Mother." I knew my request would annoy her further, but I could not resist. It had become our custom to have large platters of food deposited in the centre of the table, causing great commotion as they were passed around—no servants placing plated

187

dishes in front of each of us, none of that pretentious nonsense my mother cherished.

Refusing to pass any food, she turned to my husband, an expression of extreme concern on her face. "Oh, really Charles, are you happy with such poor service? I fear my daughter has brought you down."

Charles beamed at me and grasped my hand. "Actually, I think it is perfect."

A while later, after we had finished our meal, the boys were excused, and we were left alone with my parents. With great deference, Father requested a meeting with Charles in the privacy of his study. I swallowed my curiosity until Mother and I had relocated to the parlour. She sat on a wingback chair, and I sat opposite her. She surveyed the room, looking for something more to criticize.

Unable to contain my curiosity any longer, I blurted out, "So, why is Father meeting with Charles?"

Admiring a large emerald ring balancing somewhat precariously on her stubby finger, she answered in a vague, distracted voice. "I cannot possibly say."

"Would you like a sherry?" I poured a sizeable portion from a decanter on the table beside me and handed it to her. After two glasses of sherry, and indulging Mother in her favourite pastime of idle gossip, I brought the conversation back to the topic of most interest to me. "Please tell me what's going on. Why is Father speaking with Charles?"

Maybe, it was the sherry or, perhaps it was the thrill she experienced from gossiping, but Mother now looked me squarely in the eyes and, after glancing down the hallway toward the study, leaned toward me. "I have been hearing rumours about Charles."

Mother had enunciated each word, using her loud whispering voice. "What rumours?"

She lowered her voice. "Oh. You know how fond I am of Charles, I hate to say anything, but the rumours persist. They say…" she leaned closer to me, "… that he invests in highly irregular ventures."

"Such as?" I downed a full glass of sherry, waiting for my mother to answer.

Her eyes narrowed to slits. "Oh, I do not know exactly, rumour has it that he provides loans to men the banks have refused."

"So, what's wrong with that?"

Mother glanced down the hallway, again. "Well, the banks must have refused these men for a good reason. Too risky, too immoral, maybe even…illegal." Her eyes rounded at the last word. "Why would Charles loan them money, then? It seems like a very bad idea to me. Although I also heard he charges usurious rates."

I avoided her curious stare. The risk of bad debt affecting our personal finances was worrying enough, but if Charles's business were ever found to be immoral or illegal, it could ruin the dairy. Customers would cancel contracts and it would be impossible to carry on. Of all people, it would be my mother who added fuel to my worries over Charles.

"You believe the rumours are true?"

"Oh, I don't know. You know Charles has always been a rather mysterious sort. A little of the Devil in him." She snickered and looked at me in a coquettish way. "That's why I thought he was perfect for you."

"What does that mean?"

She shrugged her shoulders and looked away, smirking.

"What is Father doing? Confronting him?"

Just then, we heard the men coming down the hallway. Mother leaned toward me and whispered. "Your father is asking Charles for a loan."

"But, why?"

I was interrupted by Father and Charles walking into the room, broad smiles on their faces.

***

The next morning Mother harrumphed into the dining room at a shockingly early hour for her. "There you are," she said, when she spied me at the sideboard filling my plate with eggs and sausages.

"What is it?" She was wearing her favourite gown for travelling, with a broad-brimmed hat atop her head.

"We are leaving. I have had it with your husband." She turned to leave.

"What has happened?" I said, racing after her and pulling on her arm.

At my touch, she stopped, and her stare drilled into me. "Why don't you ask your husband?"

Charles came down the hall from his study, with Father. "Alice, I am sorry if you are offended, but there is no other choice."

Her glare was harsh and unyielding as she stomped out the door. Father hurried to shake my husband's hand. "She'll come around, Charles. Thank you for your help." He turned to me. "Sarah, we are so happy to see Junior home. I'm sorry to leave like this."

"But. . .?" He was gone before I could form a question.

I turned to Charles. "What was that all about?" Looking more closely at him, I noticed he was wearing his riding clothes. "Are you going too?"

"Just overnight. See you tomorrow."

"Wait," I shouted after him. "What's going on?"

When he did not stop, and strode away without a backward glance. I shouted to the empty space he left behind, "Very well!, I will find out for myself." I dashed down the hallway toward his study. Reaching the door, I rattled the doorknob and found that Charles had forgotten to secure the lock.

My hand hesitated on the door handle, remembering what happened when the key had fallen out of Joe's trousers on the day I opened the strongbox. Would a shattering truth be discovered about *this* husband too once I opened the door? Fully aware of the imminent violation of my husband's privacy, I turned the handle. It was his own damned fault keeping things from me like that. I was tired of secrets.

Holding my breath, I pushed the heavy oak door open, crept in, and closed it softly behind me. I leaned back against the hard wood. Letting my breath out slowly, I looked around the room, at the overstuffed leather chairs, walls of books, and the vast oak desk. Seeing our wedding picture on his desk, my stomach lurched. Was I about to head down a path that could ruin our amicable marriage?

The thought of abandoning my subterfuge pricked at my brain, a tiny voice encouraging me to stop before going any further. But I refused to listen. This was my only chance to learn more about Charles and I could not abandon it, not after he ran off like that.

I was soon standing at his desk eagerly rummaging through the papers neatly stacked in two piles. In the first, there was correspondence, but nothing of particular interest. Moving on to the second pile, there were articles clipped from local papers with notes attached to several, none of which provided any insight into Charles's affairs. Frustrated, I started opening his desk drawers, discovering little until I reached the bottom. There, pride of place in an otherwise empty drawer, was a brown leather-bound journal.

I paused to calm my breath and glanced out the den window, worried Charles would make a sudden return. Summoning my courage, I extracted the journal and placed it gingerly on the desk. Swaying slightly, I reconsidered going further. How could I ever ask him about anything I might find, without first confessing I had gone through his desk? It would be much more difficult to hide my knowledge of the truth than to conceal my unfounded suspicions.

Standing rigidly at his desk, afraid to sit in his chair, I opened the journal. On the first page, the left column was filled with dates that predated Charles's arrival to Canada; he must have started this journal in England. The next column contained names, and beside each an amount was recorded along with notes that appeared to be in code. On the facing page, each column was headed by one of the twelve months of the year, with corresponding amounts; most had check marks, but a few did not.

This was a record of loans Charles made and the monthly payment schedules. Those without a check mark must be outstanding. Flipping through the pages, it was clear that the tallies of the payments were significantly greater than the original loans. Charles must be charging staggering interest rates. Scanning the numbers and adding them up in my head, it soon became apparent that my husband had accumulated a fortune.

I relaxed a little. My family and Edenwae appeared to be financially secure, although the unethical nature of his business was troubling. My husband was taking advantage of desperate men who had no other option than to pay his exorbitant rates of interest. But it was not a crime.

My finger continued down the rows of names. Four pages on, I came to an abrupt halt, and sat down with a thud, as I stared at the name *Joseph Drury*. My finger stayed planted upon Joe's name, holding it in place while I considered what this could possibly mean.

Following the columns to the right, I saw the monthly payments beside Joe's name. All had check marks beside them, until a few months before he died. Was this where our savings had gone? Had they been funding loan payments to Charles? But why had Joe borrowed from Charles in the first place, and where had the borrowed funds gone?

My finger kept moving down the page. Four names below Joe's, I saw *Bertrand Denton,* but the date was two years ago, not yesterday. Below it was *Albert Whittingham.* None of the debt had been paid off by either my father or my brother-in-law.

Something must be terribly wrong.

Chapter 23

The afternoon of Charles's return to Edenwae, I stood outside his study struggling with the memory of my illicit entry through the door I now stood before. I felt sick over it. Trying to ignore my roiling stomach, I knocked loudly.

"Enter." His voice did not sound surprised. He had been holed up in his study since his return.

I strode in, ready to confront my husband.

Charles was settled into the large leather chair behind his desk and was shoving papers quickly into the middle drawer. "I expect you wish to talk about your parents."

I stood in front of his desk, refusing to sit. "I have a right to know."

His face was guarded, an aloof attitude unseen before. "Your father asked me to be discreet."

"I know he asked you for a loan. Mother told me. And he looks so dreadful these days. I'm very worried about him. If you know anything, please tell me."

"I'm not certain I should," he said, looking away.

He would tell me nothing if we remained this tense and distant. I walked around the desk to pull his face close to mine. "He is my father. My only concern is his wellbeing."

Relaxing his shoulders, he took my hand and kissed it. "Very well, then. I am only telling you because I suspect you'll never stop badgering me if I don't."

The room started to swirl around me, and I wobbled. Charles caught me in his arms and guided me to a chair. "You're not well. We'll continue this discussion another time."

"No. I'm fine. Really. Please I want to know." Looking up at him I struggled to appear much better than I felt. Queasiness and feeling lightheaded were often my first signs of pregnancy, but now was not the time to confuse things.

He sighed deeply. "Shortly after your father and I met, he told me of his concern for the future of the foundry once the railway construction moved further away. He was looking for an investment to offset the losses he envisioned and hoped I might recommend one."

"Yes, he told me of his worries."

"Nothing came to my mind immediately, but I promised to look into it for him. Before I did, he'd found an opportunity through Albert, who introduced him to a Scottish lord, by the name of Gordon. This Lord Gordon headed up a conglomerate that was to purchase land along the proposed route for the new railway line, and then sell shares to Scottish immigrants, once the rail line had been completed, generating an enormous profit. Lord Gordon promised a quick return on the investment. With the credibility his title brought, your father had been sure of this investment. He took out a loan at the bank, using the foundry as collateral. A few months later, it quickly became clear that he'd been ruthlessly swindled."

"Oh my God. Poor Father."

"Yes, without the promised return, the bank threatened to seize the foundry. All of this happened within months of him loaning you the money for the dairy. When he saw your dairy's success, he asked for immediate repayment hoping it would satisfy the bank for a while. Bertie negotiated a few months' grace from the bank, praying that you could repay his loan and give him sufficient funds to avoid losing his livelihood."

"But I didn't pay him back. Oh, how I wish he'd told me."

"How could he? He was so humiliated he couldn't even tell your mother to cut back the household staff or to stop spending money on gowns and chinaware. It was not until she proposed the purchase of an adjacent mansion as a new guest house that he finally confessed. Of course, you can imagine how angry your mother was."

I nodded slowly, thinking about Mother's fury. "No wonder Father looks so defeated."

"In desperation he also told her about your outstanding loan and his hope that it would save the foundry from being taken by the bank."

"Then why would he tell you?"

"When I approached him about your debt, he leapt at my offer to pay him what you owed, then he took me into his confidence about Lord Gordon and borrowed the rest of what was owed on the foundry."

"Oh, thank God." Then I realized something. "Wait. What you're telling me about Father happened years ago, you still haven't answered my question about why he was asking you for a loan the other night?"

"I was about to get to that. Lord Gordon was a complete charlatan and has bankrupted many gentlemen across Canada and America, under the guise of various schemes. Some of the victims have been trying to track him down in the hopes of recouping their money. Your father is determined to join the group hunting for him but needs more funds to do so."

"Do you think he will be found?"

"Perhaps." I could tell by the look on his face that he thought it unlikely. "I have insisted that your parents cut back spending. Your father had been correct about the downturn in his business, and they can no longer afford such a lavish life."

"So that's why Mother is so furious with you." I pulled his hand toward me, and he knelt at my feet. "Did you really think you could keep this from me?"

"Not really. I'm sorry I rushed off, but your father was eager for the funds." The sensuous curve of his lips as they rippled into a smile, pulled me to him.

"I know I promised to never ask about your business. But... it's just... I've been hearing rumours."

His eyes narrowed into slits as he stared down his nose at me. "What sort of rumours?"

"People are saying you loan money at exorbitant interest rates. That you are usurious. You can't keep your business a secret from me forever. I am your wife."

He rose to his feet with hands on hips. "Perhaps I've been wrong in keeping my affairs from you."

I kept perfectly still, holding my breath.

"I do charge high interest rates for my loans. Some call it usurious, but there are good reasons why. My approach holds great risk, which is why I kept it from you. I'm the lender of last resort, if you like. Often my customers are desperate by the time they seek me out."

"Are you in danger?"

"No. They are desperate men, but not criminals. Sometimes I might strike against an unseemly character, but that's why I employ good men like Roy and Sam."

"Is that why you go away?"

"I don't want my customers coming here. I want my home to be a safe haven for you and the boys."

Pausing for a moment, I asked, "Why could you not tell me all this before?"

He knelt beside me again. "Maybe I'd been a bachelor for too long. I'm used to keeping everything to myself."

"I am afraid your secrecy may have had the opposite effect," I began, but fell silent.

"What is it?"

"I don't do well when secrets are kept from me."

He drew closer. "Yes, I am beginning to see that now."

I probed further. "Did you invest with Lord Gordon?"

"No, I wasn't so easily taken in by his title. I'm not convinced it's even genuine. If only your father had told me about it in time, I would have talked him out of investing. I know Lord Gordon's type, and they're not to be trusted."

"What about Albert? He introduced Father. Did he invest?" I said, remembering his name in the journal. "And. . . there were other rumours about you investing in irregular ventures, whatever that means?"

Charles patted my hand and stood up. "That's enough for now. I'm putting you to bed for a rest."

As he helped me up, I reached up to frame his face within my hands. "Please, Charles, is there anything else you wish to tell me? Something I should know?" If only he would tell me about Joe.

He gently removed my hands. "Not now. You must rest. You don't look well at all."

Chapter 24

That night as I lay beside my sleeping husband, I could not settle my mind. Why had he ended our conversation so abruptly? We agreed no more secrets. Had we not? Joe's name in Charles's journal nagged at me like a persistent sliver embedded in my finger.

What bothered me most, even more so than whether I could trust my second husband, was whether I had been a complete fool to trust my first. If Charles were to tell me what he knew of Joe—why he had needed to borrow money—then perhaps I would finally find out why the strongbox had been empty. Four years after Joe died, I still needed my love for him to be vindicated.

***

The next morning, after a fitful night's sleep, I sat in Tabitha's dressing room, perched upon her vanity stool, my riding pants covered in dust from the journey here. My blouse, wet with perspiration, was now stuck to my skin. I had lied to Charles, claiming the nausea had disappeared, for he would not have let me leave Edenwae. The ride here through the hot morning, thick with humidity, had not helped my stomach.

Tabitha sat on the chaise longue opposite me, looking anxious. I had asked to speak with her in private when I arrived, just moments before a vicious storm struck. Rain lashed against the windows and a crash of thunder made us jump.

"I thought you'd be happy now that Junior has returned. What's wrong?" Tabitha said, deep wrinkles appearing in her brow.

"Have you heard rumours about Charles?"

She pursed her lips. "Why do you ask?"

"Well, it all started with Mother."

Her eyebrows shot up in an expression of exaggerated surprise.

"I know. I should know better than to listen to Mother's gossip. But hear me out." I proceeded to tell her everything about my worries, the rumours, my trespass into my husband's study, my discussion with Charles, and what I had learned about Father.

"My God. How horrible. Surely Albert had no idea what this *lord* was up to."

"But Albert's name was also in Charles's journal. It's very likely your husband has been defrauded too, just like Father. And if I am correct in what I saw, Albert hasn't paid back any of the loan. I asked Charles about Albert, but he avoided answering me."

"I know nothing about any of this. I never ask Albert about his business. Perhaps it would be better if you do the same with your husband." My sister's eyes grew dark. "Although, I must confess that I've always wondered about Charles. He seems a bit too. . . oh I don't know. . . enigmatic. He doesn't seem like any other gentleman I've known."

"I wish you'd told me about these doubts before I married him."

"And would you have listened to me? Just like you did with Joe?" We both smiled. "Anyway, don't be ridiculous. We women are better off if we don't know what our husbands are up to."

Ignoring her comment, I pressed on. "Joe's name was in that journal too. The fact that Charles lent money to Joe and has never told me about it is very unsettling. But I couldn't ask him without first confessing that I'd rifled through his desk."

"Really, Sarah, you must leave the past behind. We need to be concerned about Father. And now I am forced to find out what Albert has done." Her voice was sharp and tense.

I moved to sit beside her. "I can't leave it behind. I never told you why Father loaned me the money to start the dairy. Joe and I had been saving for years to expand the dairy and buy the land from Duff. Just before he died, I discovered our savings were gone, and from what I surmised from the journal, Joe was paying Charles with our savings. It's all too much to simply forget."

Tabitha shook her head in disgust. "I am not at all surprised that Joe lost all your money, nor that he needed a loan." Her hand shot up to her mouth as though to hold something back that had suddenly occurred to her. "Oh. I shouldn't say anything more."

She tried to stand up, but I held onto her arm. "Please. What else do you know? Tell me, for God's sake."

"Are you sure you want to know?" She clasped my hand in hers and squeezed it.

"Of course, I do. I am so sick of secrets. They keep us apart. Can't you see that?" I had spoken too harshly and patted her arm. "I'm sorry for snapping at you, I just want the truth. Please tell me."

Her face softened. "What I am about to tell you will come as a great shock. I have wanted to tell you ever since he died, but you'd been so blindly in love with him, I didn't know how to say it." She paused for a moment before continuing, "Oh Sarah, Joe was not the man you thought he was." In a gentle voice, my sister proceeded to tell me the truth about my first husband. "Joe gambled your money away. Albert only told me in a fit of outrage at your grief over losing such a wastrel husband. His words, not mine, I hasten to add." She squeezed my hand. I was beginning to feel ill again, her words tearing at my heart. "Albert had wanted me to tell you, hoping you would see how foolish you'd been to believe in Joe and stop carrying on about staying on the farm and move back to town."

I remembered the evening when Albert had refused to help me. How tempted he must have felt to complete my humiliation by telling me the truth about Joe. "But you never did," I said, in a soft voice.

"All I knew was that I couldn't add to your heartbreak. I convinced Albert to keep silent and told him it wouldn't change your mind anyway."

My heart in my throat, all I could say was, "Is there more?"

We sat in silence for a moment, the sound of the raging storm filling the room, then she quietly continued. "The card games were held in private men's clubs. Most men, whether gentleman or farmer, have gone to one of these establishments at some point, according to Albert. But

Joe was different. He couldn't stay away. And… he visited the rooms above the gambling rooms, where there were women…" She blushed.

"You mean prostitutes?" I began to choke on bile.

Her face was now crimson. "According to Albert, Joe ran up enormous bills drinking, and so on… and he mostly lost at the card table. That's why I'm not at all surprised that Joe's name was in Charles's journal. That loan along with your long-lost savings probably disappeared down the dark well of Joe's disgusting depravity." My sister had kept the worst secret of all to protect me from the ugly truth. My head and my heart struggled to absorb the magnitude of what she had just said.

With shocking clarity, everything fell into place. The nights Joe did not come home, he had been squandering our hard-earned money on gambling, on drink, and on whores. That odd smell on him when he returned home. That must have been one of those *women*. How could I have trusted him so blindly, never suspecting anything? I finally knew the truth about Joe, and it destroyed everything. Sliding to the floor, I balled my hands into fists and pounded my forehead, my cries obliterating the sound of thunder crashing against the windows. I had been such a fool!

Once my fury was exhausted, I looked up weakly at my sister. "Thank you for telling me." My voice was raspy from screaming. "Love truly is blind." I leaned my head against her sturdy legs while she stroked my head, smoothing my rumpled curls as if I were a small child. "To think I blamed myself for everything that happened."

"Oh hush. I should not have told you. I am—"

"I've shed far too many tears for a man who didn't deserve my love." Finally, the anger I felt toward Joe found its rightful place, no longer restrained by the grief of losing him, my one great love. The weight of that burden finally lifted and my eyes were now wide open.

Never again would I be fooled by love.

***

An hour later, I left Grandview, and took the main street out of town. As I passed Victoria Hall, its grand entrance marked by four tall columns, I thought of the day when at the age of sixteen I first laid eyes upon Joe. Should I have looked the other way that day? But that would mean wishing my children away. And I could never do that.

Riding out of town a few minutes later, I found the old trail that led to Duff's farm. At first, the trail was hard to find, so overgrown from lack of use. The first time I had ridden this path, I followed Joe to his promised land and fell in love with the idea of Edenwae.

The rain earlier today had left the trees dripping and soggy, alive with the buzz of insects and the smell of sweet pine. I found Duff easily, just near the path at the south end of his farm. He was chopping logs from fallen trees, looking rumpled and sweaty.

Hearing me, he stopped swinging his axe and turned to me. His face hardened into a grimace, and he stared. "Weel, Mrs. Bulmore, I didna ever expect to see ye again."

When I reached him, I stayed on my horse and looked down at him coldly. "Duff, I need answers."

"I only deal with Mr. Bulmore." He turned back to his wood pile.

Sweat trickled down my back and the stink of him made me nauseous. "Did you know about Joe? His gambling?" My words gulped out.

Duff raised his axe and brought it down with a loud thud. Leaving the axe embedded in the chopping block, he turned to me. "Aye." The sun was on his face as he looked up, illuminating the mess of deepened wrinkles and black pores.

"Is that why you let me stay, because you felt sorry for me?"

"Ye are so full of yerself. Na. I needed you to stay. Anyway, ye were puttin' up such a fuss. I had no stomach for a fight with ye."

"What do you mean—you *needed* me to stay?"

He just smirked at me. "Now ye have found a rich man fer a husband, bringing the soft life out here, building ye a monstrous mansion to live in." He laughed with surprising bitterness.

"Why would you never tell me who owned the land?" I hoped my voice did not really sound as weak as it did to me.

"Because it was none of yer business. Now, I've work ta do." He turned his back on me and started swinging the axe, crashing it forcefully into a log.

Not giving into his hostility, I waited until he stopped chopping. "Did you promise Hamish that he could buy the land if I married him?"

He turned on me suddenly, his face twisted by a grimace. "Maybe I was tryin' to help ye. I've had it with yer questions."

No longer intimidated by him and driven by a sudden rage, I lashed out. "Hamish became obsessed with owning that land. He tried to force me into marrying him by raping me. He threatened Junior. He is the reason Freddie was hurt. All because of you."

He raised his axe. "Ye do na come on my land... and insult me. That score's been settled."

"What does that mean?" I roared.

He starred at me belligerently. "Ask yer husband what he does to men who cross him." Duff seethed with anger. "Ask him what he did to Hamish."

My heart in my throat, I kicked my horse into a full gallop, and raced back to Edenwae.

Chapter 25

Arriving home, sweating and still nauseous, I swiftly made my way to the manor. Before I could reach the main stairway, Charles intercepted me on the pathway. "There you are. Did you not see the boys on the road?"

I drew back when he tried to embrace me. "What's happened?"

"Nothing. I didn't mean to startle you." He looked at me quizzically. "I sent them to your parents for the weekend. They were to find you at Grandview and give an invitation to Albert and Tabitha to spend the weekend with us. Albert and I have business to discuss. I can't understand how the boys missed you." He eyed me suspiciously, and my heart started to pound in my ears.

Not meeting his gaze, I said, "Oh. . . I took the trail down by the lake. It's cooler. I wish you'd given me more warning. I'm a mess. And dinner—"

"Do not concern yourself. I've made all the arrangements. Everything is ready for our guests and the meals are planned." When he saw my worried face he said, "I thought you'd be delighted to spend more time with your sister. With no children around."

"Oh, of course, but I must bathe and put on a clean dress. I'll be down soon." I ran upstairs, eager to be away from him, my head swirling. I reached the bathing room just in time to vomit into a basin.

***

An hour later, when I came downstairs, I found Charles at the front door. Hearing me, he turned. "They arrived a few minutes ago and are freshening up in the guest house before dinner." He wore the loose-fitting cotton shirt and trousers he wore on hot days. I wore a light linen dress that flowed breezily around my body. The day was still unbearable hot.

Just then, the front door opened, and Tabitha and Albert walked in. Rushing to her, I took note of her formal attire. "Oh dear, you should have brought cooler clothes." I embraced her and noticed over her shoulder that the men were now engrossed in their own conversation. "Did you find out about Albert?" I whispered into her ear.

She whispered back to me, "It is absolutely terrible. We are ruined."

We only had time to share a look of panic before Charles said, "Ladies, please join us," and ushered us all into the dining room. "We have an informal dinner laid out on the sideboard for us. Please help yourselves and be seated."

Throughout the meal, Charles was cordial and pleasant as always, the conversation light and inconsequential. Fortunately, my stomach had settled for the moment. Albert drank many glasses of wine, appeared increasingly agitated, and was inebriated before long. After we finished the dessert course, Charles startled us with an abrupt change of subject. "Albert, I am so pleased we will finally have time to talk." His voice had a contemptuous edge to it.

Albert dabbed his mouth more than was necessary, then fidgeted with his napkin. "Yes, old boy, I have been meaning to see you."

"Oh really, it felt to me as if you have been avoiding me." There was now a sharp edge to Charles's voice and the room felt suddenly chilly.

Albert did not look directly at Charles, choosing instead to focus on folding his napkin. "No, of course not. Not at all. It is just that I have—"

Charles interrupted him. "Oh, never mind. Now we are here. All together." We remained silent, waiting for what he would do next. The tension in the room was unbearable. "Please join me in my study?" he said, standing up and waiting for Albert.

Albert downed yet another glass of wine, pulled himself up, and with a bowed head wobbled down the hall after Charles. He reminded me of a naughty boy about to face his punishment, and I tried not to think about what that might be.

Once our husbands were out of earshot, I pulled my chair beside Tabitha to whisper in her ear. "What the devil was that all about?"

Looking down the hallway through which our husbands had disappeared, she said, "Not here. Come down to the guest cottage where we won't be overheard."

***

At the guest cottage, Tabitha and I sank into a chesterfield in front of the dark fireplace, sitting together just as we had when we were little girls about to share secrets. The cottage was cool with a gentle breeze blowing in through wide open windows. "What's going on?" I asked.

"As it turns out, you don't have the only husband who keeps secrets. Albert lost a huge investment in the northern railway. When Lord Gordon came along, he borrowed from Charles to invest in the land scheme hoping it would save him. When the fraud was discovered...Oh Sarah, we may have to forfeit Grandview to pay Charles back." Her voice had shaken at her last few words.

Putting my arm around her shoulders, I tried to say something to make her feel better. "Surely, Charles would never do that." My reassurance felt hollow. I had no idea what my husband might be capable of.

Her eyes were brimming with tears. "I don't know what to think any more. Albert was so agitated on the way over. And his drinking. I think there is something else he's keeping from me." I reached over to wipe a tear from her cheek, but she brushed my hand away. "Anyway, if Charles is willing to help anyone, I would rather it be Father," she said.

"I am so sick of men making bad decisions that destroy *our* lives." I said.

She sighed and leaned against me. "Oh, my darling, me too."

"Tabby, what is it?" She turned away. I took her by the chin and made her look directly into my eyes. "If there is another secret, you must tell me. I don't want anything else to stand between us."

She shivered slightly even though we were warm. I drew closer to her. "I have kept something horrible from you, about Albert… about why I can't conceive a child."

"Go on," I murmured, the same way I would encourage a frightened child.

"Albert… well… he's not able to bed me. At first, I thought it was me. God knows, Albert blamed me. On our wedding night he couldn't even become aroused, claiming the… *smell* of me repulsed him. There were other nights when he tried, then exploded with anger and left Grandview. Often, he'd stay away all night. And his drinking all day, all evening until he passed out. Then I started to notice how he looked at other men and wondered, and when I overheard the servants…Oh, Sarah…Albert prefers to bed men. If anyone finds out he is a sodomite. The scandal! He would go to jail!"

I pulled her to me. "You could have told me."

"How could I? I was embarrassed for so long, thinking I was deficient as a wife. Ever since I realized the truth, I have loathed him for depriving me of the joys of being truly loved by a man, and for making me believe it was my fault. Thank God for Robert. Now that he has a son, Albert has stopped trying. It was awful how angry he'd get, always blaming me…" Her voice trailed off.

Holding her close, I stroked her hair. "I wish you'd told me sooner. Maybe I could have helped you."

She started to tremble, resting her head on my shoulder. "I just couldn't…"

We hugged in silence for a long time until I felt myself growing drowsy. Suddenly, we were startled by the sound of Charles's voice calling to me. He pulled open the door, loudly calling, "Sarah!" and rushed in, dragging a very inebriated Albert beside him. "Help me get him to a chair."

Once seated, Albert's head lolled back a bit as he stared at us, closing one eye to see us better. "I am so, so sorry," he said, then bowed his head and started to sob. I sat beside Tabitha and clasped her hand while Charles, staying near Albert, pulled up a chair to face us.

"Albert is being blackmailed."

"By whom?" said Tabitha, her eyes round and frightened.

Charles averted his gaze. "I can only guess that you know about Albert's predilection for. . ."

Flushing bright red, she said, "Yes I do." Albert looked up in bleary astonishment. With a harsh stare she said, "I am not a complete fool, Albert."

Albert started to blubber an apology, but Charles interrupted. "I know you must be furious with him, but he needs our help. He's in a terrible state."

"Is someone threatening to expose him?" I said, my voice cracking.

"Yes. It seems a disreputable scoundrel had been stalking him and caught him in the act with another man. That's when the blackmail began." The way Charles looked at me when he said *disreputable scoundrel* made me think instantly of Hamish.

"Oh My God. We will be ruined!" Tabitha rushed to her husband. "How could you be so. . .so. . . careless?" She knelt beside him and took his hand.

"I will take care of it," Charles said, sitting next to me.

"How?" I drew away from him, unsure of whether I wanted him so close.

"That's not important. What worries me now is Albert. You can see his state."

When we turned toward Albert, we were met by Tabitha's fierce and determined stare. "I know he owes you money Charles. I am so embarrassed that he hasn't repaid you. Was it because of the blackmail?"

"Yes, he's been paying off this man for months. Each time, the scoundrel asks for more. Tonight, Albert had been drinking so heavily, I encouraged him to take a walk with me to sober himself up a little. He was upset and embarrassed. When he heard the train coming, he started running toward it. I think he intended to throw himself across the track. Thankfully, he was so drunk he fell before he got there."

Tabitha looked at Albert with surprising compassion in her eyes. "You should've told me. I am your wife. I will stand by you no matter what."

"After the way I treated you?" He looked at her piteously.

"I hate you for blaming me and keeping this from me."

Albert nodded and bowed his head again.

"Now, we need to find a way to avoid scandal," Tabitha said, clear-headed and in charge. "Charles, thank you for taking care of the blackmailer. Are you certain he will never bother us again?"

"My men are very good. This man will no longer be a problem."

I shivered at the thought.

"Good." She turned to Albert. "Without this threat, will you be able to pay Charles?"

Albert was beginning to sober up. "Yes, if it's the monthly payments, we originally agreed to. Would that do, Charles?"

Charles nodded. "But I implore you to be more discreet in your liaisons. Any whiff of scandal and your business will be ruined. And your life at Grandview. Think of little Robert. And you must stop your drinking, it helps no one."

Sitting up straighter in his chair, Albert ran a trembling hand through his messy hair and nodded in a fashion that was not convincing.

"And you will treat me respectfully and give me my own funds," Tabitha said. When he nodded, she turned to us. "I need to get him to bed."

***

A few minutes later, when we reached our bedroom, I pulled Charles close. "We need to talk. I told you before that I don't do well with secrets."

"Right now? I'm exhausted." He headed toward the bed, but I pulled at his sleeve and swung him around.

"Yes, we do. Can't you see how secrets destroy lives? Look what nearly happened to Tabitha and Albert. Was it...Hamish blackmailing Albert?"

He nodded, then searched my eyes. "But we have nothing like that, do we?"

"I'll go first and tell you what I've been keeping from you," I said.

He led me over to the chairs by the window and remained silent while I told him about Hamish's marriage proposal, my rejecting him, his vicious attack, and the terrible consequences for Freddie and Junior. After I finished, he squeezed my hand, the pain of what I had told him reflected in his dark eyes. "I knew."

"What? How?" I felt a rush of heat to my face.

"Let us not speak of it further..."

The clipped manner of his voice warned me not to ask more about Hamish. I paused to collect my thoughts and calm my breath. "Earlier today, I saw Duff." Charles's face darkened, as if a cloud had blocked the sun. "What other secrets are you keeping from me, Charles?" When he said nothing, I knew I had no choice. "I know you lent money to Joe."

His eyes rounded and took on a new fierceness. "Did Duff tell you that?"

"No!" I looked away, then took a deep breath. "When you left the other day, without any explanation about what was going on with my parents, I searched your desk and found your journal. And I saw Joe's name in it." At his look of shock, I added, "I know it was wrong, but your silence infuriated me."

He shook his head, looking pensive, though a little relieved. He gently took my hand in his. "I suppose I am partly to blame. You warned me that you don't like secrets."

"Why didn't you tell me about your dealings with Joe?"

"Because it was... complicated."

"Tabitha told me about Joe's gambling... and whoring. If that's what concerns you, I already know the worst." I cast my eyes down.

He touched my quivering chin and lifted my face to his. "That's only part of it. Joe suddenly stopped paying and I tried to seize the land only to discover Duff owned it."

"Joe owned none of it?" The full weight of the truth sunk me further.

"None. I had no choice but to take the loss on Joe's debt. Later on, when I visited you at Edenwae, saw the land, what you were doing with the dairy, and I met your boys, I bought the land from Duff and planned to propose on my next visit. Then Hamish derailed things..."

I drew closer to him. "How did you find out what Hamish did to me?"

His eyes softened. "It didn't take much to figure out something awful had happened to drive Junior away, hurt Freddie, and traumatize you. The nasty scratch across Hamish's face confirmed it for me. Once I bought the land, I got rid of the hideous man."

"What did you do—" I cut myself off and pressed a finger to Charles's lips, "No. Don't tell me. Just assure me that I will never see Hamish again."

"As I said before, my men are very good."

I felt a sinful rush of satisfaction slither up my spine as I thought about the possible ways in which Hamish might have been made to pay for what he did to me and my boys. With it, a new strength grew within me. "But let that be the last secret you keep from me. Is there anything else I should know? You never explained the other rumours," when he arched an eyebrow, I added, "remember? Those rumours about you owning *irregular ventures?*"

"That sounds like something your mother would say."

I nodded.

He smiled and continued, "You see, I have more than a loan business. I also own buildings in which some of those...er...*irregular...* enterprises operate—houses of pleasure, gambling, and the like—they pay rent to me. The way I look at it, I'm not promoting immorality, I am simply facilitating it." His smile had turned into a grin. "And even when times are difficult, I always make a profit. Immorality is a growing business."

"I wish you had told me all this earlier."

He lifted my hand and kissed it. "Does it bother you? I mean, the nature of my business?"

Grasping his hands in mine I gazed into his soft eyes. "Actually, I think you are quite brilliant. And I believe it is high time I benefited from the depravity of men."

He leaned towards me. "I was right about you."

"How so?"

"We do make ideal partners in life. Definitely cut from the same cloth."

Leaning into him I said, "You know, I never really understood what you meant by that when you proposed."

"Just like you, I would never accept my position in life. You did whatever it took to get what you wanted."

"But you're wealthy—"

"I wasn't always rich." He pulled me closer, caressed my cheek, then drew back. His eyes clouded with the memories from a distant life. "My father was a hard man. He always regarded me as inferior to my elder brother. That's why he disinherited me."

"You mean he gave you nothing?"

"At first, he sent me a small stipend, probably at Mother's urging. But really, everyone was against me—"

I cut him off. "So, you did whatever it took to build your fortune. I see your point. Perhaps we *are* alike." I kissed his waiting lips. Then something dawned upon me, and I drew back. "But your brother hasn't produced an heir…"

His fine lips curled back into a knowing grin. "Exactly."

"Then I expect you'd be delighted to hear…" I placed his hand on my belly, "… that I am pregnant."

Author's Note

This novel is a work of fiction inspired by history. Several years ago, I wrote and published a memoir for my late mother-in-law, Joan McArdle, as a gift for her 95th birthday. It was during Joan's retelling of family stories that I became intrigued by her Grannie Sarah. The facts about Sarah were scarce, but they sparked my creative imagination—the intrigue was that Grannie Sarah lived during the Victorian Era, when women were viewed as inferior in intellect and unable to do anything beyond the duties of wife and mother. Yet, when Sarah's first husband fell to his death leaving her as a pregnant widow with five young sons, she refused to flee to her parents' home. Instead, she managed the farm, and eventually married an English gentleman rumoured to be a loan shark.

The historical setting of a small town on Lake Ontario was purposely vague in its location, as this fictional story could have taken place in any of the small towns of Northumberland County. Wealthy English immigrants to the colonies during the nineteenth century, along with the United Empire Loyalists, brought with them a class riven, sexist society which flourished in the small towns lining the northern shores of Lake Ontario.

The main characters are all fictitious, inspired by the realities of life for women in nineteenth century Canada. Below are the resources I found particularly useful about women in the nineteenth century, and the local history in Northumberland County. As most history books were authored by men, it was often challenging to find a female historical perspective. I am grateful to the female authors and academics I discovered, who made important contributions to our historical knowledge.

Women in 19th century Canada:

Backhouse, Constance. *Petticoats and Prejudice, Women and Law in Nineteenth Century Canada.* Women's Press, 1991.

Minhinnik, Jeanne. *At Home in Upper Canada.* Stoddart Publishing Co. Ltd, 1994.

Mitchinson, Wendy. *The Nature of Their Bodies, Women and Their Doctors in Victorian Canada.* University of Toronto Press, 1991.

Neering, Rosemary. *The Canadian Housewife, An Affectionate History.* Whitecap Books, 2005.

Traill, Catharine Parr. *The Fugitive Writings of Catharine Parr Trail.* University of Ottawa Press, 1994

Traill, Catharine Parr. *A Tale of The Rice Lake Plains.* Carlton University Press, 1986

Ross, Cecily. *The Lost Diaries of Susanna Moodie.* Harper Avenue, 2017

Gray, Charlotte., *Sisters in the Wilderness, The lives of Susanna Moodie and Catharine Parr Traill.* Penquin Canada, 1999.

Gray, Charlotte. *The Promise of Canada.* Simon and Shuster Canada, 2016.

Gray, Charlotte. *Canada, a Portrait in Letters.* Anchor Canada, 2004.

Cohen, Marjorie Griffin, *The Decline of Women in Canadian Dairying.* Social History, Vol. XVII, No. 34 (November 1984) : 307-34

Beeton, Isabella. *Mrs. Beeton's Household Management.* Ward, Lock & Co., Limited, first published 1861.

Northumberland County history:

Climo, Percy L. *Early Cobourg.* Percy L. Climo, 1985.

Cruikshank, Tom. *Port Hope, A Treasury of Early Homes.* Bluestone House Inc., 1987.

The Rolling Hills of Northumberland, A County History. The County of Northumberland, 2000.

Guillet, Edwin C. *Cobourg 1798-1948*. Goodfellow Printing Company Limited, 1948.

Martin, Norma, Milne, Catherine, McGillis, Donna S. *Gore's Landing and The Rice Lake Plains*. Clay Publishing Co. Ltd.

Montages, Ian. *Port Hope, a History*. Ganaraska Press, 2007.

Cobourg: Early Days and Modern Times. The Cobourg Book Committee, 1981.

Acknowledgements

A special thank you to the individuals who were instrumental in bringing this novel to life.

- Donna Morrissey for your substantive editing skills. You shaped my writing and toughened my skin. I regard the mentorship of an International Award-winning author as a high point of my writing career. You are a gifted teacher.

- Tom Cruickshank for your insight into local history and architecture, your historical accuracy editing skills, and your connection to local farmer and historian, Tim Farquhar, whom I would also like to thank. Your advice and critique helped me create an authentic and believable story world. You are a generous friend.

- Linda Hutsell-Manning for being the first to believe in my writing, for showing me that it is never too late, and for being a constant source of encouragement. You are an inspiration.

- Shane Joseph for your belief in my manuscript, your insightful editing skills, your tremendous support as a publisher of emerging writers, and for never holding back an opinion. You are one of a kind.

I would also like to thank the teachers at the University of Toronto and fellow writers at the Spirit of the Hills Writer's Group, and author Liz Torlee, for their advice and support.

Special appreciation to Gordon Penrose for his father's copy of Mrs. Beeton's Household Management.

Thank you to my promotional team of fellow writers, family and friends who spread the word about this novel.

Most of all I wish to thank my wonderful husband, Ian, for his unfailing support, his good-natured weathering of my mood swings, and for his courageous editing. None of this would have happened without you, my love.

Author Bio

Pam Royl has thrived on creativity her whole life, embracing visual art, ceramic art, and her latest passion of creative writing. Graduating from The Schulich School of Business, she began a long career in marketing and advertising working for international marketing companies and advertising agencies, as well as in a leadership position at George Brown College. In 2003, she retired from full time employment, started a consulting firm, and began pursuing her writing interests.

Pam was inspired to write her debut novel by an ancestor she discovered while writing family memoirs. Developing her fiction writing skills through courses at the University of Toronto, and the mentorship of International award-winning author, Donna Morrissey, Pam set her story within the fascinating history of Northumberland County where she lives with her husband Ian. Whenever she isn't writing, Pam loves playing piano and guitar, and walking her dogs.

CPSIA information can be obtained
at www.ICGtesting.com
Printed in the USA
BVHW050620090223
657947BV00001B/3

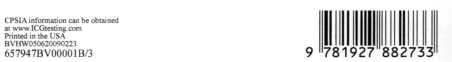